The TROUBLE
with MIRRORS

OTHER TITLES BY CHARLOTTE AND AARON ELKINS

The Alix London Series

A Dangerous Talent
A Cruise to Die For
The Art Whisperer

The Lee Ofsted Series

A Wicked Slice
Rotten Lies
Nasty Breaks
Where Have All the Birdies Gone?
On the Fringe

The TROUBLE with MIRRORS

AN ALIX LONDON MYSTERY

CHARLOTTE & AARON ELKINS

THOMAS & MERCER

Published by Thomas & Mercer, Seattle

www.apub.com

Amazon, the Amazon logo, and Thomas & Mercer are trademarks of Amazon.com, Inc., or its affiliates.

ISBN-13: 9781503940437
ISBN-10: 1503940438

Cover design by Janet Perr

Printed in the United States of America

CHAPTER 1

Good afternoon. I am speaking with Ms. London?"

"Yes, this is Alix London."

"This is not a bad time? I am not inconveniencing you?"

"No, I was just trying . . . no."

She was just trying to come up with some way of cramming one more pair of shoes into the carry-on bag that lay open on her bed and thus avoid the necessity of checking luggage on her flight to what Seattleites called "the other Washington." But both sides of the carry-on were already heaped so high that closing it, even now—assuming that was possible—was going to risk springing the zipper.

Packing for this particular DC trip had been trickier than usual because it was a mix of business and pleasure. The business part was a consulting assignment with the FBI's art squad, which desired her counsel on whether a painting being held by Customs was a twentieth-century copy based on an early seventeenth-century Rubens, as its owner had declared when trying to get it into the country from Belgium, or was instead the genuine article. If it was the former, he would get it through with a relatively minimal duty payment. If the latter, he would owe an enormous duty and would be in big trouble to boot—on both sides of the Atlantic.

The pleasure part involved spending time with the current—and, she was beginning to think, future—man in her life. The problem was that different wardrobes were required. She didn't want to stand around all day in three-inch heels, but she also wasn't about to wear flats to the fancy dinner Ted had promised her at Citronelle. Absolutely not. That dinner was the reason she'd splurged so inexcusably (she still couldn't believe it) on the Bottega Veneta pumps that were taking up all the room in her bag, because you couldn't put a pair of shoes like that in a suitcase without their box and some protective cushioning. Well, could you?

It was looking more and more as if the carry-on just wasn't going to do the job and she'd have to lug the big suitcase instead, and it had made her cross.

"Forgive me," the voice on the other end said, "but you sound a little distracted, yes? Perhaps another time, it would be better? If that is the case—"

"No, this is fine."

It wasn't the grumpiness that had made her more curt than usual. She'd heard only a handful of sentences from whoever this was, but already she didn't like him. It wasn't his words per se that got under her skin, it was that he was too smooth for her, too self-assured, his cultured Italian accent urbane and sly to the point of caricature. He called to mind some bewigged, berouged, knee-breeched dandy in the court of the King of Naples.

This guy, she said to herself, is an art dealer if I ever heard one.

"My name is Alessandro Ferrante, Ms. London. I am calling from Italy. I am a dealer in fine art—"

Ha.

"—and I am calling to you because I have a client who saw a most excellent article about you in the new *Art World Insider.*"

That surprised her. "Really? I didn't think it'd come out yet."

"Ah, but it has. He received his copy this morning, as did I. Perhaps it arrives earlier to Europe? I myself found it fascinating, by the way. To read of a person like yourself, so accomplished at so young an age, and if I may say, so beauti—"

"Uh . . . you wanted . . . ?" The more he talked, the stronger her aversion grew. There was something about the unctuous way he spoke, a subtly nuanced quality that gave you the feeling that what he was talking about wasn't really what he was talking about.

"Yes, forgive me," Ferrante said quickly. "I know your time is valuable. May I come to the point? My client was very much taken by one of the objects on the wall behind you in the photograph. He felt—"

"The small mirror, yes," Alix said, hurrying him along. It had been an easy enough guess. Other than the mirror, everything on that wall was poster art. The mirror was a one of a kind.

"Exactly. And so I was hoping that you might be amenable to parting with it—for a substantial consideration?"

"No, I wouldn't be, Mr. Ferrante."

"I assure you, the terms would be very—I should say, *extremely*—"

"No. I'm sorry." The guy was as oily as a quarter-pound of butter two weeks past its sell-by date.

"Ah, that is what I feared. It is indeed a most beautiful piece, and to my knowledge a unique one."

"That it is. Well, *signor* Ferrante—"

"I wonder, then, if you might happen to know the artist who crafted it and if this person would consider a commission to make a similar one? Not a duplicate of your own, of course, but one employing similar, ah, stylistic conventions."

"Yes, as a matter of fact, I do know who made it, and, truthfully, I doubt if he'd want to do that. It was a personal gift. It was done a very long time ago and he's pretty fully employed now. Really, I'm sure he wouldn't be interested."

"Ah," murmured Ferrante despondently, and Alix was hit with a pang of guilt. Was she really being honest, or was it simply that she hated the idea of Tiny making a second beautiful mirror for some other little girl—or big one, for that matter?

No, an act of contrition was called for. "But you know, Mr. Ferrante, it's my father that Tiny works for, so I can certainly pass your message on to him, although not for another few days. I'm sure I'll see him when I get back, though. How can he reach you if he'd like to take you up on this?"

"Do you mean it, really?" he said. "To telephone me would probably be best. You have a pen? Yes? You are ready? Here is the number: 390 10 275 45 06." He repeated it. "Please tell him my client does not expect it to be inexpensive. Thank you so much, *signorina*."

She hung up with a sense of unease. The oily Italian had left her with the feeling she'd just been conned out of something, but she didn't know what. She shook her head to brush the feeling aside, picked up the pump she'd had in her hand when the call had come, and put it into its plain and understated shoebox. Only a second later, with a faint, nostalgic smile on her face, she took it again from its tissue paper nest and ran her hand down the creamy black leather of the three-inch heel. She was thinking of her sixteenth birthday, the wonderful day her mother had taken her shopping at Saks Fifth Avenue for her first pair of grownup shoes. Alix had chosen a pair of Bottega Venetas for the then-extravagant price of almost four hundred dollars, and she had come away feeling extravagantly, delightfully decadent and mature—a woman at last.

These new shoes were the first Bottega Venetas she'd bought since then (at considerably more than four hundred dollars), and they were as much like the old pair as she could find. They revived too many precious memories—no way would she leave them behind. But she wasn't going to haul that humungous, hard-sided Samsonite monster of hers with her either, not if she could help it.

Fixing the carry-on with her most intimidating glare, she returned to battle with it.

CHAPTER 2

At six-fifteen in the evening, two days after Alix received this call, the creator of the mirror in question, one Beniamino Guglielmi Abbatista, known to one and all as Tiny, effortlessly shoved open the thirty-pound steel door of his place of employment—Venezia Fine Art Imports in South Seattle—and heaved his imposing, six-foot-four, three-hundred-and-five-pound frame out into the parking lot, tired but pleased with his long day's work and looking forward to tomorrow's. Foremost on his mind, though, was whether he still had half a bottle of Chianti sitting on the kitchen counter to go with his dinner or if he'd better pick some up on the way home. Better safe than sorry, he thought, besides which, if he stocked up today he wouldn't have to do his grocery-shopping the next day, which was his usual—

"Hey, mister, are you Tiny?"

He glanced up. The question came from a cocky, skinny kid lounging on the hood of a car, trying his best to look like a streetwise young hood (and doing a good job of it). He was wearing shredded jeans, beat-up sneakers, and a grungy T-shirt with a logo that read:

UNCLE ED'S POT PALACE
611b Third Avenue South
Hey, at least it's not crack.

Tiny didn't like his looks but he answered amicably enough. "Yeah, kiddo, I'm Tiny. What can I do for you?"

The kid jumped down (on the other side of the car that was safely away from Tiny), yelled, "Dude, if you're tiny, I'd hate like hell to see a big guy!" and took off running. There were only two other cars in the lot and as he passed one of them, a blue Toyota, Tiny thought he saw a quick glance, a single, jerky nod, from the boy toward the car.

Beniamino Abbatista was not notably big on brain, but he had a well-honed ability to intuit when something wasn't right, and he sensed that something was off here. How did this kid know his name? The sun was on its way down, but the car was only thirty feet away and he could see the driver clearly. A fleshy guy in a flat tweed cap, an old-fashioned newsboy's cap. He wasn't as big as Tiny, but he looked formidable enough. When he saw Tiny looking in his direction he quickly averted his eyes to stare with great interest at the totally blank, two-story concrete-block wall of Gionfriddo & Abrams Machine Works. His lips were pursed as if he was whistling to himself and Tiny was the last possible thing on his mind.

That, Tiny *definitely* didn't like. He considered walking up and asking what was going on, but maybe there was nothing to it. It wouldn't be the first time his imagination had run away with him. Sensing trouble was one thing, actively looking for it was another. Besides, his bus, the 106, was just pulling up to the corner. With a last look at the car—the driver was still scrutinizing Gionfriddo & Abrams's wall—he hopped on the bus and headed north.

When it reached the Pioneer Square area fifteen minutes later he got off and went into Chong's Kwik Stop Market. From the market's shadowy interior he searched for the Toyota or the man in the cap, but saw neither. He hadn't spotted them from the bus either.

Still, he wasn't convinced that all was well. He'd seen the *Art World Insider* yesterday and the cover had come as a shock. Ever since, he'd been half-expecting the appearance of unwelcome callers. The guy in the car certainly looked like one, and what was that business with the kid? It continued to bug him.

A few minutes later he emerged with his bag of groceries and walked two blocks to Occidental Mall, the tree-lined, pedestrian-zoned block of Occidental Avenue South, where he had an apartment above one of its several art galleries. Once through the street door he jogged up the stairs and looked through the hallway window, which had a view of the street below and of the entrance to the building. Nothing, just the usual strollers, and diners, and street people. He began, very slightly, to relax.

Nevertheless, instead of having his dinner in the apartment, he left through the building's rear door, went down the back alley to the corner, came back around to the mall, and slipped into a wine bar across the street and several doors down from where he lived. There he took a candle-lit window booth from which he could unobtrusively keep an eye on his building.

Nothing.

He'd downed a couple of glasses of Pinot Grigio to go with his double-order of smoked mussels with cucumbers and he'd gotten to feeling pretty good. His uneasiness seemed silly now, a touch of paranoia. After all, what were the chances of anyone even noticing an insignificant, two-inch-square image in the background of a magazine cover, let alone connecting it to the events of almost thirty years ago? And *then* connecting all that to him? Zip was about what they were. It was ancient history; there was probably hardly anybody around who even remembered it. He thought about another glass of wine, got a takeout cup of coffee and a hunk of apple cake instead, and went back to his apartment. At ten-thirty he turned off the lights and got into bed. He had taken no extra precautions. Ten minutes later he was snoring away. The night slowly progressed.

•   •   •

And nothing happened. Not until the next morning when, wearing the pre-work tracksuit he put on to go down the block for his daily breakfast, he was enjoying his usual sixteen-ounce *caffè al cacao*, two almond croissants, and two brioches at one of Caffè Umbria's outdoor tables under the trees. With the Umbria being the only place on the street that was open so early, it was particularly pleasant, the only time of day when the café- and gallery-lined block was quiet. It made the air fresher, crisper. He was sitting with a few of his Italian-American cronies, chatting away about nothing in particular, in a convivial patois that was three parts English and one part Italian, when he happened to look up the block. Whatever he'd been about to say flew out of his mind. There he was again, the guy with the newsboy cap, but on foot now, and this time he had someone with him, a near-lookalike; two bulging musclemen who couldn't have been acting more like a pair of strong-arm thugs if they'd tried. They were at the street door to his building, fumbling with a set of keys. As he watched, they got it open, slipping furtively (they thought) inside and shutting the door behind them.

He didn't doubt for a second that there were shoulder holsters under the baggy tweed sport coats they were wearing on this warm September morning. He also had no doubt, not anymore, about what was going on and what he needed to do, and that he needed to do it in a hurry.

"*Devo andare*," he said abruptly. *I have to go.*

Frowning, one of his friends pointed wordlessly at his plate. Go? When he'd eaten only a single brioche and had yet to touch a croissant?

He didn't answer. They watched in astonishment as he lumbered down the street in a heavy-legged jog that for him passed for running, heading not in his usual direction, toward his apartment, but the opposite way.

That day, for the first time in five months, he failed to show up for work.

CHAPTER 3

One week later.

"Okay," Chris said, turning the car onto the airport expressway and heading north toward downtown Seattle, "enough mystery. Spill the beans."

Alix, in the passenger seat, had been looking out her window. "What beans? What are you talking about?"

"Well, *talk* to me. How did things go in DC?"

"Very well, thanks."

"And how's Ted?"

"Ted's fine."

"And how are you two getting along?"

"Oh, fine."

Chris laughed. "Well, thanks for all the news. No need to go into all that detail, though."

Alix smiled at her and continued to look placidly out the window at the darkened streets. Chris left her to her woolgathering for a while, but five minutes was all she could stand.

"Oh, please, give me a break. You look like a kid who just found a new puppy under the Christmas tree. So tell me, what really happened back there? Hey, wait . . . you're not going to tell me that so-called Rubens turned out to be the real thing, a brand-new, previously unknown, honest-to-God Rubens?"

Alix laughed. "Better."

"*Better*?" She waited, but Alix just continued to smile. "Come on, Alix, you may as well tell me. You know you're going to."

"Yes, but not till we get to my place. Over a cup of tea."

"Now you've got me really—"

"What were you doing waiting for me at the airport, anyway? It's practically the middle of the night. I was all set to catch the shuttle."

"Ten-thirty is not the middle of the night, and you know me, the original Vampire Lady. I don't come fully alive until after dark. Anyway, I just thought you might prefer to ride in comfort in a nice, new, smooth, luxurious, silk-gray BMW 740i, that's all."

Chris's wealth (from stock options when Sytex, the "health care information technology advisory consultancy" she'd worked for, had gone public) was still so new that, given the right company, she made no bones about showing it off.

It was this wealth that had first brought them together a couple of years ago. They were a natural fit: Alix London, newly minted art consultant just getting her professional feet under her and hunting for clients, and Christine LeMay, former techie itching to put some of that lovely money to use building an art collection, and thus in need of knowledgeable consulting. Since then, Alix had provided just that, keeping her away from dubious—and in one case downright fraudulent—purchases and encouraging her in a direction that had by now resulted in a minor but credible and growing collection of early American Modern paintings and drawings by the likes of Georgia O'Keeffe and Childe Hassam. And in the process they had become close friends, wonderfully easy in each other's company.

"Well, I appreciate it most sincerely," Alix said, letting herself descend into the buttery gray leather. "This is wonderful. Thank you!" After which she fell into the wandering, cobwebby daze into which six hours in the air and a three-hour time change had put her. Her internal clock was still on DC time—going on 2:00 a.m.

This time Chris managed to go almost ten minutes in silence before she gave up again. "Alix, if you're just going to keep mum while we drive, you might as well have something to read. Have you seen the new *Art World Insider* yet?"

Alix slowly surfaced. "No. I heard it was out before I left, though."

"There's a copy in the side pocket. Have yourself a look."

Alix took it out. "Yikes!"

One look at the cover made her sit up as taut as a piano wire. Other than the magazine's logo, the front cover was all Alix; a color photograph of her sitting on her red living room sofa and looking—to her own critical eye—revoltingly smug. "The Art Whisperer," read the legend beside her. "Forgers Beware."

"Chris . . ." she blurted, waving the magazine at her. "The *cover*? How . . . ? I thought . . ."

"I thought so too," Chris said, grinning. "It was supposed to be an interview buried in the 'People Going Places' section, right? I didn't know it was the cover story until I saw it myself. I'm guessing it's because of that forgery bust in Miami a couple of weeks ago."

"But I didn't have anything to do with that."

"I know, but art forgery was in the air, and I guess they figured the story about you would be a winner."

"Sheesh," Alix said, sinking back into the seat.

Chris glanced over at her. "I can't tell if you like it or you hate it."

"I'm not sure myself. It's flattering, and I suppose it'll bring me some clients, but this whole 'art whisperer' business . . ." She shook her head. "I don't know."

The term had gotten stuck to her as a result of the art world's growing awareness of her finely honed "connoisseur's eye"—the ability to determine, at an intuitive level, the authenticity or lack of authenticity of a disputed painting. It was what had gotten her the FBI consulting assignments, along with an increasing number of private commissions, but it had outlived its welcome a long way back. Most of the time the term was applied positively, but by now it had come to make her grind her teeth with its not so faint implication of snake oil at best, or unadulterated shysterism at worst. Any references to the hard-won expertise that grounded her gift, or the years of apprenticeship in Italy that had polished it, tended to get lost in the mix.

"Learn to live with it," Chris said cheerfully. "Fame is a lonely and terrible burden."

"Thank you so much. That's incredibly helpful."

"Besides, who reads *Art World Insider*?"

CHAPTER 4

When they got to Alix's Green Lake condominium building, Chris helped her transport her luggage to the second-floor condo. Her help was needed: in the end the big Samsonite had gotten the call. "So," she said as Alix put the key in the lock, "I'm about to hear this big secret, right?"

"Absolutely. Once I make the tea."

"Don't tell me they finally made you an honest-to-God special agent, with a badge and a gun, and all that other cool stuff? Burberry trench coat, Gucci aviator sunglasses . . ."

Alix smiled. "I don't think Burberry and Gucci are on the FBI's approved vendor list. And anyway"—the smile widened—"it's better."

Chris laughed. "Better than a badge and a gun? Boy, this must really—"

"Something's different," Alix said when she pushed the door open, the key still in her hand.

Chris spotted what it was before she did. She pointed at the right-hand wall of the small vestibule into which the condo opened. "Didn't you used to have something hanging there?"

It took a second for Alix to remember what it had been. "A poster. From the Met. For an old Caravaggio show. I bought it on sale for ten dollars. I didn't even have it mounted. It was just stuck up there with stick pins. Why would anyone . . ."

Chris had stepped around the corner of the vestibule into the living room and come to a stop. "Look."

Alix came around behind her and sagged. "Oh, boy," she murmured.

The red sofa, the one she'd been sitting on for the *Art World Insider* photo, had been pulled away from the wall and toppled forward onto the floor, its rear legs in the air. The wall itself, on which she'd hung a dozen artfully arranged pictures—the nearest thing she had to a show-case area—was now bare except for picture hooks, squares of double-sided tape, and some ugly gouges in the cream-colored surface.

"Damn them," she said.

With Chris's assistance, she turned the sofa upright, which made things better, but only marginally.

"The pictures, were they insured?" Chris asked.

"I've got some general homeowners', but not specifically on the pictures. They're not worth insuring. They're certainly not worth stealing. Really, they're just mementos that wouldn't have any value to anyone else. Huh, some burglars."

"Well, maybe they got something else that *is* worth stealing. We'd better check the place out."

They went separately through the rest of the condo, with which Chris was familiar from previous visits. "Your laptop and things are still here," she called from the den alcove.

"I don't see anything missing here either," Alix called back from the bedroom. "TV . . . clothes . . ."

"Here's how they got in," Chris said. She was at the rear of the condo, where two windows and a glass door opened out onto a small deck overlooking a neat, shared garden, and farther off, the lake. When Alix joined her, Chris pointed at the marred wooden frame of one of the windows. "It's been jimmied."

"I see," Alix said. "And then once they got in, they could open the door to make it easier to cart things out. But how did they get up on the deck in the first place?"

"Are you kidding?" Chris led the way outside. "What are we here, ten feet above the ground? They could have made it with a stepstool, or even one guy getting a boost from another. Hey, you'd better call the police, don't you think?"

Alix nodded and went back in to the telephone. She wasn't feeling the usual things that people are supposed to feel when they walk into their homes and find that uninvited strangers have fingered their possessions and made off with whatever they happened to like. She didn't have a sense of having been violated, she didn't suddenly feel unsafe or vulnerable, and she wasn't even particularly shocked. What she was was annoyed. What a pain in the neck this was going to be: police report, insurance report, get the window fixed, repaint the wall, and tell her father about it and calm him down when he got all parentally stressed out about it. With the phone in her hand, she hesitated.

"Chris, I don't know if I want to make this call or not. It's not as if anything valuable was taken, and it won't take much to repair the damage. Honestly, I'm not sure getting the police involved is worth the hassle. You know, I don't really think we should—"

"The hell we shouldn't," Chris said, whipping out her own phone and dialing 911. Brushing off a few feeble protests from Alix, who knew at heart that Chris was right, she explained what had happened, was transferred to a non-emergency operator, explained again, and was told a police officer would be there shortly.

"All right, satisfied?" Alix said. "I'll start the tea in the meantime. Finally." But on the way to the kitchen she couldn't help looking at the denuded wall, and it stopped her short.

"Oh, no . . ." she said suddenly, so softly it was almost a whisper. She dropped onto the sofa, cradling her forehead in her hand. "Oh, Chris."

Chris was suitably alarmed. "Alix, what is it?"

"I just realized . . . they got . . . they took . . . Tiny's mirror."

"*What*?" She stared at the blank wall. "Oh, my God, that's right, it was hanging right . . . oh, Alix, I'm so sorry. I know how much that mirror means to you."

"A lot, yes. I—" But Alix was unable to get out any more than that. The breath had been knocked out of her as thoroughly as if she'd taken an elbow to the middle of the chest. This, she understood, was what people meant when they said "heartache," a hurt every bit as real as a toothache, and as all-consuming.

"Is that what they were after?" Chris was musing. "Did they see it on the *Art World* cover and think, what with you being the famous Art Whisperer and all, it had to be worth a lot of money? And the rest of the things they took, they were just cover, to make it look like a routine smash-and-grab, a kind of drive-by—"

She stopped when she saw Alix, who'd seemed to be nodding rhythmically along with her as if in agreement, was in reality somewhere far away. Gently, Chris squeezed her shoulder. "I'll take care of the tea," she said quietly, going toward the kitchen. "I know where everything is."

Alix continued her vague nodding.

Tiny's mirror.

It was her oldest possession. She'd had it well over half her life, ever since Tiny—she had still called him "Uncle Beni" in those days—had crafted it himself for her twelfth birthday, at a time when she still adored angels. It was one of the very few possessions she'd kept with her when she went through what she thought of as the Dismal Time in her early twenties.

Tiny—more properly Beniamino Guglielmi Abbatista—had found an old oval hand mirror somewhere, evocatively time-flecked with spots and veins of gray and rust. He had set it in the center of a rectangular wooden panel and painted the wood surrounding the glass with fat little cherubs with tiny wings, frolicking among pink-tinged clouds. He was a superb craftsman of great delicacy despite his lumbering three-hundred-plus pounds and a set of fingers like a clump of knockwurst, he had done a wonderful job making it look like something you might see on a wall in the background of a fifteenth-century portrait of some elegant Florentine lady, by Botticelli, say, or Ghirlandaio.

Tiny, in fact, could brilliantly imitate just about any artist of any era you chose to name, and it had gotten him in a great deal of trouble in his younger days, when he'd pursued a career as an art forger. Not being over-endowed with smarts, however, he had wound up serving three terms in jail, almost a decade altogether. But that was something Alix hadn't learned until much later, and it hadn't changed her feelings toward the lovable lug, who had always returned all of her affection and then some. One of her earliest memories was of sitting on his knee when she was three or four and listening, enchanted, while he sang old Italian songs to her in a surprisingly soft, sweet falsetto.

Chris came back with the tea and set the cups on the corner table between the sofa and an armchair. "I put some sugar in it. Don't argue, you can use it."

"It was so beautiful . . . he'd done such a wonderful job on it . . . oh, I feel so, so . . ."

Alix took her first sip of the hot tea. Chris was right; the shot of energy and general uplift from the sugar were welcome. A second and third swallow got her thinking a little straighter too. Things weren't as bad as all that. Yes, the mirror meant a great deal to her, and no, she didn't expect ever to see it again, but on the bright side, she knew Tiny well enough to know he'd insist on reproducing it for her, and with his astonishing skills, in a few weeks the new one would be up on her wall, with even Alix hard-pressed to tell the difference.

She smiled. So, after twenty years Tiny was going to have *two* commissions for his "one-of-a-kind" mirrors. Nice that at least one of them would be paying him, and apparently paying him well. Hadn't *signor* Ferrante implied that his client . . . his client . . . Suddenly she jerked her head. *"Wait a minute!"*

It made Chris jump, jiggling her cup and splashing tea on her slacks. "Jeez, Alix! You practically—What is it?"

"It *was* the mirror. Of *course* it was!" Alix exclaimed. "That smooth, greasy bastard who called me—that's what he was interested in, the mirror! He didn't want another one, he wanted *this* one. He was just trolling for information." She slapped her forehead, like an actor in a silent movie. "And I *gave* it to him! I practically told him I was going to be away—I *did* tell him I was going to be away. Damn, a phone call about it one day—the only phone call I've ever gotten about it—and then, inside of a week—it's gone. If that's a coincidence, then I'm, I'm—"

"If I sit here long enough," Chris said to a nearby wall as she dabbed at the tea stain on her thigh, "I wonder if she'll eventually notice me and tell me what the hell she's talking about."

"Sorry, Chris." Alix explained about Alessandro Ferrante (if that was really his name) and his phone call.

When she'd finished, Chris thought it over. "You're right, that's got to be it. Way too much of a coincidence. I can't see him coming over from Genoa to burgle your place himself, but how hard would it be to get some of our delightful homegrown thugs to do it?"

"It's completely my fault. I did it to myself," Alix said wretchedly, "with my big mouth. Dumb, dumb, dumb—"

"Please—don't whack yourself again!" Chris said when she saw Alix's hand on its way up. "That last one probably cost you a couple thousand brain cells. Anyway, if you're looking for somebody to blame . . ." She raised her hand, like a kid in class. "Hello."

"You? How do you figure that?"

Chris rummaged in her bag. "This," she said, pulling out another copy of *Art World Insider* and slapping it onto the table. "Look at that cover one more time."

Alix looked. There she was, bright and sassy (and smug), sitting where she sat now. Behind her was the wall that was behind her now, but it was covered with art prints, ten all together—Dürer, Turner, Renoir, other favorites of hers—and with Tiny's mirror in pride of place, smack in the center. "I'm the genius who set this interview thing up and then talked you into it, remember?" Chris said unhappily. "If not for me there wouldn't have been any photo, and without the photo there wouldn't have been any Ferrante, and without Ferrante there wouldn't have been any stupid break-in."

"That's ridiculous, Chris. You were doing me a favor. If I didn't want to do it, all I had to do was say no."

There was a crisp double tap at the door and Alix got up. "The police?"

She had expected a uniformed cop, but instead it was a man in a sport coat and tie, a grizzled veteran in his fifties, who brought with him a reassuring aura of competence and command. But Detective Ernest Durando was friendly too, accepting the offered cup of coffee (Alix knew he wouldn't be a tea-drinker) and joining them in the grouping of living room chairs.

He was efficient and sympathetic with his questions, but they could see his prioritizing of the case shift from high (when he saw that Alix's picture was on the cover of the magazine that lay on the sofa beside him) to moderate (when the details of what had happened became clear to him) to the absolute bottom of the list (when Alix gave him her estimate of the probable market value of the stolen objects: five hundred dollars, of which the mirror probably accounted for four hundred and seventy-five. And that was no more than a guess at what it was likely to bring on eBay. If anybody was interested).

He did show interest when she told him about the phone call, bringing out his iPhone and punching in the number Ferrante had left with her. The result obviously surprised him. "What do you know, it's a real number. And a real art gallery: Galleria Ferrante, proprietor A. Ferrante."

He slipped the phone into his shirt pocket. "Now, you understand, we can't pursue anything over there ourselves, but we can contact the Italian police—what do you call them, the *carabinieri*—and see if they'll look into this guy for us. That's always an iffy proposition, though. Sometimes a request like that works out, sometimes it just falls through the cracks and gets lost. They've got plenty of their own stuff to keep them busy. So I can't promise anything."

"You know, I might have a better way of doing that," Alix offered. "I'm a consultant for the FBI's art squad in Washington, DC. That's where I was when this happened. If I mention this to them, I'm sure they'd have some good contacts there."

"That'd be fine. All donations willingly accepted. You'll let me know what they turn up?"

"Of course."

"All right, then. There's one thing about all this that's got me wondering, though, Ms. London. Why would this art dealer character have wanted a five-hundred-dollar mirror enough to set up a break-in to get it? If his client—if there was a client—was ready to pay big-time because he loved it so much, why wouldn't Ferrante just go to some crafts guy in Italy, show him the picture, and have him make one? No law-breaking required, and probably less expensive too. But no, he had to have the real thing. How do you explain that?"

"I don't know, Detective. Are you getting at something?"

"I am, yes." He was looking down at his cup and revolving it in slow circles on its coaster. "I was wondering," he said, looking up, "if that mirror might bring a whole lot more than that five hundred bucks you think it's worth."

"I have no idea, really. This kind of thing—well, art in general, for that matter—has just about no inherent value. It's worth what the buyer thinks it's worth. If somebody likes it enough he might be willing to pay five hundred dollars, maybe more. Who knows, maybe a thousand. But even if he was—"

"No, ma'am, I'm thinking a whole lot more than that." He picked up the magazine to show the mirror more clearly. "I'm way out of my league when it comes to art, but this sure looks to me like something you'd see in a museum, something from the fifteen or sixteen hundreds."

"I can see why you'd say that, and plainly, that was Tiny's intention. But I can assure you, it was made in the 1990s by my friend."

"Can you? How positive are you that it isn't the real thing—some genuine, really valuable old piece by some artist from back then?"

"Completely."

Chris cut in. "Anyway, why would anybody give something that valuable to a twelve-year-old girl?" she asked Durando. "Especially without even bothering to tell her what it was."

"That I don't know. But I do know that people have a way of seeing what they expect to see, and if you were told when you were twelve that your uncle or whoever made it for you, and you believed it—and why wouldn't you?—well, then, from then on, wouldn't you—"

Chris had begun to laugh. "Detective, I don't think you realize who you're talking to here." She tapped the magazine's cover. "This is the Art Whisperer herself. She can tell the difference between the real thing and a fake at forty yards."

Alix demurred. "Twenty yards, maybe."

"Okay, twenty yards. In fact, that's exactly what the FBI uses her for. When *they* don't know what they've got, they call Alix."

Durando held up both hands. "Okay, you win. It was just an idea. Who am I to argue with the Art Whisperer? Either of you got any explanation for what was behind this, then?"

They didn't.

He nodded, picked up his cup and drank most of what was left, although it must have been cold by then. "Well, ladies—"

"Do we need to keep from touching anything?" Chris asked, seeing that he was wrapping up. "Are we expecting some crime scene people?"

His expression went from poker-faced to a sort of tolerant resignation. This was something he heard a lot—the *CSI effect*, cops called it: the unfortunate perception, derived from TV programs, that police forces had available to them an infinite supply of DNA analysts, crime scene analysts, forensic chemists, pathologists, anthropologists, and every other kind of *-ist* that you could name, and that they were used as a matter of course.

"Ma'am, I have to tell you," Durando said, "our crime scene resources are kind of stretched at the moment. In a case like this, where nobody's been threatened or harmed, and there's not much probability of catching the guy, and the only property damage is a bent window catch and some holes in the wall, and according to you the value of the missing items is pretty minimal, well—"

"We shouldn't expect them any time soon," Chris finished for him.

"That's about it, but don't tell my sergeant I said so. It's a question of resources and priorities."

"Detective," Alix said, "that mirror I was talking about has an awful lot of sentimental value to me. Would you truthfully say there's any chance at all of getting it back?"

He gave her a friendly, apologetic smile. "Well, to be perfectly honest . . ."

"That's what I thought."

"Don't get the idea that I'm saying we won't be on the lookout, ma'am. We'll do what we can, really, and who knows, things might work out. You wouldn't have a photo of it you could let me have, would you?"

"No, I'm afraid—"

"Sure you do," Chris said. "Right here." She picked up the magazine. "You can have this, Detective."

He took it. "Pretty piece, that mirror," he said. "I'd miss it too." He stood up. "Okay, I'll keep an eye out, I promise. Hey, thanks for the coffee, that hit the spot." He gave each of them his card and was gone.

"Whew," Alix said. "This is really exhausting. Ah, well, I guess I'd better call Geoff now and tell him about it."

"Alix," Chris said, in a change of voice that indicated she was assuming the role of Elder and Wiser Sister, which she took on when she felt it necessary. "Your father is no doubt fast asleep, and there is no reason in the world why he has to know at this particular moment. It'll hold until tomorrow."

"You're right," Alix said gratefully. "I'll drive over in the morning and tell him in person, so he sees for himself that I'm all right."

"Good thinking. Right now, what you need is dinner: a good, healthy, nutrition-packed meal to renew those depleted energy resources. Did they give you any food on the plane?"

"I don't know that I'd call it food. Just the usual bag—"

"I didn't think so. What are you in the mood for, that might be open at midnight?"

"Truthfully, I don't feel up to going out, Chris. Besides, I need to do something about the window."

"That won't take much. It just needs to be wedged with something so it can't be slid open from the outside. While you do that I can go out and pick us up something. We'll eat here. What sounds good to you?"

"How about Mama Wu's? I'm pretty sure that's a twenty-four-hour place. But not a whole dinner, I just want a bunch of appetizers we can graze on—egg rolls, rumaki, crispy wonton . . ."

"Excellent choices all. Salt, sugar, and fat, nature's three essential food categories." She grabbed her bag and Alix's keys. "You grab a shower and get comfortable. Back in twenty."

"And barbecued ribs, don't forget the barbecued spare ribs," Alix yelled after her, but the door had already closed.

"Rats," Alix grumbled on her way to the shower. This was definitely not her day.

CHAPTER 5

But luck was with her this time. Chris had heard, after all. Alix could smell the barbecue sauce from the bathroom, where she'd just finished showering and had changed into a comfortable T-shirt and roomy sweatpants. When she came out she saw that Chris had found the place mats and was setting out dishes, plastic utensils, and opened cardboard cartons in the dining nook.

"What a feast!" Alix exulted when she saw it all laid out on the table.

Those were the last words that were spoken for a while. Alix was hungrier than she'd realized, and Chris, a rangy, raw-boned six-footer (six-two in her bare feet, actually), was a reliable trencherman, so a few minutes went by in which their only utterances were grunts and murmurs of appreciation.

It was Chris who made the return to intelligible speech. "All right, time for the important stuff. Now you have to tell me. What's better than getting a badge and a gun?"

Alix looked up serenely from using her chopsticks to haul in her third wonton. "Getting a *man* who has a badge and a gun."

Chris looked back at her with a slight frown and with her head tipped to one side, like a dog that's trying its best to figure out what you're saying, but not having any luck. "Um . . . I'm not sure I understand?" The doubtful uptick at the end seemed to mean she thought she did understand, but couldn't quite believe it.

"Chris, I'm *married!*"

Chris eyed her, continuing her thoughtful chewing. "You're serious."

"Oh, yes."

"And it *is* Ted you're talking about."

"Well, *yeah.*"

Chris put down her chopsticks. "I don't believe it."

"Chris, take my word for it. We were married in Maryland on Saturday morning. By a deputy clerk of the circuit court. We had a two-day honeymoon over the weekend. In Virginia."

"No, I mean I believe it, all right. I . . . just . . . don't . . . *believe* it, if you know what I mean."

Alix, who was enjoying this immensely, knew very well. She would have been amazed if her friend hadn't been amazed. Ted Ellesworth, Alix's husband of three days and eighteen hours now, was the FBI special agent in charge of the Bureau's art squad, and it was he who had recognized the value of Alix's unique skills and gotten her onto the approved list of FBI consultants. They had first met a couple of years ago in New Mexico and had taken instantaneous gut-level dislikes to one another. It hadn't been pretty, and Chris had been right there to see it. Their relationship improved a little with the passage of time, but then took another nosedive a few months later, when they wound up together on assignment on a Mediterranean cruise—so much so that, afterward, both had gone to extreme and sometimes excruciatingly elaborate measures to avoid encountering one another on any of the next three FBI assignments that she had taken under his nominal supervision. A mutual attraction had been there, all right—in spades—and both of them knew it, but a slew of frustrating misunderstandings, misperceptions, and mistaken assumptions had kept them at loggerheads.

More recently, only two months ago, they'd been more or less thrown together again in Palm Springs, on a matter involving a suspect Jackson Pollock painting. They'd taken advantage of the situation to sit down with one another and try to figure out what had gone wrong. They'd succeeded, too, with heartfelt *mea culpa* from both sides for the misapprehensions they'd held or inadvertently fostered. And the result had been—well, the result had been that they'd gone and gotten married this past weekend, on Alix's very next trip east.

"It's not that I'm not happy for you," Chris said, "because I am—I think it's wonderful. And you know how much I love Ted. But isn't it a little, uh, rash? You've just gotten back on speaking terms after staying miles away from each other for months and months. Okay, you took that sailing trip together after Palm Springs—for what, a week?—but is that enough to get married on? You hardly know each other."

"Well, you know, I'm a little on the conservative side when it comes to . . . um, affairs and such—"

Chris honked. "No kidding, tell me about it."

"—and, believe it or not, Ted is too."

"I do believe it, and that's what's so surprising about all this. I would have expected a couple of poky old straight-arrow types like you to be a bit more, well, prudent."

"Prudent how?"

"Well, I believe I've heard somewhere that people who want to get married sometimes get engaged for a while first. Now there's an idea for you."

Alix shook her head. "We're not a couple of nineteen-year-olds, Chris, who don't know what they like or what they want out of life. We weren't halfway through dinner that first night in DC before we came to the conclusion—both of us did—that there was no point in putting things on hold. We couldn't be more right for each other and we knew it. So the next morning we went over to Maryland—you can go through the whole process in one day there—got our license, went to the local courthouse, and we got married." Just hearing herself say those last few words brought another smile to her face.

"Okay, that's hard to argue with," Chris said, "but here's my next question, and this one I'm almost afraid to ask. Does this mean you're going to be leaving Seattle for DC?"

"Absolutely not. I'm not going anywhere." She popped one of the two remaining spring rolls into her mouth.

"Ted's getting himself transferred here?"

"Unfortunately, that's not possible, not with him being in charge of the entire unit. It's got to be done from Washington. So—" She gave a resigned sigh. "—We're both staying where we are, on opposite sides of the country."

Chris put down the barbecued rib she'd been gnawing on and stared at her. "It's going to be a long-distance marriage, then? Is that what you're telling me?"

"Come on now, don't look at me like that. I don't like it either, and neither does Ted, but it's the best we can do under the circumstances. Me, I love my life here, and I do *not* want to live in the DC area. As for Ted, the DC area is where his work is—and he loves his work—so that's where he lives. Besides, that work of his is anything but a forty-hour-a-week job, and when it's undercover it can keep him away and incommunicado for weeks at a time. He couldn't really commit to anything like a normal marriage, not right now, anyway."

"So . . . ?"

"We'll alternate. I'll go back east once a month—more, if I can line up a consulting job that takes me there—and Ted will just come on out here and be with me whenever he can get away for a few days. As long as we can afford it, anyway."

"I guess that's fair enough. So how long will it be now before the newlyweds get to see each other again?"

"Well . . ." Alix hesitated. Even to her own ears, the more she got into the details, the more untenable they sounded. "The fact is, I don't exactly know. I don't even know the next time I can talk to him. He went out on an assignment this morning, an undercover one, which probably means he's going to be completely out of touch for at least—well, I don't really have any idea."

"You mean you're not even allowed to talk to him on the telephone?"

"Unfortunately, that's exactly what I mean. You know Ted, he does it by the book. And the book says that while you're undercover you don't break that cover, except in an emergency. A *real* emergency."

"Like what, if somebody's life depends on it?"

Alix nodded. "That's it."

"But I thought you told that detective you were going to tell Ted about the burglary. How are you planning on doing that?"

"Not Ted himself, Chris. I don't even know where he is, let alone what he's doing. I'll call Jamie Wozniak at his office in the morning, though. She'll get the ball rolling in his absence."

"You don't even know where he is," Chris echoed wonderingly.

"Right."

"And you don't know when he'll be back."

"Right."

"And you're totally out of touch for you don't know how long."

"'Fraid so."

"And you've been married for all of three days."

Alix sighed. "Look, Chris, we'll just have to play it by ear and see how it goes. I certainly don't expect it to stay this way forever."

"Well, I hope it works for you, kid." Alix could see that she was trying to play down her doubts. "You know I wish you both the very, very best."

"I know you do, Chris, thanks. If we can have anywhere near as good a marriage as you and Craig have, I'll be happy. And after all, you two have pretty much the same problems, and you deal with them just fine."

Chris's husband was a pilot with ShareJet, a fractional jet ownership outfit. Although he was based in Seattle, his schedule was anything but predictable, and he was often off to destinations all over the world, sometimes for eight or ten days at a time, while he shuttled clients around or laid over waiting to make the return trip.

"Oh, sure," Chris said, while trying to snag a steamed mini-dumpling with her chopsticks. "We have *exactly* the same problems—except that I always know just where he is and what he's doing, and when he'll be back, and we're in touch three or four times a day the whole time, with texting, or telephone, or email, and . . ."

Alix knew all that, of course, and she was all too aware of how much more difficult the path that she and Ted had taken was going to be. It must have shown in her expression, because Chris, a first-rate reader of moods, stopped in the middle of her sentence. "Forgive me, Alix, what am I doing? Look, I know you and I know Ted, and I have no doubt, no doubt at all, that the two of you will make a go of it. Okay?"

"Okay."

"Good. Oh, the hell with it." Chris tossed one of her chopsticks onto the table and speared the dumpling straight through the middle with the other one, then dipped it in hoisin sauce and popped it into her mouth. "What do you know, tastes just as good this way."

They ate quietly for another minute or two, and then Chris suddenly sat up straight. "Whoa, it just struck me—wasn't Ted part of the team that got your father convicted?"

"He was, indeed."

"So how does he feel about having him for a son-in-law, or have you told him yet?"

"Nope, haven't told him yet."

"Oh, my. It was a long time ago and all, and long before you and Ted knew each other, of course, and Geoff is the sweetest man in the world, and I can't imagine anyone who spent eight years in jail bearing less of a grudge about it—"

"But?"

"But I think there may be a teeny-tiny little difficulty there, a slight fly in the ointment."

"More like an elephant," Alix said.

"And is that why you're not wearing a ring? I've been wondering."

"Well, two reasons. Ted did give me a beautiful ring, an antique, and I love it, but it's too big, it'll have to be resized. A jeweler's got it now, and, truthfully, I'm not going to be putting any pressure on him to get it done. I need to figure out how to break the news to Geoff before I start walking around with it on my finger."

How Geoff was going to take the news was the one concern she'd had about her newly changed circumstances and it had been chafing away at her all weekend. Her father, Geoffrey London, had been a prominent and respected art conservator—at the Metropolitan Museum of Art, no less—before morphing into the "most notorious forger of the decade" (thank you, *New York Times*), throwing away his reputation, eight years of his life, and every penny of the once-substantial family fortune in the doing. Alix had been nineteen at the time, and for a while it had seemed to her that her life had been destroyed as well. But now she was back on her feet, a long way from rich, but an even longer way from destitute. And quite astonishingly so was he, the owner and founder of not one but two perfectly legitimate (knock on wood), flourishing, art-related businesses in Seattle—with his old friend and fellow ex-forger, ex-con Beniamino "Tiny" Abbatista, her "*zio* Beni," working productively alongside him.

How strange, she thought. She had loved—truly loved—only three men in her life, and two of them were jailbirds and the third one was a cop. The cop knew about the jailbirds (having helped put one of them away), but the jailbirds knew nothing about the cop.

And therein lay the elephant. For years after the catastrophic debacle of her father's self-inflicted disaster, she and Geoff had been estranged—admittedly, not by his choice, but by her bitterness—but now she'd grown so close to him again that she couldn't bear to think of causing him pain. He was aware that his daughter did a little consulting for the FBI's art squad and he appreciated the irony, often joking about it. But a deeply personal relationship—and how much more personal did relationships get—with its top guy? That couldn't help but distress him, and from it he had been most carefully shielded.

"So for how long are you planning to keep it a secret?"

"I don't know. For now you're the only one I want to know. I'm sort of newsworthy at the moment, thanks to that damn magazine, and if word got around that I was married, it'd be bound to reach him. He has the most amazing pipeline in the universe when it comes to art world gossip." She thought for a moment. "Well, the second most."

"I'll take that as a compliment," Chris said, then peered at Alix for a long time before delivering her honk of a laugh. "Alix, God bless you, you are really one of a kind. I ask you, who else in the world would blithely walk into a marriage to a man who can't be reached, and who's God knows where, doing God knows what, for God knows how long— and, oh, incidentally, just happened to be the man who put her father in the slammer for eight years?"

"He wasn't *the* man, just one of the men."

"Oh, yes, right. Well, I can certainly see how that would make all the difference in the world."

CHAPTER 6

"Good morning, sweetheart."

Ted. Alix had been sleeping soundly, but she came instantly awake. *Sweetheart.* The homely, everyday word thrilled and soothed her at the same time. "But aren't you supposed to be on assignment?"

"I am, yes, so, technically, this is strictly against the rules, but . . . well, I couldn't help it, just had to hear your voice. Believe me, I've taken all kinds of precautions."

Her maddeningly by-the-book husband flouting the rules, though? Amazing, totally out of character, and wonderfully endearing. She pressed the cell phone against her cheek to be closer to him. "I'm so glad to hear *your* voice. I was already missing you . . . terribly."

"Same here," he said warmly, then laughed. "But my God, look at what a terrible influence you are on me, and we haven't even been married a week yet. I didn't wake you, did I? Your voice sounds a little muffled. It *is* almost eight o'clock there, isn't it?"

"Yes, ordinarily I'd have been up hours ago, but I had kind of a long night."

The next twenty-five minutes were given to her telling him about the burglary, the visit from Detective Durando (whose name and number Ted took down), and the earlier call from Ferrante (ditto).

"I can probably find out some more about this Ferrante," he said. "I'll check with Durando and see if he has any objection to my horning in at the Italian end."

"I already mentioned it to him as a possibility. He's all for it."

"That's good. I'll get going on it as soon as we're done. Uh, Alix, you *are* okay, aren't you? I know how traumatic something like this can be. You'd tell me, wouldn't—"

"I'm fine, Ted. Honestly. It's just the mirror that has me a little down."

"Okay, I believe you. But do me a favor and get that window taken care of right away, will you? Today. And make sure the others are secure. And the door too. And—"

"Sir, yes sir!" Alix barked into the phone and heard a forbearing sigh from his end of the line.

"Now. Let's talk about the mirror," he said, cooling things down a bit. "There's something that's got me wondering." He then asked the same question Durando had. Was it possible that it was worth more than she thought?

"I really don't think so, but Ferrante might have thought it was."

"An art dealer make a mistake like that? Pretty doubtful."

"I don't see that that necessarily follows, Ted. You know as well as I do that you don't exactly have to take an exam and get a license to call yourself an art dealer. All you have to do is put a sign in your window, and *voila*, you're an art dealer."

"Well, sure, but then how do you explain the burglary any other way than *somebody* thinks it's valuable?"

"Ted, consider: You're imagining that little mirror is some kind of masterwork by some artist-craftsman like—I don't know, somebody like Benvenuto Cellini? Worth hundreds of thousands of dollars, or maybe millions—"

"I don't know about Cellini, but yes, that is exactly what I'm thinking."

Alix was getting tired of having to contend with this line of argument. "A masterpiece," she said testily. "Worth millions. That Tiny's just going to blithely leave with some little girl he knows, and forget all about it. Aside from how ridiculous that is, where would he even *get* something like that?"

She clamped her teeth together, but the words were out, and Ted jumped on them.

"Are you serious?" He had picked up the edge in her voice and was reacting in kind. "Where would *Benny Abbatista*"—Ted typically referred to Tiny this way when he had something critical to say about him, probably because it sounded more like a gangster's name—"get hold of a stolen piece of art? How would *Benny Abbatista* even know somebody he could get one from? I sure can't imagine. Come on, Alix, I know you love the guy, but you seem to be forgetting that he was once—"

"And don't you think it's time to forget?" she snapped. "That was all a lot of years ago."

"Yes, and a lot of years ago is when he gave it to you!"

Neither of them spoke. The prickly exchange thrummed in their ears.

"Ted?" Alix said meekly after a few seconds. "Are we having our first fight?"

"Is that what that was? Yes, I guess so. Oh, hell, it was my fault for being so snarky, and I apologize."

"No, I was the snarky one, and I apologize. My fault."

"No, my fault," Ted insisted.

"No, my fault. I started it."

"Alix?" Ted asked. "Are we having our second fight?"

That got them both laughing. "Let's just hope they never get any worse than that," Alix said.

"And they never will, not if I can help it," Ted told her with conviction. "Look, I'd better hang up now. It's late afternoon in Italy, and if I want to get hold of the *carabinieri* today I should call right now. I probably shouldn't call you again, honey, but if I have anything to tell you I'll pass it on to Jamie and she'll fill you in."

They finished with a sweetie-pie, lovey-dovey kind of goodbye that neither of them, only a week ago, could have stomached hearing, let alone actually participating in.

Alix was smiling as she hung up. *Boy, love really makes you goofy*, she was thinking.

•   •   •

Later that morning Alix drove down to the old warehouse that was headquarters for her father's primary business enterprise, Venezia Fine Art Imports, "purveyor of imported, high-quality reproductions of fine *objets d'art*, in quantity and at reasonable prices." That the main countries from which these high-quality *objets* were imported were Guyana and Bangladesh, Venezia's website neglected to mention.

In real-world terms, Venezia was in the business of supplying cut-rate, cost-conscious hotel and motel chains with framed prints and items like ashtrays and soap holders to tone up the rooms of their establishments. Unlike the wares of other such purveyors, each picture from Venezia came with four pre-attached metal eyelets so that it could be screwed to the wall in the event that some guest might mistakenly think he had brought it with him. This inspired innovation had made Geoff one of the leaders of the pack.

The two-story warehouse, which he now owned, was in Seattle's forever gentrifying but stubbornly grungy Industrial District, a warren of rail yards, grimy, brown-brick warehouses, and mysterious manufacturing establishments south of downtown. (One of Geoff's neighbors had an ancient sign on its facade: Buffalo Sanitary Wipers. What exactly these might be, Alix had chosen not to ask.)

Geoff's living quarters were on the floor above the no-frills ground floor occupied by the company. As Alix pushed her way through the dented steel street door and traversed the ever-dank, raw-concrete corridor toward the packing and storage areas, her heart was in her mouth.

This was where Tiny worked, and her throat had dried up at the prospect of telling him his beautiful creation was gone.

She needn't have worried; he wasn't there. Instead, Alix was greeted by another of Geoff's rehabilitation projects, one Frisby Macdowell, ex-professor of art history and, according to Geoff, an astonishingly good forger of early twentieth-century Neoplastic and Constructivist art, an ability it had taken him years to perfect. It had then come as quite a blow to him to find that no one since the 1960s had any interest in buying even a *real* Neoplastic or Constructivist painting. Concluding that a career change was called for, Frisby had turned to faking Marcel Duchamp and George Grosz instead, both of whom were still in vogue. The problem was that he didn't have quite the same knack with these two artists, and he'd wound up in prison for four years on multiple charges of fraud. On his release, a job from Geoff had been waiting for him. Like Tiny, he had taken it up with sincere gratitude and he had now been there for almost a year. And he had seemingly taken to the straight and narrow path.

He looked up from the partitioned carton he was loading with Venezia's "Aztec-style faux onyx soap dishes" (made at a family sweatshop in the Bangladeshi village of Jhara Barsha). They were Geoff's biggest seller, being extremely popular with departing motel guests but cheap enough to be reordered by the gross. "Hello there, Alix. Looking for your pater? He's upstairs in his lair."

"Thanks, Frisby."

She walked through the work area to the waiting freight elevator, pulled the gate closed behind her, and punched Up. After a creaking, grinding ride of twenty feet or so there was another depressing concrete corridor, lit, like the one below, with two bare sixty-watt bulbs that hung from the stained ceiling. Then there was another forbidding steel door, the kind you'd see leading to the death chamber in an old prison movie, except that this one had a modern keypad on the wall next to it.

Only two people other than Geoff himself had the code: Alix and Tiny. Even Frisby and the part-time workers couldn't get in without being invited. Geoff wasn't hiding anything or especially worried about intruders, he just valued having a space to himself—merely one of his many contradictions. He was a thoroughly outgoing, friendly, sociable man who also loved his privacy. Or maybe it wasn't such a contradiction. After eight years in a ten-by-twelve cell shared with another prisoner, she supposed, anyone would long for a space that was his alone.

She punched in the code, the lock clicked, the door swung open, and she stepped into another world, as up-to-date—and even trendy—as the rest of the warehouse was tired and antiquated. Geoff's living quarters were sunlit and airy, took up the entire upper floor, and consisted of a high-ceilinged, three-thousand-square-foot loft, brightened by big arched windows and more than a dozen skylights, and broken into "rooms" by handsome, movable fabric partitions.

Only one corner, with its truly gargantuan window facing the northern sky—for centuries the artist's preferred source of light—was a real *room*, with actual lath-and-plaster walls and a door, and that was Geoff's studio, recently constructed and outfitted to accommodate his newest venture. Genuine Fakes by Geoffrey London had begun as a lark, but was now a profitable business of its own. And an enjoyable one. Geoff relished the delicious fact that he had come up with a way to capitalize on his unique attributes: he had been both a distinguished and sought-after restorer and (far more famously) an internationally known forger, in both of which he took great pride. It was the best of all worlds. He was painting his meticulous fakes, which he loved to do; he got to sign his own name to them, which he loved even more; and he was getting paid for them ($5,000 to $15,000), which he *really* loved. And it was all perfectly legal. Which absolutely took the cake.

She rapped on the inside of the door and yelled "Hello, Geoff, it's me!"

No answer. He was in his studio, then, at work on another master-piece and oblivious to the world. The familiar, pungent, oily smells of paints and solvents verified that, and she headed directly there. Even before he came into view through the open studio door she could tell what the current project was from the many enlarged, high-definition detail-photos that were taped to the walls: the *Arnolfini Marriage*, painted by Jan van Eyck in 1434 and generally credited with being not only the foundation of the Flemish school, but also the first major Western artwork to use oil paints as its medium, egg tempera having ruled since Egyptian times. Alix had stood before the original in London's National Gallery many times, bowled over by its luminosity and translucence after almost six centuries. A heck of a technique, never surpassed, but if anyone could come close, it was Geoffrey London.

Once through the studio doorway, she found Geoff himself at his easel, studying his fake-in-progress with great intensity, the handle of a slender brush clenched between his teeth. She rapped on the doorjamb. "Good morning, Geoff."

He glanced over his shoulder. Then he extricated the brush so that his fixed expression could relax into the happy smile her appearance invariably brought.

"Good morning, my darling, how lovely to see you. I didn't know when to expect you back. Welcome home!"

Somehow, the old scandal and all those years in jail that had followed it had failed to dull the crisp, bright edge of the English accent that had never left him despite his forty-year stay in America. It had shrunken him, though, so that where once he'd looked like a merry, youthful Santa Claus with a prematurely gray beard, now he looked like what he was, a bent old man with a white beard, who looked a decade older than his actual early seventies. As usual her first sight of him after she hadn't seen him for a while made her heart sink, but the moment he spoke the twinkling, cheery, old Geoff was back.

He stepped to the side of the easel so she could see it, revealing that the new painting had hardly any paint on it yet, just a few tentative dabs of malachite and russet on the wife's dress. The intricate pencil sketch, however, was extraordinarily thorough.

"The underdrawing's wonderful," Alix said. "I didn't think you usually did such a detailed one."

"I don't, but van Eyck did. And you know me, when I say 'genuine fake,' I mean *genuine*. Tell me what you think about it."

"Well, let's see." She came closer. "I do notice a few little deviations from the original. Their faces—"

"Are the faces of Mr. and Mrs. Ernst Schulte of Hamburg, Germany, drawn from photographs of thirty years ago"—he gestured at a grouping of black and white photos among the pictures on the wall—"in accordance with the Schultes' wishes. Does your eagle-eye detect any other differences?"

"Well, the new bride seems to be not quite so pregnant as the old one."

"Yes, also in accord with their wishes. Understandably so."

Whether the new Mrs. Arnolfini of 1434 had actually been pregnant or was showing off a stylish, high-waisted fashion of the times was still a bone of contention among art scholars, enough so that, in an apparent bow to propriety, the National Gallery itself was no longer calling it the *Arnolfini Marriage*; it was now simply the *Arnolfini Portrait*. Whatever the lady's marital status, she certainly *looked* pregnant—about seven months' worth, would have been Alix's guess. About the fashion theory Alix had her doubts.

Geoff seemed to be waiting for her to say something more, but when she didn't, he cleared his throat. "Ah, nothing else?"

She shook her head. "No . . ."

"Nothing different about any of the other faces?"

"What? There are no other faces . . . Wait . . ." She focused on the small, convex mirror that hung on the wall behind the couple and reflected not only their backs, but beyond them several little figures, one of whom was generally thought to be the painter, van Eyck himself. But in Geoff's version the tiny face was nothing like that of the lean, somber, clean-shaven van Eyck, but a rounder one, somehow made to look merry, with a small, neat beard drawn in. It was all done with a few pencil strokes, but there was no mistaking who it was supposed to be.

Alix burst out laughing. "Did the Schultes request that too?"

"No, that was my own contribution, made, may I point out, at no additional charge."

"How generous of you. And I'm sure it's got nothing to do with your ego, it's just a clever way of ensuring that no future crook ever gets away with erasing your signature and putting in van Eyck's in its place. Correct?"

"Exactly! The thought of that slacker van Eyck getting credit for my own brilliant work would be intolerable."

She had continued to look at the drawing while he spoke. "You know, Geoff, I really am impressed. Not many . . . people"—she'd almost said "forgers"—"would take on a van Eyck. I had no idea you could do him."

He drew himself up. "My dear girl, have you forgotten? You are looking at the most celebrated forger of the decade."

"Am I mistaken, or wasn't the usual word of choice 'notorious'?" She knew that he would regard it as a compliment, unlike almost anybody else in the world.

He replied with a shrug. "Six of one, half-dozen of the other. In any case, of *course* I can do van Eyck." He *hmphed*. "Really."

And now, still smiling, he finally came forward to hug her. "Enough about my poor efforts. I want to know how things went in Washington. I'll put up some coffee or pour some orange juice if you like, and you can tell me everything that happened."

Oh, no. Not bloody likely, as he himself might say. She mumbled a few words about the Rubens that turned out not to be a Rubens, then leaned over the easel, searching for something to talk about before he probed any further. She settled on the "ground"—the foundation layer laid down on the canvas, or in this case the panel, to provide a good base for the pigments to adhere to. "Geoff, that's a chalk and glue ground, isn't it? But it's sort of . . . yellowish. Why is that?"

"That's not the ground, Alix, that's a film of drying-oil that I've applied *over* the ground—"

"To make it less absorbent? But there are so many more efficient, less time-consuming ways to do that now. Who uses drying-oil anymore?"

"Nobody, but—"

"—van Eyck did," she finished for him. "Got it."

"Exactly. And Mr. Schulte, who commissioned this work, has requested the deluxe $15,000 treatment, which means it is being executed *precisely* as van Eyck himself would have done. Well, as nearly as I can approach his technique," he added in a rare show of modesty.

"I understand, Geoff, and that's commendable, but when it's finished no one's going to be able to see the ground. Seriously, what difference does it make what's underneath?"

Geoff's chin came up. "It makes an ethical difference, as I would have expected you of all people to understand. The man is paying for the treatment to be as authentic as possible, and I am honoring his wishes. And what, may I ask, brings that dubious smile to your ordinarily lovely face?"

She was smiling because it always struck her as funny, and charming in its way, that a totally unrepentant old rascal of a forger could be as dedicated to a set of uncompromising ethical standards as her extraordinary father was. What made it so charming, and *him* so charming, was that it was true. He *had* been a forger—maybe he still wasn't quite a hundred percent straight; she'd never entirely gotten rid of her last lingering doubts on that subject—but he was also (with the possible exception of Ted) the most moral, principled man she knew. It was still hard for her to believe that a combination like that could genuinely exist in one person. From what she'd seen of the world, her father was the only living example.

Alix wasn't about to go into this, though. The yellowish ground had served its purpose of diverting him from hearing about *everything* that had gone on in Washington. "Geoff," she said, "I had a bit of a shock yesterday when I got home."

Over a pitcher of fresh orange juice—Geoff got it delivered daily from a local grocery supply—in a grouping of chairs that overlooked a surprising and lovely brick-pathed, brick-walled little garden he'd put in behind the warehouse, she told him what she'd come home to.

She succeeded at downplaying it, so that his reaction was nothing more explosive than a natural parental concern, along with some predictable tut-tutting about the way things were in the world today.

"They didn't really do any damage, and nothing that they took is worth very much," Alix said. "But Tiny's mirror . . . that really hurts. You know how much I loved that thing."

"I do, indeed."

"I dread telling him it's gone. If I can summon up the nerve, I'll ask him to make me another after a little time passes. I'm really going to miss it."

"There's no need for nerve, my dear. Tiny would jump straight out of this window if you asked him to, so I expect he'd be happy to comply."

Alix finished her orange juice and stood up. "Is he around, Dad? I may as well face it now."

Geoff had remained in his chair. "As a matter of fact, he isn't." A tiny frown creased the space between his eyebrows.

"He's not here today?" Alix felt herself growing tense. Something was wrong.

"Alix, I haven't seen him since Friday."

"Four days?" She sat down again. "That's longer than usual, isn't it?"

"Longer than *ever*."

She was aware that Tiny, while a loyal and efficient employee, was a bit . . . different . . . in a number of ways, one of which was his habit of occasionally disappearing for a couple of days at a time. When he returned to Venezia, always ready to more than make up for the lost time, he offered no explanation and by mutual agreement was asked no questions. But *four* days? Now there was a scowl on her face too. Tiny's mirror stolen . . . Tiny himself missing . . . ?

"That's worrisome," she said.

"More than you realize." He was looking down at his steepled fingers. It had been a long time since she'd seen him so somber. "He doesn't have any money, you see. Well, no more than a couple of hundred dollars, surely. I can't imagine what he's living on."

"But he's only been gone a few days. Couldn't he use checks, credit cards?"

"He doesn't have a checking account, he doesn't have any credit cards, no stocks, no savings account. Tiny . . . well, he doesn't like to leave a paper trail. It's an old habit—from the ah, mm, old days—that he's never quite shaken."

The *old days*. As generally used by Geoff, the phrase meant what it meant to anybody: some period in the more or less distant past. But that telltale "ah, mm" in front of it—that signified that he was talking about the very particular time period during which he and Tiny were on the wrong side of the law and often not more than a few steps ahead of it. Back then, the need to "get away for a while" popped up quite a lot, in Geoff's case as well as Tiny's. Alix remembered very well her mother's frustration with his absences, although, as children do, Alix herself took them for granted. Didn't everybody's father disappear for a few days every now and then?

"I still don't understand," Alix said. "He must have plenty of *cash*, then. I've always assumed you paid him pretty well."

"Of course I do," Geoff said, bristling just a little. "His current salary is thirteen hundred dollars a week, with another few hundred when he's assisting me with a Genuine Fake."

"But that's more than sixty thousand dollars a year—"

"Closer to seventy, actually. There's quite a lot of Genuine Fake work these days."

"So how can he not have any money?"

Geoff sighed. "All right, let me explain the situation. Let's simply say that Tiny isn't much of a money manager—which puts it extremely mildly. And he knows it. He prefers *not* to have a lot of cash available. So, at his request, he receives about eight hundred dollars a week in cash, the greater part of which probably goes for his rent."

"He pays his rent in cash?"

"I told you, he pays *everything* in cash. To continue: Another two hundred goes to his family in Italy—he has me send it directly to the post office in Pieve di Teco, which Wikipedia says is a tiny village in the Ligurian Alps—and the rest is put, by me, into a mutual fund, for which he's the beneficiary—but it's in my name, so that he has to ask me to get access to it. So yes, he's been building up a nest egg, but by his own choice, he can't get at it on his own."

"Well, have you tried at all to get ahold of him?"

"How? I have no phone number for him, no email address."

"You *don't*?"

"Alix, you have to understand. Tiny is his own man, one of a kind in more ways than you know. And he prefers to keep, as they say nowadays, a low profile."

"Well, what about going to where he lives to check on him? For all we know he might be—" The expression on Geoff's face stopped her. "You don't even know where he lives?"

She really didn't know why she should be surprised. Geoff and Tiny were both wonderfully sunny, open men in most respects, but there were chapters of their lives that remained sealed up tight, even from her—even from each other, as she'd just learned. A common trait among ex-cons, probably.

"No, I don't," Geoff said. "Tiny is a very private person. I don't like to infringe . . ." He brightened. "Wait a moment, I *do* know something that might be helpful. I know where he has his morning coffee. The most authentic *prima colazione* in Seattle, so he claims. Not only true Italian caffè latte, but almond croissants and brioches that are the closest thing to Milan. It's called . . ." He tapped his lower lip, trying to remember the name. "No good. Senior moment, can't think of it, but I know that it's up near Pioneer Square, on that pedestrian street, the one with all the galleries—"

"Occidental Mall?"

"That's it, yes! They might know where he lives."

"Caffè Umbria, I think you mean."

"Right!"

"Okay, good, but if he doesn't let even you know his address, why would he tell the people who work at a coffee shop?"

"Well, he might not have done. But if he's there most mornings, they might have gotten to talking, and who knows, it might have popped out."

"You're right, it's worth a try."

"Yes," Geoff said. "We're probably making a mountain out of a mole hill about the whole thing, though."

"Yes, we probably are."

"Coincidences do happen, after all."

"Yes, they do. All the same . . ."

Now they both rose. "We'll take my car," Geoff said.

"No, thank you. I've driven with you before. I consider myself lucky to still be among the living."

Geoff gave his head a rueful shake. "How sharper than a serpent's tooth—"

"Thank you, King Lear. My car's in the lot. Let's go."

On the slow, rumbling descent in the freight elevator, something occurred to her. "Wait a minute. If you pay him in cash, and he doesn't leave a paper trail, how does he pay his taxes? How do you pay his Social—"

Geoff's face clouded over. "Er . . ."

"Or don't I want to know?"

He was silent for a few moments, but as he swung open the elevator gate, he said, "Alix. Tiny—my oldest, dearest friend Tiny—*insists* that he has to have it this way . . . for reasons of his own, I should add, to which I'm not privy . . . and I can assure you that I'm not going to send him on his way for the sake of a few trivial rules. So, yes, Tiny's employment is off the books."

"A few trivial rules?" She wasn't exactly surprised, but she was disappointed. "Don't you realize how much trouble it could get you into?"

"I realize it perfectly well, but I should think you would see that the ethics of loyalty and friendship do not permit me to let the man down."

Ethics again. She couldn't help sighing.

How in the world was she ever going to juggle her relationship with the two most important men in her life, and the relationship between them? It was one thing when they occupied separate compartments in her existence, but as of last weekend they were in the same one, and it was the most important of all: family, the only real family she had. Two men with sincere, deeply felt views on morality, views that governed large parts of their lives, but oh, what a difference! Of course, only one of them knew they were related now, and that made it easier, but that would have to end some day (well, wouldn't it?). She foresaw a rocky road ahead.

When they got to the car, he spoke again. "You will be glad to know, however, that Frisby and the others are strictly on the books, and I do rigorously pay all my own taxes, business and personal."

"You're right," she said, her smile coming back. Maybe there was hope after all. "I am glad."

CHAPTER 7

Occidental Mall is a one-block stretch of Occidental Avenue, in Seattle's generally scruffy Pioneer Square district, that has been converted to a handsome pedestrian-only zone. A tree-shaded, sun-flecked passageway surfaced with rose-colored paving stones, it is lined with mostly upscale galleries, boutique shops, and, near its southeast corner, Caffè Umbria. Alix had been in the coffee shop a few times for a mid-afternoon latte, and she agreed with Tiny's evaluation of their coffee, to say nothing of the gelato, which she rated Seattle's best. Outside were sun-dappled tables populated by contented-looking people who were enjoying coffee, conversation, and newspapers, and looking as if they'd been there awhile and meant to stay a considerable while longer. Just as in Italy, indeed. If she and Geoff hadn't been there on more serious business, she would have suggested that they take one of the tables and have a cappuccino themselves.

Inside it was as she remembered: roomy, pleasant, not too crowded, not too vacant, with just the right amount of quiet, coffee-house buzz.

"Good morning, we're trying to contact an old acquaintance," Geoff told the barista. "Unfortunately, we don't know where he's living at the moment, but we do know that Caffè Umbria is a frequent breakfast stop for him. A rather large gentleman, Italian—"

"You mean like Italian from Italy?" the barista said, pausing in his work at the machine.

"More like Italian from Little Italy," Alix supplied.

"Big Italian-American guy who comes in here for his *prima colazione*," the barista said. "Well, that gets it down to only about a thousand or so. Could you maybe narrow it down a little more for me? *Espresso con panna!*" he yelled, setting two small cups on the counter. "*Espresso macchiato!*"

"His name is Beniamino Abbatista," Geoff said. "Everyone calls him Tiny."

The barista was shaking his head. Near him, the employee at the register, who was working with a line of customers but had overheard their conversation, was doing the same. "Old guy or young guy?" she asked.

"Young," said Geoff.

"Old," said Alix.

The cashier laughed. "I guess it's a question of perspective. How old?"

"Late fifties," Geoff said, smiling. "Ancient as far as you three are concerned."

Both of the employees shook their heads some more. "As I said," the barista said, "that still describes a lot of people, and I doubt if I know any of their addresses. How about you, Carla?"

"Could be that he pays with a credit card," she offered, "so you might be able to track him down through that, but you'd probably have to go through the police to do it."

Geoff sighed. "Well, thank you for—"

Alix had an inspired thought. "He's got this pocket watch that plays music when he opens it. He takes it out about once every ten minutes."

"Once every bloody minute," Geoff amended under his breath.

"Oh, him!" The barista chortled. "When you said 'rather large gentleman,' you meant 'large,' as in 'UPS-truck-large.' Yeah, he's opened that thing in here a couple of times, and you have to love it. It's like a sing-along. All these other old *paisanos*—excuse me, middle-aged Italian gentlemen—hum right along with it. Seems like a nice guy, but as to where he lives, I don't have a—"

"*I* might know," Carla said. "Be back in a sec, Monte," she told the next person in line and motioned Geoff and Alix to the front window.

"You see, up the block, Perigord Galleries? That green doorway right before it? That goes up to the apartments and studios and things they have on the upstairs floor. Well, I've seen your man go up there sometimes after he comes out of here in the morning."

"Thank you," Alix said. "We'll give it a try."

"It'll probably take a key," the barista put in. "You'll need to ask at Perigord." He twirled an imaginary mustache and put on a French accent. "Monsieur Jean-Denis de la Porte. Oo, la la."

◆ ◆ ◆

As it turned out, neither the mustache nor the accent was imaginary. M. Jean-Denis de la Porte possessed both: a fussy, waxed, jet-black, *moustache* worthy of Hercule Poirot and a rich, fruity accent not heard since the demise of Maurice Chevalier.

"I have not seen him to come or to go for several days, but this is not so unusual. Always he returns, eventually."

"Yes, I know," Geoff said, "he's the same with me, but in the past if he were going to be gone more than a day or two he always checked with me to see if I needed him."

"Needed him?"

"Yes, he works at my business." Geoff took a business card from his wallet and handed it to the gallery owner, who scrutinized it with care, looking from the card to Geoff and then back again. "London, London . . ." he mused, trying to place the name.

"Correct, I'm Geoffrey London," said Geoff a little impatiently. "Do you suppose it would be possible for us—"

"And *you*"—de la Porte turned to Alix with a sudden, smiling burst of recognition—"you are the Whisperer of Art, is that not so? From your photograph I know you!"

Alix managed to convert the resultant instinctive grimace into something that she hoped might pass for a smile. "Yes, that's me," she agreed, resolving afresh to swear off publicity "opportunities" for the foreseeable future, or better yet, forever. "And we're both very concerned about Mr. Abbatista. We're afraid that he might be ill or that something might have happened to him. Would it be possible for us to check on him upstairs?"

He hesitated. "I have a key, of course, but, you know, we don't like . . ." A hesitation and then an elaborate Gallic shrug. "Ah, well, for the Whisperer of Art, an exception, it can be made." With a snap of his fingers he summoned an assistant and spoke in rapid French, of which Alix could only follow the gist. The assistant, Moira, was to show the lady and the gentleman to M. Abbatista's apartment upstairs, and if there were no response, to open the door for them and accompany them inside for a brief time. Did Moira recognize the lady, by the way? No? Had she not seen the new *Art World Insider*? No? Well, treat her with every courtesy. We have a celebrity in our little shop.

It wasn't necessary to go back to the street to get to the stairwell. There was another door that led to it from the gallery, and as they followed a few steps behind Moira, Geoff said: "This is a day of mingled pride and sadness for me, Alix. A watershed. The torch has been passed. My daughter is now the family *célébrité*. The child has become more renowned than her aged and passé parent."

"For maybe one more week," Alix said, "until the next issue of that damn magazine comes out."

"But, really, that man had *no* idea of who I am. Wouldn't you think the owner of a prominent art gallery would at least . . . ah, well, fame is fleeting, my child. Enjoy it while you may."

Alix was laughing. "Most people would be thrilled *not* to be instantly recognized as the world's most notorious forger. Not my father. Him, it makes crabby. Amazing."

"It's only that people forget so quickly. Three or four years ago, he would have recognized me the second I walked in."

"I'd say that's a moot point. Three or four years ago you wouldn't have been walking in. You were still doing time at Lompoc."

"Well, yes, there is that," Geoff allowed.

The stairs led up to a pleasant, carpeted hallway with several open storerooms and a single polished door with an empty nameplate on it. There was a buzzer, which Moira pressed, and then, after a few seconds, pressed again. When there was still no answer she inserted her key and turned the knob. Alix felt a knot forming in her stomach. Please, God, don't let . . .

Her unfinished prayer, if that's what it was, was answered. No body on the floor, no body in the bed. She breathed more easily.

The wood-floored, brick-walled apartment was monklike; sparingly furnished, but spic-and-span, with nothing out of place. Bed crisply made; no dirty dishes in the kitchen sink (or even clean ones on the drain board); no clothes lying around. Depressingly neat, really, like a motel unit that had just been through its between-guests servicing. All it needed was that germicidal deodorant smell.

The living room closet was filled with clean, tidily hung shirts, trousers, and jackets, and a shelving unit held socks and underclothing, all smartly folded. A partition in the closet separated the clothes from a washer-dryer combination. On the little shelf above it were an opened box of Tide, a measuring cup, and a plastic bottle of Downy Spring Lavender fabric softener. She realized suddenly and with shame that she had never, not once in all these years, given any thought to where or how Tiny might live, and the sight of these homely instruments of domesticity moved her. Did that big-hearted, slow-moving, slow-thinking, oversized lunk really troll the supermarket aisles with his cart, searching for his favorite Spring Lavender fabric softener—as opposed, say, to the April Fresh line? The image made her want to laugh and cry at the same time.

Moira had gotten antsy. "Everything looks all right to me," she said as they walked through the bedroom. "There's no sign of any problem. Are you ready to go?"

As she spoke, Alix noticed a small leather tray on top of the bedroom dresser. In it, in addition to a comb, a few coins, and a couple of ballpoints, was an object that made her breath catch in her throat. She touched Geoff on the arm to point it out. His barely perceptible nod told her that he had already seen it for himself.

"Yes, thank you, we can go now," he said to Moira.

CHAPTER 8

Once out in Occidental Mall again, Alix was the first to speak. "Not good."

"Not good at all," Geoff answered. "He'd never have left it behind."

"Not willingly, no."

What they were talking about—what had so seized her attention on the dresser—was the nineteenth-century musical pocket watch Alix had mentioned at the Umbria. It had been a gift to Tiny from her, and he had very clearly treasured it as much as she had the mirror that he'd given to her so many years earlier. It had taken her months of Internet searching to find just the right one: gold, engraved, and—most importantly—with a tiny music box inside that tinkled *Vieni sul Mar*, the lilting old Italian barcarolle that Tiny had so sweetly sung to her while she'd sat on his lap as a four-year-old. He loved the song a lot, he'd told her, because when he'd been even younger than she was, his grandfather had had a pocket watch that played it, and *Nonno Luigi* had taught him the words and had delighted him by letting him open the cover and play the music all by himself.

When Alix had given it to him last year and he'd pressed the tab that opened it, and the lovely melody had come floating out, she'd seen how his Adam's apple pumped and his eyes glistened. Ever after, he was a changed man. Until then one of the least time-conscious people in the world—he didn't wear a wristwatch—he now rarely passed up an opportunity to haul out the old timepiece and check the time. Alix loved watching his slow, closed-eyed grin whenthe lid clicked open and the tune began to tinkle out.

That he might sometimes leave the watch in his room when he went to the Umbria for breakfast was believable; that he would leave it behind if he were going away for days was not.

"Unthinkable," said Geoff, as if he'd been tuned directly into her thoughts. Then he stood there looking a little muddled, as if he'd lost track of what they were talking about. Alix's throat suddenly tightened. She worried about him these days. He'd come out of prison a lot frailer—a lot older—than he'd been when he'd gone in. His mind was certainly still sharp; he was as witty and charming and seemingly capable as ever. But there was about him now a vulnerability, a fragility, that hadn't been there before. It didn't surprise her—prison would do that to a person, she supposed, and so would being in one's seventies. Still she couldn't help cosseting him a little, although she did her best to hide it.

Casually, she pointed to a couple of folding chairs that someone had placed near the two decorative totem poles in the center lane of the mall. "I could stand to get off my feet for a while, Dad. Why don't we sit down for a minute and go over what we know and see if we can figure out what we're dealing with."

"Why, certainly, if you need to rest," he said, lifting one eyebrow to let her know the old boy knew when he was being patronized.

She laughed. Hiding what she was thinking—especially from Geoff—would never be among her strengths. "All right," she said as they sat down, "we know that, wherever Tiny's gone, and for whatever reason, he left unwillingly—and suddenly. The watch tells us that much. And the closet full of clothes."

"Unwillingly, yes, but not involuntarily," said Geoff. "No one dragged him out of that apartment—kidnapped him—without his cooperation. He left of his own volition."

"I don't follow you. Why would you think that?"

"The apartment. The place was neat as a pin; I'm surprised you didn't notice. No sign of a struggle at all."

"I did notice, but how much struggle would there have been if some-one had walked in on him with a gun? Or two or three guys with guns?"

Geoff smiled. "It could have been six men with guns, as far as that goes, or ten. Tiny wouldn't have gone quietly, I assure you. The place would have been a wreck."

She sensed he was right, although the only side of Tiny she'd ever seen was the amiable, tame-bear one, the *Zio* Beni one. If he'd ever been angry about anything in her presence, she had no memory of it.

"I hope you're right, Geoff."

"I'm right. I'll tell you what I think. I think that, for reasons of his own, Tiny is running away from something. Or someone."

Alix hunched her shoulders. "Could be. So where does that get us?"

It didn't get them anywhere. Neither of them wanted to suggest that he might have been waylaid, not in his apartment but elsewhere, and that he might perhaps already be lying dead in some out-of-the-way drainage ditch, although these possibilities were in both their minds. Tiny had been on the wrong side of the law for a long time, and even Geoff didn't know all the details. Who knew what his associates had been like, who knew how many people were out there with scores to set-tle and payback to be collected? And once you got beyond those awful possibilities, everything else was groundless speculation, and dead-end speculation at that. No, they agreed, best to stick with their working hypothesis: Tiny was alive—alive, and on the run.

"Which implies," Alix said, "that he doesn't want to be found, even by you. Otherwise, he'd have called you, if only to let you know he was all right."

Geoff nodded. "Nor by the police, I would suspect. Perhaps *especially* not by the police."

"What do you mean? Why especially not by the police?"

Geoff gave her his quizzical look, peering skeptically out from under his brow, with his chin dipped. "You haven't considered the pos-sibility that it might be the police from whom he's running?"

Alix stared at him. "Geoff, are you saying that Tiny still . . . that he's still engaged in . . . in some kind of . . . of . . ." But she couldn't get the words out for fear of what he might answer.

"Some kind of nefarious behavior? Back to his old misguided ways, you mean? No, no, that's over and done. But, you know, there are still a few, well, let us say, unresolved matters from his past that, perhaps, it might be time for you to know about. You see—"

"I don't care about what he did or didn't do back then," Alix said to head him off. She didn't want to hear about his past. She knew who he was now, who he'd been for the last twenty years, and that was more than enough to earn her love and her trust.

"I understand, but isn't it possible the police may have some unanswered questions—lingering questions that he would prefer not to have put to him?"

"I suppose so," she allowed. "But I don't see that that makes any difference."

"Well, good for you, my dear. And neither am I, by the way," he added with a smile.

"Excuse me?"

"Back to my old, misguided ways—just to put your mind at ease. In case you were wondering. Not, of course, that you were."

Another socko performance of his mind-reading act, because that was exactly what she'd been wondering. It was something she never stopped worrying about: that the two of them might veer off the straight-and-narrow and forge a painting or two, not out of malice or greed, but out of, well, mischief. Fun. To see if they could still pull it off and get away with it. They both had that rascally streak in them that was never far below the surface.

"In any case," Geoff went on, "I think Tiny would prefer that we didn't bring the police into it."

"All right, I'll go along with that—for now, anyway. But I'm still concerned about him."

"And you think I'm not?"

"No, I know you are. And so I'm going to call my . . . my contact at the FBI."

Now both his eyebrows shot up. "The FBI! Didn't you just agree—"

"Relax, a strictly informal call. Nothing official—not to get them to do anything on their own, but maybe find out things for us that we could never find out by ourselves. Maybe give us a lead on where he is."

Geoff was shaking his head. "Alix, really, don't you think—"

"Whether you approve or not," she said sharply, perhaps a little more so than intended.

It stopped him cold, but then he surprised her with an agreeable laugh. "Well, that certainly puts the old fellow in his place."

"Dad, I'm sorry. I didn't mean to sound so—"

Geoff waved her apology aside. "I must say, though . . . the FBI. You're certainly becoming awfully chummy with your dad's old nemesis, aren't you?"

You don't know the half of it, Alix thought. "Well, they do have a lot of resources," she said, "and we can use whatever help we can get. We're kind of stuck right now. I mean, where do we go from here?"

"I have an idea," he said brightly. "If you think you are sufficiently rested—"

"Ha, ha."

"—then why do we not return to the Umbria? One of their double-shot lattes would go a long way toward sharpening my thinking processes, I can tell you that."

Alix smiled. "And one of their almond croissants too, maybe?"

"Definitely. And one for you as well. This will be my treat. Our spirits can stand a lift."

◆　　◆　　◆

They found a table that sat a little removed from the others, alongside a wide brick pillar that separated the café into two sections, and sat down with their espressos. Geoff had his croissant too. Alix had settled for the little gold-foil-wrapped square of dark chocolate that came along with the coffees—one more typical touch of *il madrepatria vecchio*, the old country. On the way from the counter Alix caught a glimpse of her own face smirking back at her from the magazine rack on the wall. "Just a minute, Geoff," she said, setting the cups down on the table. She grabbed the well-thumbed magazine (this was an arty part of town), returned, and slapped it down beside the cups.

He looked at it fondly and smiled. "My daughter, the celebrity."

But she was serious. "Geoff, it's got to be this."

He tore his eyes from the image. "What's got to be what?"

"Tiny's disappearance . . . whatever happened to him . . . everything." She thumped the magazine with her knuckles. "It's the magazine. Consider. Everything's fine, no problems. Then this thing comes out, and before the week is out, Tiny disappears, my condo's broken into, and the mirror's stolen. Surely, that can't be mere coincidence."

"What are you suggesting, Alix?"

"I don't really know, but . . . well, I've been denying this ever since it happened, but now I'm starting to wonder if everybody else could be right—"

"Everybody else? Who might that be? And right about what?"

"The detective who talked to us, for one, and . . . well, just the detective, I guess. He thought that the mirror could be something more than we think it is—something *worth* stealing. Maybe Tiny *didn't* make it. Maybe it's real. Maybe—"

"A real what? A real mirror? Well, what if it is? If there's any high value market for that sort of thing, I'm not aware of it."

"No, I'm not talking about the mirror itself, the glass part. That probably came from a second-hand store. It's old, but not *that* old: no bubbles in the glass, no wavy distortions, and only a little veining. But it's the panel that it's set in that I'm talking about, the painted part—the cherubs, the clouds."

"Alix, I have to tell you, you're barking up the wrong tree. Look, have you ever heard of a competent forger spending his time faking the ornamentation on old mirrors? No, you haven't and the reason is there's no money in it. One doesn't find an old mirror in an art gallery, one finds it, as you say, in a second-hand store, and second-hand stores are not where the big spenders go. That's the trouble with mirrors: they're simply not worth the effort."

But Alix had gotten herself into high gear and pushed on. "What if it's not just the borders that are painted, what if the entire panel—the part behind the mirror—is painted too? You know, if it's all one painting and the mirror was just glued over it with removable adhesive. It's beautiful, isn't it?"

He hunched a shoulder. "In its own way."

"Couldn't it be . . ." She thought for a moment. "Couldn't it be . . . I don't know, a Boucher, a Fragonard, or one of their followers? Or even a Tiepolo? A genuine one, I mean. And once Tiny stuck the mirror to the front of it, nobody ever thought about what might be behind it one way or the other? Don't you see? *That's* why it would have been worth stealing."

Geoff smiled throughout her little speech. "A twelve-by-sixteen-inch Tiepolo? Now that would be something."

"I'm not saying it's a whole painting. It doesn't look like one, but I do think it could be a fragment of a larger panel. I can easily imagine—"

"No, my darling daughter, I'm sorry. It's quite impossible, I assure you."

His smug certainty had gotten under her skin. "I don't agree. How can you make a blanket statement like that?"

"I can make it," Geoff said mildly, "because I was there. I saw him paint it. I stood at his shoulder and watched."

Alix stared at him. "You . . . you . . ."

"Watched him paint the thing, yes. I . . . was . . . *there*."

Talk about demolishing a plausible, well-reasoned hypothesis with three one-syllable words. Alix blew out a breath and fell back against her chair. "Damn."

"And the reason I remember," Geoff said, "is because I took him to task over it. I asked him—a bit tartly, I admit—if he realized that he had French Rococo cherubs floating around on Italian Mannerist clouds."

"He did?" Examining the mirror in her mind's eye, she frowned for only a moment, then nodded. "Yes, you're absolutely right. I just never gave it any thought before. The clouds, the sky—they couldn't be any more Mannerist if they tried, could they? That coloring—purples, grays, whites—lurid, harsh, and gloomy all at the same time. The clouds themselves look like they're in pain, stretched out beyond endurance. The whole sky is . . . unquiet, threatening."

"Indeed it is. It could be the morning of Judgment Day."

"But those cheery, rosy little cherubs, they belong in a bright pastel sky, all pinks and cornflower blues with puffy white clouds, and ribbons, and birds, and—"

"Correct, but nobody painted them like that until Fragonard and Watteau and the rest of that crew came along, and that was in another country and not for another two hundred years."

"You're absolutely right," she said again. "What is it, Geoff? You look . . . concerned."

"No, not really," he said a little diffidently, "but, well, you've had the mirror since you were twelve years old, Alix, almost twenty years. And until today, this minute, you never realized this before? I should have thought, with that famous connoisseur's eye of yours, that it would have jumped out at you long ago. I'm a little surprised, that's all."

"Geoff, I've never *studied* that mirror, never analyzed it, never deconstructed it into schools of art. I simply loved it and took it for what it was, a beautiful present from my Uncle Beni."

"Which is what it was, my dear."

Alix swallowed a minute sip of her coffee while she thought this new development over. "Why *did* he combine Mannerist and Rococo elements like that, do you know? He certainly would have known better."

"Well, I can tell you what he said to me when I called his attention to it. 'I don't give a fig,' is what he said. 'These are the kind of angels Alix loves, and these are the clouds she thinks are so beautiful.' That's an exact quotation."

Alix managed a faint smile. "Fig?"

"All right, I may have paraphrased just a bit, but that was the substance of it. Was that the case? Did you love the Mannerists' treatment of clouds?"

"Did I? They do seem a little gloomy for a twelve-year-old, but maybe I did. I really can't remember."

"Well, whatever the case, I *was* there, my dear. I watched him paint it myself. Truly."

"I just wish you'd told me that in the first place instead of letting me blather on like that."

"Not at all, your speculations are always entertaining," Geoff said with no trace of sarcasm. "And this was a reasonable one. It just doesn't happen to be the case."

They finished their coffees without saying more, and continued to sit there a few moments longer, sunk in their own reflections.

"Geoff," Alix said as they gathered themselves to leave, "if Tiny *is* running away from something, where would he run to? Does he still have family in New York?"

"Yes, but I believe he's estranged from them. I do know that he has some contacts—old friends, family, I'm not sure what they are—in San Francisco. There was a Wilfred . . . a Wilmer . . . something like that, whom he used to talk about—in North Beach, Little Italy. That's where he'd go when he needed to get away for a while in the, well, in the—"

"The ah, mm, old days?" Alix suggested.

"Exactly." He tipped his head to one side and frowned. "Dillard? Could it have been Dillard? No, I don't think so. Wallace . . . ?"

"Dad, let me ask you: what chance do you really think we have of finding him?"

Geoff considered. "I think the more pertinent question is: should we be trying to find him at all? Isn't it possible that by searching for him we might be bringing him more trouble than he's already in? As you implied, if he wants our help, all he need do is call us—either of us."

"No, I'm sorry, Geoff, that's just not good enough. If Tiny is in trouble—and he *must* be in trouble—and especially if it has something to do with that mirror, I can't simply sit here and wait until he calls. Any lead I can find to him, I'm going to follow."

"Such as going to San Francisco yourself, do you mean?"

"If that makes sense, yes."

"And if you were to find him, what would you do?"

"See that he has some money, I suppose, or help him however I can. Advice, information . . . I don't know. You said yourself, the man would jump out of a window for me. Don't you think this is the least I can do for him?"

Geoff sighed but said nothing.

"If you're worried that I might do something stupid—dangerous—don't be, because I won't. I promise. Trust me on that."

He nodded, seemingly as much in approval (she hoped) as in resignation. "That's my daughter," he said. "One would think I'd be used to her by now. Go to it then, my dear. You have my blessing. If you can think of any way that I can help, you'll tell me."

"I will, and thank you." She covered his hand with hers. "Come on, I'll drive you back."

"I wish you luck in this, you know that," he said as they walked to her car. "But FBI help notwithstanding, I have to tell you that if Tiny doesn't want to be found"—he slowly shook his head—"nobody's going to find him."

CHAPTER 9

I have to tell you that if Tiny doesn't want to be found . . . nobody's going to find him.

But Alix thought otherwise. As soon as she got back to her apartment, the naked walls of which shocked her all over again—she'd have to get something up on them as quickly as she could—she climbed up on the step stool in the entry closet and rummaged on the messy overhead shelf. She had to shove out of the way a tennis racket that hadn't been used in a year, a non-functioning printer, and a small cork bulletin board still in its wrapper (now why had she bought that?) in order to extract an old shoebox, softened and sagging with age, from behind them. Then she took the box to her dining room table with more care than beat-up old shoeboxes generally got.

For this was no ordinary shoebox, this was the very box in which those original Bottega Venetas had come, the ones her mother had bought her for her sixteenth birthday. Like Tiny's mirror, this box was one of the very few things that she'd managed to keep with her all these years—a treasured possession, laden with memories. She hadn't thought about it in months, though, not since the day she'd moved into the condo, and handling it now brought many of those memories back.

That day in 2000, when she'd watched so proudly as the clerk gently nestled those shoes back into the box, had been even more meaningful than she'd realized at the time. Until then, until that very day, she'd seen herself as her daddy's girl, captivated by Geoff's wit, flamboyance, and raffish irreverence for convention. Her decorous, unostentatious mother, Rachel, on the other hand, was old-money New England stock—a van Hoogeren, no less—and acted like it, her natural liveliness dulled by rules of proper behavior for every conceivable situation, rules that Alix had heard so many times that she'd stopped listening—stopped hearing, even—by the time she was ten.

And that day was to be no different. Alix had fallen in love with the shoes the moment she'd seen them, but she'd been raised to be frugal despite the family wealth, and when her mother asked if those were the ones she wanted, Alix had expressed her hesitancy.

"Yes, but four hundred dollars for a pair of shoes? It's so much . . ."

"I have a rule for clothing purchases, Alix," her mother responded. "Now that you're a young lady, it's time for you to begin following it. And that rule is . . ."

Alix barely managed to stifle the by-now automatic urge to roll her eyes. Rachel's "rules" were invariably less like rules and more like mini-sermons.

"Buy infrequently," her mother intoned, "but when you do buy, never look for the latest frippery. The more popular the style, the sooner it will be out of fashion. Buy quality, both in manufacturing and in quiet good taste, and take care of it. It will last you for years, it will simplify your life, and you'll be the happier for it, I promise you."

The funny thing was that, whatever the reason, for once her mother got through to her, and all the other long-disregarded rules fell into place behind it. It was the "quiet good taste" part that had done it. At base, wasn't that what all of Rachel's rules were about? And what was so bad about that?

It was at that moment that she began to understand that, while she adored Geoff and his ways and had even made some not very successful efforts to emulate him, at heart she herself was more her mother's daughter, valuing privacy, simplicity, refinement—and yes, quiet good taste—more than the restless exhilarations of her father's brilliant world.

The realization had been a life-changer, freeing her to be her own person from then on.

She looked lovingly and nostalgically at the box as she set it on the table. In it was not the usual hodgepodge of rubber bands, paper clips, out-of-date grocery coupons, and canceled checks for which retired shoeboxes were generally put to use, but only memorabilia in the truest sense of the word: things genuinely worthy of remembrance. As a result, there wasn't that much in it—personal photographs, significant post-cards and letters, ticket stubs and programs from outings with people who'd been important to her.

Thus, she quickly found what she was looking for. It was a photo taken inside an old-fashioned Italian delicatessen, its shelves crammed with bottles and jars going up to the ceiling, and in front of them, hang-ing from hooks, dozens of variously sized salamis thickly coated with rich white mold, and interspersed with russet-brown smoked hams in string netting. Simply looking at the picture, you could practically smell the place. And in the immediate foreground, standing in front of a long sales counter and brandishing a squat, straw-basketed bottle of Chianti by the neck in one gigantic paw and a foot-long hero sandwich in the other, was Beniamino Guglielmi Abbatista. From the goofy, lopsided grin on his face, Alix had concluded that there probably wasn't much left in the bottle. From behind the counter, a young blond clerk at the slicing machine was laughingly shouting something at him.

It was the only photo of Tiny she had—in fact, the only photo of him she'd ever seen. He'd mailed it to her when she was twelve, during one of the several times he had disappeared from her life for a few weeks without warning. (This was in the, ah, mm, old days.) There had been no letter with it, only a penciled note on the back, painstakingly—and somewhat painfully—printed in block letters. It was easy to imagine him sitting with his tongue peeking from the side of his mouth while he worked at it with the stub of a pencil.

Dear Alix,

I am fine. I thought you would like this nice phota-
graph of me and my freinde Waldo. This is my favroite
deli in the whole world and is right around the corner
from my house where I live for a little whiole. Lucky
me, huh? I hope evreything is alright with you and
your mamma and papa. I miss you very much. Soon
I see you.

   Your loveing Zio Beni. XXOO

She studied the picture for a while, smiling to see him so young.
With his black, organ-grinder's mustache and a nose like a potato,
he'd have fit right in with the Mario Brothers. He still had the potato-
nose, but the mustache was gone and his hair had thinned and now
had more gray than black in it. And she'd forgotten how dense (and
delightful) his accent had been then. Although he'd been raised in
New York, his parents could barely get along in English, he'd told
her, and Italian had been the only language spoken in the Abbatistas'
apartment. As a result, Tiny spoke both languages, but each heavily
accented by the other. Since then, she realized now, his English had
come a long, long way.

But it wasn't to look at Tiny that she'd gotten the picture down.
What she was interested in was a proprietary placard that she thought
she remembered being on one of the shelves behind his left shoulder.
And she was right; there it was, big and bright: *G.G. Zappa & Figli, dal
1896*, in the proud red, white, and blue of the American flag. Now, if
Geoff was right about San Francisco being where Tiny went when he
needed to beat a retreat . . .

On her laptop she opened up Google Search, reasoning—hoping—
that if a delicatessen had already stuck it out for almost eighty years at
the time of the photo, it just might still be there.

"Yes!" she exulted when it popped right up on Fodor's San Francisco Shopping page: *Zappa's Delicatessen, established in 1896 in San Francisco's Little Italy, may well be the last of the true Italian salumerias . . .*

She sat back, much satisfied and flushed with elation. If this was his "favorite deli in the whole world," and he was a familiar enough face there that one of the clerks would be mugging so openly with him, wasn't it just possible that some old-timer in an old-timey place like that might know something about him, even have some idea of where he was now?

And even if there wasn't anybody there who still knew him, there was another clue on the back of the photo. Assuming that "right around the corner" wasn't just a figure of speech—and the literal-minded Tiny wasn't much for airy locutions—then that meant the house he'd been staying in was . . . well, right around the corner, and how hard would it be to check on the buildings that met that description? She knew what those places in North Beach's residential Italian neighborhoods were like: not big tenement-style apartment buildings, but modest little houses converted in the fifties and sixties to hold two or three apartments each, with the occasional rambler of a Victorian that might be split up into five or six apartments.

In the best of all possible worlds, he was there now. If not, she was betting there'd be someone who could give her some kind of clue to his whereabouts—*if* she could get whoever it was to trust her. Knocking on every door in an entire block would be a big job, but it was certainly doable—especially if she had someone to help her.

She reached for the landline telephone on the table beside her and punched in a familiar number. It was picked up on the second ring.

"H—"

"Chris, hello! Listen, could you get away for a few days later this week, or even better, tomorrow, to go down to San Francisco? I'm worried about Tiny, he's been missing for days—it's got to have something to do with that mirror, don't you think? Even Geoff doesn't know where to find him. We went to where he lives, but he wasn't there, but I've got an idea, only I could really use your help. I'm afraid that . . ."

It occurred to her that under normal circumstances Chris would have said something by now. "Chris? Are you there? Hello?"

"Oh, am I allowed to speak too?"

"Sorry, I guess I'm a little keyed up."

"No kidding, really? Now. Take a deep breath, slow down, and start all over again."

It took five minutes to explain and another five to work out the logistics, at the end of which they agreed to fly down to the City by the Bay the next morning. They would start with a reconnaissance visit to Zappa's Delicatessen in hopes of digging up something on Tiny, and take it from there.

Chris tried to book a ShareJet for the flight, but despite the fact that she had a couple of "ins" with the company (she was a stockholder and her husband, Craig, was one of their senior pilots), there was nothing available on such short notice. In the meantime, Alix had found an early-morning flight on Alaska Airlines and suggested that she just book it on her laptop.

"What time?"

"Seven-thirty?" Alix offered without much hope.

As she expected, this plan failed to fly. "Are you out of your *mind*?" Chris yelled. "We'd have to be at the airport by six, which means I'd have to get up and start getting my face on at . . . at . . . my God . . ."

"All right, I get the message. Let's see." She prowled through Expedia. "Eight-ten?"

An indecisive pause and then: "Keep going."

"Well, there's one at nine-thirty, but that doesn't get there till noon, which kind of cuts our workday short, don't you think?"

"That's all right, get that one. I'll work fast, you'll see. So be downstairs ready for pickup at, oh, seven-fifteen, then. But get us first-class on the plane. I'll pick up the extra tab."

"Checking . . . checking . . ." Alix mumbled.

"Oh, and hey," Chris said, "do you know the Inn at Union Square down there?"

"I don't think so."

"My favorite place. Not real expensive—well, considering it's right off the square. You'll like it too. Is it okay with you if I get us a couple of rooms there?"

"Sure . . . Oops, sorry, no first-class available on that flight. The best I can do is a pair of coach seats together. Think you can stand a couple of hours flying like the rest of us?"

"*Quel horreur*," moaned Chris with a heavy sigh. "What I don't do for my friends."

Alix laughed. "You can have the aisle seat."

◆　◆　◆

As soon as she disconnected from Chris, Alix switched from her landline phone to her cell so she'd have one hand free to start packing while she made her next call. She brought up the FBI art squad on her contacts list. There were only two names: Ted's, of course, and Jamie Wozniak's. It was Jamie she'd be calling, but catching a glimpse of Ted's name at the top of the page sent a lovely little chill up her spine and put a tiny, self-satisfied smile on her face. How very lucky she was. What a rocky start it had been with him, and how wonderfully it had all turned out. Ted: decent, accomplished, manly, sexy, funny, caring, intelligent . . . as far as she was concerned, there weren't enough adjectives in the thesaurus to do him justice. And, ha-ha, world, he was all hers, "for as long as we both shall live," as they'd promised just, what was it, four days ago? Despite the unsettling events of the intervening days, she couldn't remember ever having four days filled with such bursting happiness.

Jamie was the art squad's "operations specialist," a laughable misnomer, since what she truly was was Ted's all-around generalist: his go-to person when computer skills were needed, or information-ferreting abilities, or cut-through-the-bureaucracy savvy when you *really* needed to get things done right now. More than that, Jamie had become a good friend of Alix's, the only person other than Chris who knew about the marriage. She'd served as a witness at the ceremony.

"Missing him already, are you?" were Jamie's first words after the *hellos.*

"Desperately," Alix replied, "although, believe me, there have been enough strange things going on around here to keep my mind fully occupied."

"Strange? What does that mean? Tell me what's happened."

The abrupt change in tone didn't surprise Alix. This was a woman who could switch to an utterly focused, all-business mode in a tenth of a second. It was one of the things that made her so good at her job. And it was tremendously reassuring. You knew at once that you were in good hands.

Alix went through it all for her: the telephone call from Ferrante in Italy, the burglary, Tiny's troubling disappearance, and Chris and Alix's plan to search for him. "And we can sure use your help, Jamie. Finding him's not going to be easy, so I'm hoping you might be able to get some additional information on him for us—anything that might help us hunt him down."

"You bet. Tell me what you do know about him."

"Not much, considering how close we are. My father's his oldest, most intimate friend, and he barely knows any more than I do." She paused to collect her thoughts. "Full name is Beniamino Guglielmi Abbatista—"

"One *b* or two *b*s?"

"Two. In his late fifties, I'd say. Big guy . . . huge, really, six-four, three hundred pounds—"

"Hence 'Tiny'?"

"Exactly. Let's see, what else . . . I remember him talking about Jerome Avenue in the Bronx as the street he was born on, but he has a pretty definite Italian accent. His parents were both immigrants and I gather they spoke Italian in the house. Oh, I think I remember his saying that they lived over a barbershop, but I'm not sure about that. I know he's got a prison record, so that should help."

"Do you know where he was, or what the charges were?"

"Well, I know he was in Lompoc at the same time as my father. And I guess there was a time quite a few years ago where he was in and out of jail a lot, but I don't know where. Mostly fraud-related stuff, I'm pretty sure—the guy was a serial forger—but I never wanted to press him on it. It's sad, really—"

"Um, Alix? You sure you want this guy back?"

"Yes. Tiny is the kindest, most generous, wonderful man in the world. I love him deeply. He's just, well, not the brightest bulb in the chandelier. He took a tremendous set of talents, and instead of pursuing a career of his own, he took to doing fake Homers and Velázquezes instead. He's over that now—"

"What was that? Did I just hear you knock on wood?"

Alix laughed. She'd done it unconsciously. "Well, he's kind of a slow learner and it did take him awhile to straighten himself out. But he *is* straight now. Really."

"Okay, I believe you," Jamie said, after waiting a second to see if there were any more telltale knocks. "Anything else?"

"My father says he's estranged from his family in New York, but he must have other family in Italy because he has a piece of his salary sent to a village there. Oh, and I also know he's had contacts in San Francisco's Little Italy in the past, so I'm heading down there tomorrow with my friend Chris to see if we can find anybody who might be able to tell us something, and . . . that's it. Anything more you can come up with, Jamie—"

"Gotcha. I'm on the case. I can reach you on your cell while you're in Frisco?"

"Yes." *Keep cell phone ON!* she wrote in her mental notebook. It was something she frequently failed to do, but from now on, *ON* was going to be its normal state. And not only because Jamie might call. What if Ted wanted to reach her?

"Thanks a lot, Jamie."

"Not a problem, you're welcome. I'm going to be doing my daily check-in with Ted in a few minutes. Do you want me to pass all this along to him when I do, or is this just between us for now?"

"No, you don't need to, Jamie. I already—" She winced. "Oops."

"You already told him?" She sounded suddenly concerned. "How did you get his number?"

"Well, I didn't exactly call—"

"He called *you*? You're telling me he called *you*? While undercover?"

"Well . . . yes, sort of . . . I guess you could say that. But it wasn't . . . that is, he didn't say where he was, he didn't—"

She was saved from continuing to flounder by the welcome sound of Jamie's rolling laugh. "I don't believe it!"

"Jamie, tell me I didn't just get him into trouble."

"No, come on, don't worry. Really, it's nice to know that Mr. High-and-Mighty-Stickler-for-Protocol is actually human under there." She chuckled a little more. "Love really does conquer all, I guess."

"You won't rib him about it, though, will you? I know he was kind of uncomfortable doing it."

"Well—"

"Promise."

Jamie sighed. "Okay, I promise, no ribbing—even though I already had my little lecture half-prepared—mostly taken from his own little lectures to the troops, I should add. You sure take the fun out of things, Alix."

"Thanks, Jamie. But I wouldn't mind if you told him that . . . well, you know, that I love him and I can't wait to see him again."

"You don't think he already knows that?"

"Well, but he hasn't heard it since this morning."

"I'll be sure and squeeze it in," Jamie said.

Alix shook her head and smiled to herself as she disconnected. A pretty weird marriage, all right, when you had to get another woman to do it for you when you wanted to tell your husband you loved him.

CHAPTER 10

Les Ports Francs et Entrêpots de Genève (Geneva Free Ports and Warehouses) is the oldest, largest free-port facility in the world, an enormous, altogether nondescript complex offering high-security, customs-friendly, tax-free storage options for anything worth storing. With over a million works of art in it at any one time, it is the world's largest such assemblage. "If it were a museum," say those who know, "it would be the finest museum in the world." But of course it is not a museum, it is the opposite of a museum: a place to hide things from curious eyes. There are many possible motives for burying fine paintings and sculptures in secret underground vaults for years or even decades, most of those motives ranging from dubious to downright illegal.

It was this practice that had engaged Ted's interest and brought him to Geneva. He was the FBI's liaison with the Spanish Guardia Civil, Interpol operatives, and the Swiss Customs Agency, and was helping to plan the interception of a shipment of twenty-four nineteenth-century paintings stolen from a museum in Barcelona in 2002. For almost the entire thirteen years since then the art-theft ring that had taken them, had kept them at the complex, waiting until—the thieves hoped—the world's investigative agencies lost interest and moved on. They were wrong; Interpol never "moves on." And now Interpol had word that it was the pictures that would finally be moving on, to shadowy intermediaries in Thessaloniki.

So far Ted's operation had gone smoothly. Even the Swiss authorities had been cooperative, which the Swiss are not known for; not when it comes to their vaunted bank accounts and their anonymous vaults.

Their attitude in this case seemed to be that as long as the works were inside a Swiss facility, their secrecy would be defended, but once they were out the door they were fair game.

As always, the schedule for Jamie's daily call to Ted changed each day. Today it was 1:30 p.m. DC time, which made it 7:30 p.m. in Geneva—convenient on both ends for a change. Making the call was simpler than ever, thanks to NSA's new telephone encryption system. No more complicated setup each time, no more codes to put in or questions to answer. You just let the mini-camera look you in the eye, and if it liked what it saw, you were on. Jamie loved it.

There was a momentary wait while the similarly equipped portable phone in Geneva checked Ted's irises, and then he came on. "Yes?"

"*Guten Tag.* How's it going in Yodel-land?" Jamie said. This sort of blithe, silly telephone greeting was her own break with protocol, but when someone was undercover more than twenty-three hours a day, possibly for weeks at a time, she thought a little lightheartedness was in order.

Ted responded in kind, with a lame quip of his own. "Not too bad, not too good," he said. "Pretty neutral here in Switzerland, I'd have to say." And then, after a beat: "Well, you could at least pretend to laugh."

"I'm smiling," Jamie said. "That's all you get. Seriously, everything's all right? Anything you need?"

"Nope, everything's right on target. A model operation. Things okay at your end?"

"Perfect, couldn't be better. You'd be amazed at how well we get along without you."

"Thank you so much." He cleared his throat. "So. Heard anything from Alix lately?"

"You mean since you called her this morning?"

"Since I . . . ? Uh-oh, I'm in hot water, aren't I? You're going to read me the riot act."

"You bet your life I would, if Alix hadn't extracted a promise from me not to."

"You're not going to tell any of the guys about it, are you? I've been kind of strict about that sort of thing, you know."

"Your secret is safe with me," Jamie said. "Besides, I think it's kind of sweet. Anyway: you know about what's been happening with her, so what are your thoughts?"

"That her father's behind it all, that's what. I'd trust that guy about as far as I could throw him."

"How can you say that? You haven't ever met him, have you? You don't know the man."

"Met? No, but I know his record, and that's good enough for me."

"Well, if you want my thoughts," she said stiffly, "I'm sure he's got nothing to do with it. What, break into his own daughter's apartment to steal something? Worry her like this about her Tiny? No way. He's not involved at all, I'm sure of it." *I'm not being entirely truthful*, she thought. She'd never met the man either and, well, records did speak for themselves, and his was spotty, to put it charitably. Still, she knew how much Alix loved him and even respected him. "And, frankly, I'm surprised to hear you make a totally uninformed prejudgment like that."

"I thought there wasn't going to be any riot act."

"This is a different subject," Jamie pointed out, "but never mind, I will withhold further comment and leave the matter to your conscience, such as it may be. Anyway, I was on the phone with her just a few minutes ago, and things have developed since she talked to you. She's found a possible lead to Tiny in San Francisco, and she and her friend Chris are flying down there tomorrow."

"What? Why isn't she waiting at least until I have a chance to check on this Ferrante and see what's up at his end?"

"So she should be sitting around waiting to hear from you before she does anything?"

"Well . . . yes. Sure."

"So that you could have given her, through me, the benefit of your wisdom in guiding her next steps."

"I wouldn't put it in quite your inimitable way, but yes, I suppose so. Is there anything wrong with that? I'm her husband, aren't I? For all we know, there might be some danger involved here."

"Let me put it to you this way, Buster—"

"*Buster?* Hey, let me remind you, madam, that there is a code of expected office behavior in this esteemed agency, among which is the rule that minions and underlings do not address their superiors in any manner that—"

"Sorry about that. I'll try again: Let me put it to you this way, Lord and Master . . . Is that better?"

Ted emitted a *so-so* sound. "Better, but your tone needs work. Now, you were saying?"

"Just this: Among the reasons you were so attracted to Alix in the first place were that she was independent, capable, self-willed, and self-sufficient. Is that not so?"

"And ornery, don't forget ornery."

"Yes, ornery too when the mood strikes her, and if you're thinking that because she now has a husband who's maybe even more ornery and self-willed than she is, she's about to become a timid little woman asking for approval and guidance on anything before she does it, you are in for a disappointment, pal—Excuse me: you are in for a disappointment, my liege."

"But at least—"

"Give it up, Ted. You're not going to change her, and she isn't going to change you. And if it was any other way, you wouldn't like it. You know that."

A long sigh from Ted. "Yeah, okay, you're right . . . as usual. Damn it, Jamie, do you have any idea of how annoying that can be?"

"I apologize. Now do you want to talk about what we're doing on our end? I have other things to do too, you know."

"Of course I do," Ted said docilely.

"Okay. I'll start by informally checking out Tiny on this end. I'm going to call Homeland Security and also someone I know at the Bureau of Intelligence and Research and see what they have on him. And I gather you're going to be checking out the Genoa gallery owner, Ferrante—not right away, I assume, since you're still on assignment."

"True, but I'm hoping that'll be wrapped up inside of a day or two. But before then, I know just who to call in Genoa to get whatever police information there is on him, and I'll do it first thing in the morning."

CHAPTER 11

A visitors' guide to the city of Genoa contends that it has more fifteenth- and sixteenth-century palazzos per square inch than any other city in the world, and that just might be so. In some places there are nine or ten to a city block. Many are very grand indeed, sporting colonnaded porticoes and magnificent facades with long rows of tracery windows. Others couldn't be plainer. The somewhat hyperbolically named Monumental Complex of St. Ignatius, sitting on the crest of the Carignano, the scenic rise in the center of the city, is one of the plainest, looking less like a palazzo than an office building—which is what it's been for the last two centuries.

Since 1817, the structure has been occupied by the State Archives, except for two unpretentious rooms at the rear of the ground floor, which now house the Genoa branch of Italy's art squad, the *Comando Carabinieri per la Tutela del Patrimonio Culturale*. The smallest of the twelve branches, the Genovese art unit currently has only one full-time *caribiniere*. *Capitano* Gino Moscoli was the most senior member of the entire nationwide team, having joined it as a simple *carabiniere* in 1979, only ten years after its inception.

Over these decades he had made many good friends in the law enforcement community, both in Italy and internationally. Among them was a much younger man, but a competent and resourceful one, pleasant to associate with, open to instruction from an older, more experienced colleague, and always ready to pitch in when called upon by the Italians. This was the American Ted Ellesworth, "Teo" to the Italians, who headed the FBI's art squad, a far smaller operation than the Italian one. This was natural enough; Italy had a thousand times more art treasures just waiting to be snatched out of remote churches and poorly guarded municipal museums. Besides, Italian art thieves—one might as well be honest about it—were more up to the job.

When his phone had quietly beeped at nine o'clock this morning, it was with pleasure that he saw Ellesworth's name on the screen. It had been awhile since he'd heard from his *buon amico americano*.

"Teo! It's good to hear from you," he said in Italian.

"And it's good to hear your voice, Gino. It's been awhile." Ted was speaking Italian too. Like many whose work required familiarity with the history of Western art, he found a grasp of the language indispensable. "I have a favor to ask."

"You shock me."

"It shouldn't take more than an hour of your time, all told. I'd just like you to ask one of your local art dealers a few questions and get back to me."

"Certainly." Moscoli opened a small notebook and jotted down the questions as Ted went through them. "Yes, it shouldn't take long at all. What's this all about?"

"At this point I don't know if it's about anything, really. I'm on kind of a fishing expedition. It's a long story, Gino, but if it looks as if there's anything to it, you can be sure I'll let you know the minute I do. Listen, I'm working undercover in Geneva right now, so when you call me back, you need to use a special number and then enter a code when you're asked for it, and you'll be put through to me."

"All right," Moscoli said, writing down the number and the code as they were read to him. "And who is this art dealer to whom these questions are to be put?"

"His name is Alfonso—no, Alessandro Ferrante. I was hoping you might know him."

Moscoli replied with a snort of corrosive laughter. And then, archly: "I do have some acquaintanceship with the gentleman, yes."

•   ◆   •

Almost thirty years' worth, in fact, Moscoli thought a little later, starting out on his twenty-minute walk to Ferrante's gallery. *Capitano* Moscoli had been stalking Alessandro Ferrante for longer than Inspector Javert had hunted Jean Valjean. Indeed, sometimes he felt as if he and Ferrante were living their own personal version of *Les Miserables*, although in Hugo's story Valjean at least had the decency to stay on the run in order to elude the dogged Javert. Ferrante, on the other hand, had been right out in the open all this time, right in front of Moscoli's eyes, never troubling to leave Genoa. His art dealership boldly bore his own name—the *Galleria Ferrante*—and was located on the city's most exclusive shopping street, the elegantly colonnaded *via XX Settembre*. And not at street level, mind you, among the shops catering to whatever riffraff happened to stroll in off the tiled sidewalk (e.g. Cartier, Rolex, Swarovski), but on the upper floor, above one of the elegant, block-long porticoes, in an airy, spacious suite of rooms with a shrub-bordered terrace atop the portico itself, onto which privileged clients could take paintings out to be studied in the clarifying light of day.

Moscoli's acquaintanceship with the slippery Ferrante had begun in 1987. At that time a *sottotenente*, a sub-lieutenant, Moscoli had been made the field chief of a team working on an important art theft in the city. *Colonnello* Tebaldi had gone against both protocol and the advice of his superiors in Rome in giving so responsible an assignment to a sub-lieutenant, and a baby-faced, twenty-seven-year-old one at that. Moscoli, grateful for the opportunity, had attacked it with all his youthful zeal, but to no avail; the case had never been resolved.

That Ferrante had planned and executed the theft, and that he had done it at the behest of the Genovese Mafia, Moscoli knew for a certainty; a dozen meaty clues had led straight to him and to his nebulous association with the Mafia. But when you had judges and juries to deal with, knowing something for a certainty was one thing and having the evidence to prove it at the level demanded in a court of law was another.

And that, Moscoli had been unable to come up with. The case was never solved and the loot never recovered. Unfairly, to Moscoli's way of thinking, it was *Colonnello* Tebaldi, not the young lieutenant, who was penalized for this failure. He was demoted to *tenente*, which was hard, and reassigned to Calabria, which was worse. But Moscoli had never forgiven himself for what he considered to be *his* failure, and the case had gnawed at him for almost three decades now, almost like a lost first love that might have been his, had he only been more perceptive, more discerning, more diligent, more . . . something.

Since then, he had called on Ferrante dozens of times, officially and unofficially, aggressively and amicably, in hopes of ferreting out some overlooked datum, some factoid that might lead to the recovery of the looted art, but Ferrante had fended him off every time.

This case, his very first major case, was, in fact, the reason he hadn't retired years ago. He had stayed on the job for a long time; too long, even in his own eyes. He was nearing sixty now, older than *Colonnello* Tebaldi had been in 1987, and any possibility of promotion to *maggiore*, let alone *colonnello*, was long gone. Even his promotion to *capitano* five years ago, he had been made to understand, was more a reward for his long and loyal service than anything else. And then there was his deteriorating health: an arthritic hip that couldn't wait much longer for an operation, and a recent, troubling diagnosis of incipient Parkinson's disease (neither of which his superiors knew anything about). It was time to go and he knew it, but the need to solve that ancient crime and, if at all possible, to retrieve the loot or at least to determine for sure what had happened to it, was still with him. He understood himself well enough to know that it was closure he was after; a deeply personal need, not an official one. But that didn't stop him from dreaming—and it was little more than a dream now—of getting it done before he retired, which he would surely be forced to do in any case before much longer.

As soon as Teo had mentioned Ferrante's name, Moscoli had peppered the FBI man with questions, hoping there might be a connection to the old theft, but no. This was something about an ornamental mirror, and no mirror, ornamental or otherwise, had been involved.

The entrance to Ferrante's gallery was an unprepossessing doorway wedged into the narrow space between a chic women's-wear boutique and a trendy new gourmet shop specializing in caviars, pâtés, and Belgian chocolates. The door itself was a dull brown, as ordinary as they come (although steel-reinforced, Moscoli knew), and the only indication of what lay behind it was a postcard-sized brass plate on the doorjamb:

Galleria Ferrante

Arte Moderna et Contemporanea

Below it was a push button, which Moscoli now pushed. From the perforated speaker came a robotic voice that explained that the gallery was open only by appointment, six days a week from 10:00 a.m. to 1:00 p.m. and then again from 4:00 to 6:00 p.m. If the caller wished to apply for an appointment, he or she need only press 1.

Moscoli pressed 1.

"*Galleria Ferrante, come posso aiutarla?*" said a familiar female voice. *How may I help you?*

"*Buongiorno*, Filomena," Moscoli replied. "It's *Capitano* Moscoli. I'd like to speak with *signor* Ferrante if he has a moment."

Moscoli recognized the scraping, shuffling noise that meant that a hand was covering the telephone. A moment later she was back on. "Please come up, *Capitano*." The lock clicked, the door opened a couple of inches, and Moscoli pushed his way through.

The neon-lit foyer was as unwelcoming as the door, its walls a sludgy, dismal olive-green. The place was a mess, with construction debris and equipment everywhere. A six-foot, paint-splattered aluminum ladder leaned against one wall, a threadbare work apron hung from a seemingly randomly placed nail, and the floor was littered with sawdust, power tools, and scraps of plywood. The air smelled of turpentine and lubricating oil, and the steel staircase to the upper floor looked as if it had been liberated from a heavy manufacturing plant.

There was no construction underway, however. This unfortunate introduction to the gallery was the gallery's latest "installation." They changed every few months. In the recent past it had been the back room of a butcher shop, a macabre wax museum, an autopsy room, and a two-story prison cell. Why these grisly, off-putting settings should put clients in the mood to buy art, Moscoli had no idea. He had asked Ferrante once, and the answer had been that "edgy" was what was selling these days. For Moscoli, that had explained nothing but had only confirmed his long-held conviction that people were unendingly perverse.

Moscoli wondered what he would do if something like this mess were stolen and he was ordered onto the case. It wouldn't be a happy assignment, he knew that much. Personally, he'd be in favor of the Carabinieri Command for the Protection of Cultural Heritage paying some gang to *steal* this brainless litter. As long, that is, as they'd promise to get it out of Italy.

Upstairs, there were two high-ceilinged exhibition rooms with Spartan white furniture and chalk-white walls. One held a show of sardonic "religious" paintings by a Norwegian artist, the other a "neo-Soviet Constructivist" exhibit by a Genovese painter. These consisted mostly of posterlike, 1930s-style representations of workers with brawny forearms, raised fists, and fervent, skyward gazes, but with wizened old faces and spotted, balding heads with wispy white hair. Snakes, lizards, and fish crawled over the ground. A woman in a black shawl sat on a kitchen chair, facing away from the viewer. Delightful.

Ferrante's office was at the rear and quite different, a tasteful, unassuming room that might have been the office of a well-to-do attorney or psychologist. On the walls were black-and-white landscape photographs of the Apennines, one to each wall. Beneath each one was a pedestal holding a flowing, abstract steel sculpture, tributes to the works of Brancusi (or maybe mockeries, who knew these days?).

By the time Moscoli got to the office door, Filomena was right behind him with a tray holding two espresso cups of *caffè corretto*—espressos spiked with a few drops of grappa—and two small glasses of water. This had become a welcome custom whenever Ferrante knew his old enemy was on his way up.

Smiling, Ferrante stood behind his bow-top, maple desk (uncluttered, as always), and offered his hand. Also as always, he was immaculate in a conservative, three-piece suit and tie. "Good morning, Gino, I wonder to what I owe this pleasure."

Moscoli shook the proffered hand and smiled back. "Why, primarily, my hope that I might be offered a cup of Filomena's marvelous coffee, of course."

"As you see, Filomena herself has anticipated you. Thank you, Filomena, you may go."

Filomena left, wearing her usual unreadable face.

Ferrante sat and invited Moscoli to do the same, which he did. One of the minuscule cups, resting on a saucer, was slid to the *capitano* across the burnished surface of the desk, and both men drank their coffee.

"Thank you, Alessandro."

"My pleasure, Gino, as always."

This was normal interaction for them now. They had known each other so long, sparred with each other for so many years, that they had eventually moved naturally to a first-name basis two decades and more ago, polite but chilly at first, but in the last few years they had become more like old friends than old enemies. Moscoli no longer had any desire to put Ferrante away, which wouldn't happen in any case, any applicable statutes of limitations having run out years ago. Over and above that, he would have been sorry now to see this urbane, sophisti-cated man spend his declining years behind bars.

In any case, that was not what he was here about today. "About a week ago, Alessandro, you made a telephone call to America, to Seattle, no?"

"True. To Alix London, an art consultant there."

"And would you mind telling me the nature of that call?"

Ferrante leaned back in his curvy ergonomic chair and folded his manicured hands at his waist. "*Signorina* London's photograph was on the cover of a magazine last week. On the wall behind her was a small mirror set in a decorative panel—a pretty thing. A client of mine, let us call him *signor* X, saw it and was much impressed. He asked me if I could find out who had crafted it and whether the craftsman might be amenable to making something similar for him. Naturally, the simplest way for me to go about it was to contact the *signorina* to see if she could put me in touch with its maker, which is what I did. Whether my appeal was successful or not, I don't yet know."

"I see," Moscoli said agreeably. "Now: Your client, this *signor* X—I don't suppose you would care to tell me his name?"

"You know my policy on that, Gino. I don't wish to be uncoopera-tive, but unless I am served with a warrant, '*signor* X' he must remain. Gino, excuse me, why are we discussing this at all?"

"Because," Moscoli said, "the lady's apartment was ransacked within a very few days after your call, and among the objects taken—the only one that might be of any value at all—was that very mirror." From beneath lowered eyelids he watched for Ferrante's reaction.

All he got for his trouble was a brief, tiny flicker of the skin under Ferrante's right eye, an itch that he scratched with a single finger and that probably meant nothing. "Taken? Stolen, do you mean?"

"Yes."

"And you think—surely, you don't imagine—that I had anything to do with that?"

"I thought that you might have some idea of *why* it would have been stolen," said Moscoli tactfully. "If I understand correctly, it wouldn't be worth much, a few hundred euros at most."

"Oh, a bit more than that, I should think. But Gino, why is this a *carabinieri* concern? I would have thought it a problem for the police in America."

"And so it is. I'm here as a favor to an American colleague."

Ferrante's hands came up to steeple in front of his mouth while he cogitated and then he slowly shook his head. "Truly, my friend, I wish I could help you."

CHAPTER 12

Half an hour after Moscoli left, Ferrante was a different man, distraught, in shirtsleeves, his tie undone, and raving into his telephone. *"Idiota! Stupido! Testa di . . . di . . ."*

Nine thousand miles and nine time zones away, in Bellevue, Washington, Gus Voss muttered "Jesus Christ, do you know what time it is here?" and hung up on him.

"What! Don't you dare—" Ferrante babbled pointlessly. "You . . . you . . ." Trembling, furious, he redialed at once.

"How could you do a thing so stupid?" he screamed when the phone was picked up again. "Do you even realize what you've done? I hired you because you were supposed to be a professional, not just another brainless—"

"Oh, man, screw this," Gus said, and then as he crammed his phone into its cradle, in a barely heard afterthought: "And screw you too, Ferrante." *Click.*

The next three tries produced busy signals. Ferrante put his elbows on his desk and with a groan laid his pounding head down on his forearms. What was he to do next?

Alessandro Lucio Ferrante rightfully prided himself on his stringently cultivated ability, whatever the crisis might be, to maintain not only a calm exterior but also an inner calm as well. But then had there ever been a crisis like this before? He was practically frothing at the mouth, and not only because he was furious with Voss; he was terrified for himself as well. Greasy rivulets of perspiration slid down his cheeks and over his jaw line, and disappeared under his shirt collar. Despite his determination to still his fingers, they fumbled as he tried to light what must have been his tenth cigarette since Moscoli had gone, most of which he'd forgotten before he'd finished them and now lay smoldering in the ashtray. At one point he'd found himself with a lit cigarette in his mouth and another one between his fingers.

What was wrong with Voss? What had he been thinking? That he could sell the mirror, was that it? *Stupido, stupido, stupido.* If word of this were to reach Don Rizzolo before Ferrante had time to straighten it out (assuming it was even possible for it to be straightened out), Ferrante was as good as dead, and so, in all probability, was Voss. (That was one bright spot, anyway.) And even if Ferrante *could* somehow make things right, the don would be seriously irked, and not many people still walked the earth who had seriously irked Don Rizzolo. And those few who did walked it with a prominent limp.

Despite the panic filling his chest like a cold lump of clay, Ferrante's lip curled at the thought of the Mafia chief. "Don" Rizzolo, indeed. It took effort not to sneer when the "don" allowed some crawling supplicant to kiss his ring, as if he were the damn pope. And who let himself be called "Don" anymore? Even in the Sicilian Mafia, the *real* Mafia, the custom had died out a half-century ago. But then came *The Godfather*, and suddenly the *capo* of every two-bit, would-be Mafia *cosca* in Italy thought he was Marlon Brando. Don Rizzolo's father, the Mafia chieftain who had commissioned Ferrante for the theft, had never gone along with the trend. His intimates continued to call him Piero. To others he was simply *signore*, as he had always been. Now there was a man who didn't require a title to be respected.

But in 1989, when the old *capo* died (at home in his bed, of pulmonary disease) and his son replaced him, it was as "Don Rizzolo." The whole thing was ludicrous, farcical; they blindly followed a movie made in Hollywood, not even knowing enough to get the protocol right. "Don" was a traditional honorific, yes—it had been in use since the 1500s—but as a form of address it was not to be paired with one's surname alone, but with the given name, as was the case with "Prince" or "Sir." Don Corleone should properly have been Don Vito, and Don Rizzolo was properly Don Pantaleone. Although with a name like that, even though it was in honor of a thirteenth-century saint greatly admired by his father, one could understand why he'd prefer "Don."

Not that Don Rizzolo himself was ludicrous, or that the Genovese *cosca* was two-bit. Far from it—it was one of the very few new Mafias that lived up to the vicious old tradition in every respect. They were smart, powerful, unforgiving, implacable, and brutal in the extreme. And it was the don—

Ferrante jumped when his telephone rang. He jammed his cigarette into the ashtray—good God, he had two of them going again. *Calm down, Alessandro, get hold of yourself.*

He snatched up the phone. "Voss?" he said, disturbed to hear how short of breath he was. He'd barely managed to get out that one syllable.

"Yeah, Voss. Okay, now you got me wondering instead of sleeping. So tell me, what's the big deal? What do you want?"

Ferrante told himself to take a deep breath but couldn't manage it; he continued to pant. "Are you . . . are you out of . . . your mind? Did you think . . . whoo . . . did you think you could . . . could sell it? Was that it? It's not . . . whoo . . . it's not worth anything, you moron. You'll be lucky to get twenty dollars for it, that is, if you can even find anyone—"

"I got no idea what you're talking about," Voss said placidly. "Call me again if and when you can control yourself. And Ferrante?"

"Yes, what? *What?*"

"Don't yell at me again, Ferrante. Not ever." Voss's voice was burred from four decades of booze and cigars, but it was icily level. "Remember what I told you when you hired me. I'm not your lousy employee, I'm an independent contractor, and I take crap from no man, least of all you. You can't be polite, I don't want to hear from you."

"Now . . . now, just one minute, my friend. You listen to me—"

Click.

Ferrante sat there, motionless, his eyes unfocused, for two minutes, three minutes. Then, surprised to find himself still clutching the telephone, he set it on its stand, went to the maple and glass liquor cabinet in the far corner of his office, and poured himself a brimming shot glass, not of the famous but insipid French champagne kept for his run-of-the-mill customers, but of the top-tier *Vecchia Romagna* generally reserved for his most favored clients. He downed it in a single gulp, tipping his head back to toss it down his gullet like a seasoned rummy, which he was not. Still, once he felt how the brandy warmed and eased him on the way down he poured another, drinking it slowly this time, in three swallows, after which he tried another deep breath and found he could do it this time. He put the glass down and studied his fingers: not shaking now, or only a very little. And the pounding in his temples was down to an almost pleasant sort of buzz. *Madonna mia*, no wonder people became drunks.

He gave himself another ten minutes to collect himself and lit another cigarette, just a single one this time, and thought about Voss while he smoked it most of the way down.

Voss had been difficult to work with from the first. Most of the professionals for hire in the illicit surveillance business were young, manageable kids—nerdy hackers or moonlighting IT specialists—but Gus Voss was a hard-nosed, fifty-eight-year-old ex-lieutenant with the Seattle police. He'd been their hacking and identity theft expert, fired when he'd made a few forays of his own to the Dark Side and had gotten caught at it. He had then served four months in jail for his misdeeds, but within only a few more months he was making more money than ever. He had morphed into one of the world's most sought-after—and most expensive—"consultants" when surveillance services were required. "Legal" and "illegal" were not terms that concerned him. He'd worked for (and just as likely against) everybody from McDonald's, to the US Defense Department, to Britain's MI5, and, now, for the Genovese Mafia.

He was worth his exorbitant price, certainly, but he was not an easy man to get along with. The American who'd been the middleman between Ferrante and Voss had described him as "your typical Yankee hard-ass." Ferrante hadn't fully understood the term at the time, but it didn't take him long to get it. This was one very tough guy, but a thin-skinned one—someone who had to be handled with kid gloves if you wanted his cooperation. And now Ferrante had stupidly let his emotions—might as well be frank, his goggle-eyed terror—get the better of him.

The brandy was relaxing him, helping him see things in a new light. He had a third glass—or was that his second? His fourth? Hurriedly, he capped the bottle, put it back in the cabinet, and locked the door. He knew better than to allow himself to get carried away. He sighed. Why had he gotten so excited? Things weren't as bad as all that, not yet. Given a little luck, a little time, they could still be resolved. Maybe. But the key was Voss. He dialed the number again.

"This better be good," Voss said in a singsong voice when he picked up his phone.

"Good morning, my friend," said Ferrante. "First let me apologize for my earlier rudeness. I did overreact, but, you see, it appears that you may have—inadvertently, it goes without saying—created a serious problem. I'm calling in hopes that, by working together, we might remedy it before it's too late."

"Hey, that's much better, Ferrante. Now you sound like the sleazy con man you are. So tell me, what's this serious problem that you got to wake me up at two o'clock in the morning for?"

"Well, it's the mirror, Gus. I understand the temptation, believe me I do. A lovely thing, is it not? But the man I'm working for—you see, also I have to report to somebody—will be, ah, displeased when he learns—and he will learn it, I assure you—that you, ah, removed it, thereby creating considerable disorder in *signorina* London's apartment, to the extent that the police became involved. It was our expectation, you see—and did not you and I discuss this in some detail?—that you would simply put the listening devices in place, nothing more. Everything would be left as you found it, so that Ms. London herself would be unaware that you had been there. But by taking the mirror, you see . . . Gus? Are you there?"

Voss sighed. "What mirror?"

This response stunned him. He'd anticipated Voss's offering to negotiate for the mirror's return. "I . . . you are trying to tell me you did *not* take the mirror?"

"I'm not *trying* to tell you anything. I'm *telling* you: *One*, I don't know what the hell we're supposed to be talking about here, and *two*, I didn't see any damn mirrors—I don't know, one in the bathroom, maybe. Look, I did exactly what I told you I did, nothing more, nothing less. There wasn't any point in putting bugs in the walls because the weird wiring in them would have screwed everything up, but there was a landline phone in the kitchen, with two extensions in the other rooms, and I bugged them all, and then I took off. Best I could do, best anybody could do. I was in and out in twenty-five minutes. And trust me, Ferrante, no way would she know I was ever there."

Ferrante's headache began to build again. "Gus, please, tell me this: what did the apartment look like when you left?"

"It looked like it did when I came in, a mess. I wasn't really looking—"

"What do you mean, a mess?"

"A mess. The whole place looked like it'd been tossed."

Ferrante jerked his head. "'Tossed' . . . 'tossed' . . ."

"Like somebody robbed the place. Tossed. Jesus."

When Ferrante tried to speak, the connections in his brain seemed to get crossed and he started blinking instead. "Why . . . why didn't you . . . why didn't you tell me that before?"

"Hey, I figured it was something you knew about, probably why you wanted the place bugged in the first place. I don't ask a lot of questions, you ever notice that? Anyway, I've seen a lot worse. Look, the bugs are doing their job aren't they?"

"Yes, they're fine, fine—"

"Don't give me 'fine, fine.' Listen, if you got some kind of problem with my—"

"No, no, Gus, they work perfectly. There is no problem at all with them." Ferrante was doing his best to sound soothing, although it was clear to him that only one of them was in need of soothing, and it wasn't Gus Voss. He doubted if Voss was stuttering and blinking away in America. "No problem at all. None whatsoever."

Hardly, Ferrante thought. There was a huge problem and he was in big trouble. But the problem was *him*. He hadn't *listened* to the damned recordings; not until half an hour ago, the minute Moscoli had left his office after telling him the mirror was gone. But it wasn't his fault; no one could say it was his fault. At the time that the critical conversations between the two women were taking place, Ferrante had been on a morning flight to Basel for an auction, and he hadn't gotten back until this morning, only two hours ago, upon which he'd come straight from the airport to the gallery. He simply hadn't had a chance to listen, and as a result Moscoli had caught him totally by surprise.

Voss replied to his last comments with an unpleasant rattle in his throat. "Yeah, well."

"Listen to me, Gus, please. You did a wonderful job, but our predicament—"

"*Your* predicament."

"—is the mirror."

"Christ, the mirror again. Okay, let me ask you something. If this mirror's only worth twenty bucks, what are you so excited about? What's the big deal? Hey, I know—how about if I send you the twenty bucks, will that make you go away?"

"Well, ha-ha. As I said, the piece has next to no monetary value in itself, you see, and is of no importance. What is important is its pertinence to another matter entirely, a pertinence which, should it become apparent to certain other—"

"Okay, okay, I'm sorry I asked. I should've known better. But I'll tell you this one more time, and that's all: I didn't mess with any mirrors, okay? Anything that was in that place when I came in, it was there when I went out, right smack where it'd been, okay? I don't know how to make it any clearer for you."

"I . . . I believe you, of course, but, well, what am I to think, that someone *else* broke in and took the mirror? I mean to say, two break-ins by two different parties within the space of a few days? No, I simply cannot believe it."

A weary exhalation from Voss. "You believe what you want, Ferrante. I put in the bugs, they work, you paid me, end of story. You got any more jobs like this, call somebody else. I don't need this aggravation."

"Gus, you don't understand who we are dealing with here—"

"Ooh, I'm so scared. I told you, Ferrante, don't call me no more."
Click.

But Ferrante did understand with whom they were dealing, and he *was* scared to death. Without his willing it, his eyes drifted to the liquor cabinet.

CHAPTER 13

A few minutes later, steadied and calmed by another *Vecchia Romagna*, he was seeing things in a different light. You *can* get away with failing a *capo*, he told himself. Hadn't he already done it? It was when the two morons that he'd hired in Seattle had lost that fellow "Tiny" after coming so very close to getting him. But the way the Mafia looked at such things, it was Ferrante, as the man who had hired them, who was ultimately responsible. He had immediately telephoned Don Rizzolo, or rather Fausto Martucci, his chief lieutenant. (One did not telephone Don Rizzolo directly without being invited to do so.) As fearful as he was, Ferrante had told Fausto everything, and to his immense relief, there were no recriminations, only a single casually uttered piece of advice:

"Next time, hire Italians."

From Rizzolo himself, nothing. But here Ferrante was, still in one piece after almost a week had passed. *Why?* he asked himself now. Because, he answered, failing a *capo* is not an unforgivable crime. No, what you cannot do—*absolutely* cannot do—is deceive one. And that meant that Rizzolo had to be told about the theft of the mirror, that it had to be Ferrante who told him, and that it had to be done now, before anyone else did it. The *capo's* reaction to this second mishap on Ferrante's part would not be pleasant, but allowing him to find out on his own that it had been stolen and that Ferrante had hidden the fact from the don would mean death for certain.

He picked up his phone and dialed Martucci's number. At the first ring he suddenly lost his courage and very nearly hit "End" before realizing that Martucci's phone would already have recorded his number. Clumsily, he reached across his desk and for the first time in his adult life gulped liquor directly from the mouth of a bottle. He promptly went into a coughing fit. For once he was glad that he was not among the Chosen, whose calls were to be answered immediately, because by the time Martucci answered on the fourth ring, his spluttering had died down.

"*Pronto.*" Hello.

"Ah, Fausto, yes, this is Alessandro Ferrante," he got out quickly, before his nerve deserted him again. "There has been a problem with the mirror, not a major problem, all things considered, but a small problem, yes . . ."

Things were different this time. Martucci listened quietly for no more than thirty seconds. "This is not good, Ferrante." Martucci was a small man and slight, but when he was displeased his voice could be every bit as wintry and forbidding as that of the don himself.

"No, no, of course it's not *good*, Fausto, I didn't mean to say it was *good*, but . . ." Breathlessly, Ferrante jumped ahead, explaining that Voss had done them some good, after all. It was from the telephone bugs he had planted in the London woman's apartment that Ferrante had learned that she was on her way to San Francisco with a friend, close on the track of this "Tiny." And so Ferrante, on his own initiative and at his own expense, had already hired a San Francisco detective agency that would have a man at the airport when the women arrived, and would stay with them for as long as it might take. Thus, when Alix found him, *they* would find him too. And of course, once they had him—

"The name of this detective agency," Martucci said.

"Di Stefano Investigations," replied Ferrante with a painfully fabricated laugh. "You see, I took your advice."

No response from Martucci.

"Fausto, if there's anything else I can do—"

"Continue to do what you're doing. Let me know immediately if something turns up."

"Yes, certainly, without fa—"

"And remain available. It may be that the don will wish to speak to you about this in the next few days."

"Of course. Thank you. Shall I—" But Martucci was no longer there.

Ferrante's heart would have plummeted if it weren't already in his shoes.

CHAPTER 14

Conversation in the 7:15 a.m. limo to the airport was constrained, to say the least. As far as Alix was concerned, it wasn't that early. Like her father, she was an early riser and had gotten a couple of work-related emails out of the way before the gleaming burgundy Lincoln had ever shown up. But Chris, cocooned and grumpy in the far corner of the back seat, was anything but a morning person. She resented being awakened by an alarm, or, really, by anything other than the morning sun (and she wasn't too keen on that), and she had no reluctance about letting people know it. As a result, Alix quit after just one stab at chatting (*Alix*: "Looks like it'll be a beautiful flight." *Chris*: "I'm trying to sleep, here.").

A stop for lattes and oat fudge breakfast bars at the first Starbucks they came to at Sea-Tac perked Chris up a little, but other than the few minutes she spent on her iPhone, she obviously remained in no mood for talking, an attitude that continued for their two-hour flight.

Alix didn't really mind. It was only a two-hour trip, she did have the window seat, and a beautiful flight it was. It was a rare, relaxing pleasure to gaze down at clouds that looked like the tufts of cotton wool you pulled from the top of a pill bottle, and leave her mind free to wander, although it didn't wander far from simply going over and over the wonderment, the happy astonishment, of being married . . . to *Ted*!

It was only during the limo ride into San Francisco to their hotel that anything got underway that might reasonably be called conversation, helped no doubt by the coffee service to be found in the elegant little teakwood bar at their knees. Chris set her porcelain cup and saucer down on top of it. "I," she announced, "have been thinking."

"I'm happy to hear it," Alix said abstractedly, still half-absorbed in happy daydreams. They were on Highway 101, a few miles north of the airport, just passing the dry, brown hillside with the giant white letters, much like the famous HOLLYWOOD sign, but even larger, only not with quite the same panache: SOUTH SAN FRANCISCO, THE INDUSTRIAL.

"About psychology," Chris went on. "You ever hear of Leon Festinger?"

"Mm, I don't think so."

"Came up with the theory of cognitive dissonance?"

"Oh, yes, something about the stress of having two conflicting perceptions in your mind at the same time. Is that the one?"

"Right, and because it's so stressful, people are prone to making dumb decisions, even irrational ones, so that they don't conflict any-more—either trying to pretend the situation doesn't exist, or making up dim-witted theories that explain it away. Back in the fifties, I think it was, he investigated this cult that believed Earth was going to be destroyed on December something, and everyone would be killed—except for them, because these aliens were going to come and take them away on a spaceship. So they sold their homes, said goodbye to their friends, and all the rest of it. You following this? You look like your mind's a million miles away."

"Just a few thousand, but yes, not only am I following you, but I can't wait to hear what happened. *Was* the Earth destroyed?"

"No, the Earth was not destroyed."

"Whew."

Chris lifted an eyebrow. "Alix, I do have a point to make. Kindly treat this seriously."

"Sorry, go ahead. Really, I'll be good."

"Well, what Festinger was looking at was how they reacted when December something came and went and the Earth was still there. And what he found was that instead of losing confidence in the cult, they wound up having *more* faith in it. And the reason for that was what he labeled cognitive dissonance. That is, they'd trusted in the cult with all their hearts and their minds, but they could see with their own eyes that the disaster hadn't really happened. How could they possibly have been that stupid? That was the dissonance, and they couldn't live with it. Well, what they did was revise their thinking so it fit more comfortably with the facts. It wasn't long before they 'realized' that it was their devotion to the cult that had done the trick. The God of Earth had been so moved by it that he'd spared the planet after all—thanks to them. Cognitive dissonance in action. Now, then—"

"Chris, I see where you're going with this. You think that all the evidence—well, the simple fact of Tiny's mirror being stolen, to start with—indicates that it must be really valuable, but that would mean that I've been pretty dumb about it all these years. And that's a perception I can't deal with, so I'm just obstinately, stupidly refusing see what's in front of my eyes."

"Umm . . . yeah, that's the general idea. That's what our detective friend Durando thought right away, remember? That it was some valuable piece of art from the sixteenth or seventeenth century. And I've come around to thinking maybe he had something. First of all—"

"First of all, forget it. I already told you: Geoff was there when Tiny painted it."

"I suppose," Chris said ambiguously, staring pensively out her window. They were passing AT&T Park, the Giants' home park, on the right, ten minutes or so from downtown. "Still . . ."

"Come on, Chris, get it out. What are you thinking? Do you think he was lying when he told me that?"

"Now don't get your hackles up, but isn't it possible?"

"That he would lie about it like that? No. My father might have his faults, he might prevaricate a little, maybe, or omit a minor detail or two, but outright lying? No, that isn't his style."

"Oh, right, Geoffrey London, Mr. I-Cannot-Tell-a-Lie."

Alix wasn't sure what hackles were or where they were located, but something certainly prickled on the back of her neck. "And what exactly is that supposed to mean?"

Chris, being Chris, answered bluntly. "When he was bilking all those collectors out of hundreds of thousands of dollars with his forgeries, he didn't lie to them? And he didn't lie to you about his doing it? Or was that just omitting a minor detail or two?"

"Chris—"

Chris put her hand on Alix's wrist. "Alix, listen to me. I love your father almost as much as you do. He's my second favorite man in the entire world. But you have to admit, his morals are a little on the, shall we say, stretchy side . . . yes?"

Alix's hackles subsided. "A little, yes," she allowed.

"What if he thought he was protecting Tiny in some way, or possibly protecting you, by keeping alive the idea that the mirror is just a worthless little trinket that Tiny tossed off in a day or two for a little girl he loved—wouldn't he do it? Wouldn't *you*, in his place, if you thought the same thing—that you were protecting *him*? I know I would."

"I suppose so," Alix said reluctantly. "But the idea that he'd lie to my face as baldly as that, after all the trust I *thought* we'd built up these last couple of years . . . it's a really painful feeling."

"It's also a pretty common kind of feeling. There's even a name for it."

"A name?"

Chris smiled. "Cognitive dissonance."

It took a couple of beats, but Alix returned the smile. "You know, you're right, and, obviously, my preferred way of dealing with it is to pretend the situation doesn't exist. Which I would like to continue to do, if it's all the same to you, so could we just drop the subject, at least for now? We have plenty of other things to do."

"Well, sure, but would you have any objection if I go ahead and keep pursuing a few avenues of my own on the mirror? Nothing that would create any problems for Geoff."

"Of course not, Chris. Go to it."

"We're here, ladies," the driver said. "Your hotel."

⬧ ⬧ ⬧

On Chris's recommendation, they were staying at the Inn at Union Square on Post Street, in the bustling heart of San Francisco's glitziest shopping, dining, and hotel district. The Inn was an exception, an older, relatively modest (by San Francisco standards) hotel, an island of *cozy* in a sea of *glitzy*. Chris claimed it was her favorite place to stay in the city, as good a combination as could be had of being in the middle of things and yet having a pleasant, truly quiet room to work and sleep in. Alix wondered if it might have been more out of consideration for Alix's pocketbook, but when they checked in, she saw that Chris was indeed a familiar figure there. She had asked for rooms 406 and 408 and they were ready for the two of them despite the relatively early hour.

The fourth floor rooms were at the rear of the building, looking out on the backs of restaurants and shops that fronted Sutter Street, so they had nothing that anyone would call a view, but they were indeed remarkably quiet, considering where they were. Since neither of them had any interest in working or sleeping in their rooms at the moment, they left their bags unopened, quickly freshened up, and met again in the lobby five minutes later.

"On to Zappa's Deli?" Chris asked brightly.

"You bet. It's only a mile from here according to Google Maps; what do you say we walk?"

"You're on. I could sure stand to stretch my legs."

"Me too. Besides that, it should put us there at about the middle of the lunchtime crush with a lot of other people, which is good. I don't think it's a good idea to stand out too much."

"And besides that, I'm hungry," Chris said, striding toward the front entrance. "Come on, kid, get a move on."

CHAPTER 15

The two men were at their easels a couple of yards from each other, each looking very much the hard-working artist that he was: paint-stained smock, brush in one hand, thumb-hooked palette in the other.

"Have you heard anything from Tiny?" Frisby Macdowell asked, not looking up from the painted oak panel before him. Frisby was even wearing a beret.

"Nothing," said his employer, Geoffrey London, entirely engaged in his own project.

"It's getting worrisome, wouldn't you say? You'd think that by this time—"

"Tiny is not the most predictable of men. I should think you'd know that by now."

His tone was meant to indicate that the topic had now been exhausted and shouldn't they be getting back to work? Geoff's fellow ex-forger, the fussy, pedantic Frisby, was on his way to becoming a confidant, but he wasn't yet a member of the inner circle, entry to which was hard to come by, having been granted so far only to Tiny, to Alix, and maybe even to Alix's friend Chris, although that was still up in the air.

As with other fusspots and pedants, Frisby also tended toward obtuseness, and he failed to get the message. "I do know that, but it's been almost a week now. In my opinion—"

"Frisby." Geoff set his brush in the can of linseed oil beside him and walked to his colleague. "Tiny marches to his own drummer. He'll be back when he's ready. Now: to the matter at hand. How is it going?"

The matter at hand was the *Arnolfini Portrait* for the German couple. It was almost done, requiring only some lightening of the linear highlights along the pleats of the lady's sumptuous green dress. Geoff himself had spent a good hour trying to come up with a color mix that exactly matched van Eyck's results, but had eventually decided his skills could be put to better use, and he had called Frisby up to the studio to try his hand at it. Since then, Frisby had been laying experimental color patches on square after square of blank canvas leaning against the painting itself.

"I'm not sure," Frisby said. "I *think* this one might do it, but . . ."

Geoff looked from the patch to the high-definition photographic enlargement taped to the wall. "No, we're still not all the way there, I'm afraid. This malachite green is certainly the right base, but . . . have you tried adding just a tad more of the Cremnitz to it?"

"Yes, I have. A tad more, a tad less." He gestured at the dozens of patches. "Nothing does it. I think I'll try a less opaque white—a zinc white is what I was thinking about. That might do it."

Geoff registered shock. "Frisby, zinc white—"

"I know, I know. Zinc white did not exist until the end of the eighteenth century, a little late for van Eyck's use."

"Only by about two hundred years." He put an avuncular hand on Frisby's shoulder. "Frisby, my boy, I thought you understood. The reputation of Genuine Fakes rests on the buyer's expectation that they will be as genuine as possible in every sense of the word."

"True, but also fake . . . in every sense of the word."

The hand was withdrawn. "I don't see that cynicism is called for. From the first I have adhered with unwavering consistency to the principle—"

"Hm, am I mistaken, or didn't somebody once say that consistency was the hobgoblin of little minds?"

"'A *foolish* consistency is the hobgoblin of little minds, adored by little statesmen and philosophers and divines' is the way Mr. Emerson put it, I believe."

"And I couldn't agree more," said Frisby, who loved a good argument. "So when a long-anticipated painting is already overdue, it seems to me that unwavering adherence to consistency becomes foolish, that perhaps a little flexibility might be in order. Especially when this particular buyer wouldn't know zinc white from cadmium red."

"That is not the point—" Geoff began sternly, but let the rest of what he was going to say drop. He shouldn't *have had* to explain it to someone who'd been working with him for more than year. This was exactly why Frisby had yet to achieve inner-circle status. "Simply do as I ask, please."

Frisby finally realized he was being rebuked, and he wilted. Good jobs were not something that came easily to ex-convicts. "Of course, Geoff. I understand completely. It was only a suggestion."

"Keep on with the Cremnitz white," Geoff said and left him to it, going back to his own easel and his new problem. It was a new commission, another double portrait, this one to be done in the style of Modigliani's *Jacques and Berthe Lipchitz*, the 1916 painting now at the Art Institute of Chicago. Geoff was no fan of twentieth-century art in general, but Amedeo Modigliani was, in his opinion, a true descendant of the post-Renaissance, his sinuous, elongated forms with their almond eyes and swanlike necks unmistakably redolent of El Greco, and Pontormo, and Parmigianino, all of whose methods Modigliani had studied as a young painter.

Geoff had already sent photos of his underdrawing to Mrs. Pulsipher in Salt Lake City, and they had met with her enthusiastic approval. Fine, but the painting part was proving tricky. Duplicating Modigliani's smooth, sweeping strokes and modeling was never easy, but this picture was particularly challenging. Modigliani had done so much tinkering, so much dibbing and dabbing, that it was next to impossible to decipher the mixing and layering of colors, even with the help of X-ray and ultraviolet photos. Geoff was now taking his fourth stab at getting merely the background right—all those overlapping russet and sienna browns.

As difficult as it was, it was work that he enjoyed, and he smiled, thinking about how this particular painting had come to be so "overworked." Years later, Lipchitz described it. He had asked his friend Modigliani to do a portrait of him and his wife. Modigliani had happily complied, and at one o'clock one afternoon they began posing for him. By sunset, Modigliani was satisfied; it was done. But Lipchitz, by then having achieved some financial success as a sculptor, wanted to do more for his impoverished friend than give him the ten francs that a single afternoon's work brought, so he requested changes and "improvements"—to which Modigliani's grumbling reply was, "All right, if you want me to spoil it, I'll keep at it." Which he did, keeping at it for two full weeks, probably the most time he'd ever spent on one painting, and resulting in the most money he ever made on one.

Poor Amedeo, Geoff mused, mixing still another brown-yellow-red paste. The man had been a virtual template for everyone's image of the romantic, starving artist in his garret. He did live in a garret; he was, if not starving, not doing very well; he was young, and handsome, and debonair; and he lived a loose, promiscuous life full of drink and drugs. More than once he was heard to say that he intended to drink himself to death. And he did, most assiduously. Before turning thirty-seven he was gone (followed in short order by his faithful, pregnant, long-term mistress, who threw herself from a fifth-story window the day after his funeral). Modigliani had died never having dreamt of the value and respect his work would one day command. To think of what he might have—

"I think I've got it, Geoff," Frisby said. "Will you have a look?"

Geoff went to Frisby and stood looking over his shoulder. After a few seconds, he nodded. "I believe you do, Frisby, I believe you do. That's perfect."

"Do you want to take over from here, then, Geoff?"

"No, no, no, you finish it up yourself," Geoff said kindly. "I couldn't do any better than you are." He was feeling guilty over his earlier harshness.

Frisby's eyes shone. He was being forgiven, or at least getting another chance. This was the first time anybody but Tiny had been delegated any substantial work on a Genuine Fake. Geoff clapped him on the shoulder again and turned to go back to his own painting, but froze after a single step. "My God," he said.

"What?" said the startled Frisby. "What is it?"

Geoff looked at his watch. "Yes, she should have landed in San Francisco by now," he muttered.

"Who should have landed in San Francisco? Geoff, what's the matter?"

Geoff was already on his way to a telephone in the living quarters of the loft. "I have to call my daughter!" he shouted back. "Right this minute!"

CHAPTER 16

Zappa's Delicatessen is in the 300 block of Columbus Avenue, a mere dozen blocks north of downtown San Francisco, an easy, pleasant stroll, but culinarily speaking, getting there takes you halfway around the world. Three blocks from cosmopolitan, quintessentially American Union Square, you walk beneath Grant Avenue's Dragon Gate and for the next eight blocks you might as well be in China, but the moment you hit Columbus, a block south of Zappa's, you have left mu shu pork and dim sum behind and are now in Little Italy, AKA North Beach. Here, and for the next several blocks, if your life depended on finding a chow mein noodle, you'd be out of luck. The cafés and restaurants (and most of the streetside establishments are cafés or restaurants) are proudly, flagrantly Italian—Trattoria Pinocchio, Calzone's Pizza Cucina, Sotto Mare, Caffè Trieste, Rose Pistola, Da Flora, and on and on.

As the world knows, the cuisines of China and Italy are unmatched for their mouthwatering aromas, so by the time Chris and Alix reached the door to Zappa's and edged by the exiting, sack-bearing customers, they were practically slavering, their oat fudge bars mere distant memories.

"Maybe we should eat first?" Chris suggested as the smells of salami, olive oil, garlic, and earthy red wine really hit them, the sentence ending with a hopeful uptick. "Before we get down to asking questions? Give us some energy, you know?"

Alix's response was a stern and withering look. Chris was not easily cowed, but they both knew that Alix held the moral high ground here. First things first. They hadn't come to San Francisco for its dining pleasures.

"Or not," Chris said with the faintest of sighs.

But the sigh was sufficiently dolorous to make Alix give way a little. "Well, I suppose we could at least order our lunches first, before throwing questions at the staff." Besides, she was starving too, and ordering food was at least a step in the right direction.

Chris perked up. "Right. Get on their good side. Excellent thinking, Holmes."

Alix had expected that Zappa's, being "the last of the true Italian *salumerie*," would have changed little since the old photo of Tiny had been taken, but she hadn't anticipated its looking *exactly* the same. Nothing at all had changed: the same shelves stocked three deep with bottles of wine and olive oil; the same long counter atop a huge deli case filled with cheeses, olives, sliced salamis, and cold cuts; the same slicing machine (or its twin), the same red, white, and blue *G. G. Zappa & Figli* plaque right where it was before and looking just as dusty. If you asked her, the salamis and hams hanging from hooks in the ceiling were the very same ones too, but surely that couldn't be true (could it?). The only difference was that a slim, serious young man with dark hair, "Gabe" according to his name tag, was behind the counter, where Tiny's blond "freinde" Waldo had once stood mugging at the camera.

"How does he stay that skinny working in a place like this?" Alix wondered to Chris as they waited behind the half-dozen customers milling about and placing or picking up their orders.

"I know I couldn't. Must be new here."

"Hope not. I was counting on someone older, someone who might know Tiny from before."

While they waited, they made their lunch choices from a sandwich menu posted on the wall: Italian salami and provolone for Alix, meatballs with marinara sauce for Chris. But watching Gabe make up a fat, fabulous-looking "Pavarotti Special" (prosciutto, sausage, mozzarella, sun-dried tomatoes, and onions on a flour-dusted ciabatta roll) for an earlier customer changed their minds, and when their turn came, that was what they both asked for. On Gabe's recommendation they each ordered a bottle of Moretti beer to go with it.

"Oh, say, Gabe," Alix said with calculated nonchalance as they watched him slap together their sandwiches. "I have an uncle, haven't seen him in years, but I know he used to live around here. Beniamino Abbatista? Uncle Beni, I used to call him. I know he used to love this place. He'd write me letters about it, you know?"

Without stopping his swiftly moving, plastic-gloved hands, Gabe glanced up, not saying anything but his expression was clear enough: *So? You are telling me this, why?*

Chris was also looking mutely at Alix. Her thoughts were equally easy to read: *You're overdoing it, making him nervous. Just get to the damn point.*

Alix quickened the pace. "So, anyway, do you know who I mean? 'Tiny,' they mostly call him—you know, because he's so big. I thought maybe he might have mentioned my name—Alix? I'd love to catch up with him, and I was wondering if you might know him. I thought maybe he still comes in."

He shrugged. "Mustard or mayo?"

Alix gave up. "Mustard," she said.

"Mayo," said Chris.

"This all gonna be on one check?"

"No," they both said together. It had taken a long time, but Alix seemed finally to have gotten through to Chris that, while she appreciated the way her newly rich friend automatically reached for whatever bill was presented, she couldn't keep on accepting it. And Alix couldn't afford to pay for *her*. So how about going Dutch as a regular thing? Chris had resisted but thus far, on this trip at least, she was going along with it and Alix was grateful.

Another shrug from Gabe as he began wrapping, after which the plastic gloves were tossed into a canister behind the counter. "Sorry I can't help you. That's $14.50 each."

"Thanks," said Chris with resignation. She was already envisioning a long afternoon of knocking on strangers' doors. "Is there a park or something around here where we could eat these?"

But Gabe wasn't the talky kind, and he was already engaged with the next customer.

A pink-cheeked, middle-aged man with receding, pale hair that seemed to float above his scalp like a cloud of cotton candy approached them as they were taking napkins from the countertop dispenser. He wore a short-sleeved white business shirt with a tie. The name tag above the pocket said only *Manager*. "Did I hear you say you were looking for a place to have those sandwiches? Why don't you try Washington Square Park? It's just a couple of blocks up Columbus and it's far and away the best place around here for a picnic. You can sit on a bench and get some shade if you want it, or out in the sun on the lawn. It's nice. Safe too. Lots of kids and families around, especially this time of day."

"Sounds perfect," said Chris. "Thanks."

"Enjoy," he said and turned to answer a question from another customer.

⬩   ⬩   ⬩

They opted for shade, seated on one of the green benches along the northern border of the block-square lawn, backed by the brooding, gray, neo-Gothic facade of the old St. Peter and Paul Catholic church and screened from the sun by a hedge row of boxwood pruned into a sort of canopy. A pair of the area's famous green-bodied, cherry-headed parrots chittered and flitted through the branches above them. When they finished their sandwiches they sat back, nursing the last of their beers and trying without much success to catch glimpses of the swift-moving birds.

After a few moments of digesting in silence, Alix said, "Chris, take a look at that guy over there, will you? Brown baseball cap, glasses, skinny. Be subtle."

"I am always subtle," Chris intoned. "Subtlety is my middle name." She followed Alix's line of sight toward a bench some twenty yards off. "Working on a crossword puzzle or something?"

"Yes, does he look familiar to you?"

"No. Do you know him?"

"No, but I think I saw him at the airport when we were getting off the plane."

"So?" Chris tilted the long-necked bottle of beer to her mouth.

"So I think he's following us."

"Because he was at the airport, and now he's here?"

"Because the reason I remember him is that I happened to notice him pretty carefully watching everyone disembark, and when he saw us, I could see the flash of interest in his eyes. I mean, he was really studying us."

Chris laughed. "You actually saw a man staring at two good-looking broads like us? How utterly amazing. The nerve of him."

When the man's head came up, they both looked away. "All right, tell me this," Alix said. "What was he doing at the airport?"

"How would I know that? Probably waiting for somebody."

"No, you can't get through security to wait for somebody anymore, you know that. You need a ticket."

"All right, then maybe he was catching a flight himself."

Alix shook her head. "No. If he was catching a plane, then what is he doing still in San Francisco? And other than catching a flight, the only way to get into the secure area of an airport is to get off an incoming plane yourself. So he must have arrived on an earlier one. Why would he be hanging around watching a later flight disembark?"

"Well—"

"And what are the chances of him showing up right here, right where we happen to be, two hours later?"

Chris stole another look at him. "You're positive it's the same guy?"

"I am, yes. The glasses, even the gawky way he's sitting, scrunched up like that, all knees and elbows."

"So what do you think we should do?" Chris was staring fixedly at the man now, with an unsettling gleam in her eyes.

"Well, I don't think we should confront him, if that's what you mean," Alix said nervously. "I might be wrong, after all. I think the best thing to do is wait and see and keep an eye out—"

"Oh, the hell with that," Chris declared, tossing her lunch bag into a trash can beside the bench and standing up. "Come on."

She strode forcefully toward the man. Alix, after a moment's wavering, jumped up and tagged along after her.

The man still seemed to be absorbed in writing something in his magazine, but when the six-foot-plus Chris LeMay loomed over you, feet apart and hands on her hips, not two feet away, she was hard to ignore. He looked up, wide-eyed and blinking through smudged, plastic-rimmed glasses.

"Something we can do for you, buddy?" Chris said.

"I beg your pardon?" He wasn't as old as Alix had thought, probably in his late twenties, a slight, bookish young man who looked as if he might be a graduate student at one of the local universities. He was sharing the bench with a heavy-set older man in a battered leather jacket, who was smoking a cigarette—holding it in the old European way, not between his first two fingers but pinched between the thumb and the first finger, palm up.

"Were you at the airport this morning?" Chris demanded. The older man, already at the far end of the bench, nervously edged even farther away. He had the look, not quite of a street person, but of someone who'd been through the wringer himself and wanted no part of anyone else's troubles.

"Yes, I was. How do you—"

"That's what I thought. I hope I'm not being too intrusive, but I'm kind of a curious person and I can't help wondering why you're following us."

He uttered an incredulous laugh, followed by a frown. "Ma'am, if I've offended you in some way—"

"Let's see some ID, buddy."

Alix's mouth practically dropped open, although she really should have known better than to be surprised. Chris had changed some as she got used to having more money than she knew what to do with. Her taste in clothes, for one thing, was less flamboyant and more fashion-conscious than it used to be. But Chris herself was as audacious, bold, and brassy as ever and this little impromptu interrogation was right in character.

"Are you . . . are you a cop?" he asked, eyes even wider.

That was enough for the old man, who quietly gathered his newspaper and paper bag and slipped away to find another place to have his lunch.

"What I am, pal—" Chris began, but Alix cut in before she could get them both in trouble.

"No, we're not police officers, but we did happen to notice you at the airport, and now again here, and so we couldn't help wondering—"

But this wasn't direct enough for Chris. "What are you doing in this particular park?"

"Doing Sudoku, not that it's any of your business." He stood up, which made Chris back off a step and seemed to increase his self-confidence. "Let me ask *you* something: What are *you* doing in this particular park? How do I know you're not following *me*? And where's *your* ID?" He was doing his best to show some backbone and establish dominance, but his pale eyes, nervously blinking away behind those smudged glasses, didn't do much to make his case.

"Look, buster—" Chris said, but in fact, she had lost a little of her moral authority and he sensed it.

"No, you look. I came here for a little peace and quiet, but obviously I picked the wrong place for it. Fine, you can have the park. I'll find someplace else. Jesus Christ."

Without waiting for a response he slammed the magazine down on the bench (and there was the Sudoku partly filled in) and tramped off, but a few yards away he turned for a final shot. "And I'm warning you," he yelled. "Stay away from me! Hassle me one more time and I'll bring the cops down on you. I mean the *real* cops!" Unfortunately, his voice had broken on the word "real." He finished with a muttered "Some people!" as he shook his head and walked away.

It was more than loud enough for those nearby to hear, and the two women found themselves on the receiving end of some strange looks, which sent them on their way. They didn't see much profit in sticking to the man in the baseball cap, so they started across the lawn, threading through the people sitting on it and having their own lunches, back toward the block that Zappa's was on.

Alix was giggling. It was something she almost never did, but she couldn't help it now.

Chris scowled at her. "What?"

"'Let's see some ID, buddy,'" she said in something like Chris's vibrant, deep growl.

Chris grinned. "You think that was maybe overdoing it a little?"

"A little?"

"Alix, he *was* following us."

"Well, you know, now I'm not so sure. What he said was true. From his point of view we could just as easily be following him."

"No, there's a difference. The odds of it being a total coincidence are zilch, right? Somebody's following somebody. The difference is, we *know* we're not following him. Therefore—"

"—it has to be him. All right, what do you think we should do? Go to the police?"

"Without a name? With no proof? I don't think so."

"He didn't seem very threatening, did he? I don't think he means to hurt us." She paused to boot a soccer ball back to a couple of kids who were kicking it around.

"Neither do I. You know what, I just wonder if the guy's a PI. Not looking like one is probably a big plus in that line of work. Why he'd be following us—or who would have hired him to do it—I have no idea."

Alix thought about that. "And I just wonder if it's not us he's really interested in, but Tiny, and he thinks we might lead him to him. I can't think of another reason."

"But how would he know we're here looking for Tiny ourselves?"

Alix shook her head. "I don't—"

"Pardon me, ladies?" The polite query came from a man coming toward them—the manager from Zappa's Delicatessen. "I hope you enjoyed your sandwiches."

"Very much," Alix said. "And thanks for recommending the park."

He stood there, chewing the corner of his lip, trying to decide something, then said to Alix: "I hope you don't mind my asking, but . . . well, are you Geoffrey London's daughter? Alix London?"

Instinctively, Alix pulled back. When a stranger brought up Geoff's name out of the blue, nothing very good was likely to come of it.

"Yes," she said tautly.

"I thought so," he said. "You don't know me—"

But to her surprise, she realized she did know him. "You're Waldo!" she exclaimed.

His turn to be surprised. "I am, yes, but how do you know that?"

She scrabbled about in her bag and came up with the old photo of Tiny in front of the counter, and Waldo, laughing and mugging behind it.

Waldo beamed when he saw it. "Oh, isn't that great! Look at Tiny. And look at *me*—was I ever really that young?" A rueful shake of his head. "Thirty or so years ago, this had to have been."

"Just twenty, actually," Alix said with a smile, "and you haven't changed that much. I'll make you a copy of it if you like."

"I would, very much," he said, handing it back, then got more serious. "You asked in the shop whether Tiny ever mentioned you, and in fact he did, many times, and very affectionately. And you're looking for him now? May I ask why?"

Alix quickly decided to level with him. "He's disappeared, Waldo—a week ago—and we're worried about him. We're pretty sure he's in some kind of trouble, and we think maybe he can use some help—money, anything. Oh, and this is my friend Chris LeMay."

"I'm a friend of Tiny's too," Chris said as they shook hands and the three of them continued toward Columbus Avenue.

"Well, I can tell you that he did come through here a couple of days ago. He stayed one night with me before taking off. I'm worried about him too."

"Do you know what the problem is?" Chris asked. "He left Seattle without a word to anybody."

Waldo shook his head. "No. I was hoping you might be able to tell me. He sure didn't want to talk about it, and I learned a long time ago not to push him. He was headed for Monterey, that's all I know."

Alix stopped walking so abruptly that Waldo stumbled over her foot. "You know where he is?" she exclaimed.

"No, just that it's Monterey and he expected to be there for a while."

"Why Monterey?" Alix asked, frowning. "I don't think I ever heard him talk about Monterey."

"Well, he has somebody down there, I know that—a distant cousin, I think it is—and Tiny seems to think he'll give him some kind of work that'll let him stay pretty much out of sight and put bread in his mouth at the same time."

"You don't know the person's name?" Chris asked. "The kind of business?"

Waldo chewed on his lip some more. "All I can tell you is that the guy's name is Tino, not that that's going to be much help."

"Why not?" Chris asked. "How many *Tino*s can there be in Monterey? How hard can it be to look them up? We can do a White Pages search on the web."

"We could, yes," Alix said, "but Tino's usually just a nickname for any name ending in *t-i-n-o*, and there are a lot of them: Albertino, Costantino . . ."

"Valentino, Celestino . . ." Waldo put in.

"Faustino," Alix added, "Juventino . . ."

Chris rolled her eyes. "Oy."

"Not that his name couldn't *be* Tino," Alix pointed out. "Sometimes it is used as a given name."

"Hey, wait," Waldo said, "I do remember something that could be useful. He said this Tino ran a seafood place down there, so I'm guessing he's going to be working in the kitchen or maybe somewhere else behind the scenes—picking up from the wholesalers, or maybe cleanup and custodial, that kind of thing." He shrugged. "I don't know any more than that. Sorry. You know Tiny; he doesn't exactly go around broadcasting his plans."

Alix smiled. "Yes, we know Tiny." Then she looked at Chris. "Well, anyway, I guess I know where we're off to next."

"Monterey, here we come," Chris responded. "Waldo, thanks a lot, you've really been helpful."

He was doubtful. "I don't know how helpful I've been. There must be a thousand seafood restaurants down there."

"It's a start," Alix said stoutly, but her confidence at this point was not very high.

When they said goodbye to Waldo, he asked them to let him know how things went with Tiny, and if there were anything he could do to help, but his last words were: "Now you won't forget to send me that picture, will you?"

◆　◆　◆

"So what do you say?" asked Chris as they watched him walk back toward the deli. "Want to fly down or rent a car and drive? Probably two hours either way under normal circumstances, but 101 can have some horrendous tie-ups."

"It sure can," said Alix, who spoke from experience. "Let's fly, then. Then we—"

She was interrupted by the ringing of a telephone, which was emanating from Chris's giant shoulder bag and playing a plaintive melody that Alix recognized but couldn't place. "Now why would your father be calling me instead of you?" Chris muttered. They sat down on the nearest bench while Chris shrugged off the bag and set it next to her, then started her usual poking around in its depths.

"What makes you think it's Geoff?" Alix asked, puzzled. "You haven't even found it yet."

"I have individualized ringtones. Different melodies for different people," said Chris, very nearly elbow-deep in the detritus that filled the bag. "Not for everybody I know, but some."

"You do? What's that one?"

"'Starting Over.' You don't know it?" The snatch of melody tinnily played a second time. Chris was now pulling things out of the bag; lipstick, mirror, Kleenex, Purell, sunscreen, wallet, keys . . .

"Don't know it," Alix said.

"John Lennon?"

"Nope. That is, I do know John Lennon, but . . ."

"Can you believe this?" Chris was grumbling at her bag. "Where did I stick that . . . Ah, here we go."

She extricated the phone and held it to her ear. "Yes, Geoff, hello. No, we're both fine and she's right here. Oh, I suspect she just forgot to take the phone off airplane mode. Here she is."

"Airplane mode, individualized ringtones," Alix muttered as she took the phone. "If these things are so smart, why didn't it know when I got off the plane?" And then, more clearly:

"Hi, Geoff, have you been trying to get me for a while?"

"Oh, no, merely all day long," he grumped. "When . . . *if* . . . you ever look at your phone again, you'll find three messages from me, or perhaps it's four; I've lost count."

"I apologize for that. I'll be more careful from now on, I promise. Is everything all right?"

"Yes, fine, but while I was working alongside Frisby this morning, I realized that I had greatly misled you. And myself, for that matter. I had him putting in some color highlights in the Arnolfini, and as I stood beside him looking at his progress, I suddenly realized that if I were there watching as a casual observer at that point, I would have assumed, quite naturally, that he had painted the entire picture. Why would I have thought otherwise? But all I really *did* see—see with my own eyes—were a few streaks of green he was laying on an otherwise finished work." He laughed. "You see?"

Alix reran his words through her mind. "I'm afraid not."

He made a frustrated little clucking sound. "Of course you do. It's precisely the same situation that existed when I saw Tiny working on the mirror. I didn't stand there watching him for hours on end; I was that casual observer. The fact is, when I told you I saw him painting the panel, I *should* have said I saw him painting the cherubs, and I more or less automatically assumed he'd done the whole thing, but in truth I have no recollection of seeing him working on the clouds or the sky, or the figures, which means . . ."

CHAPTER 17

Which means," Chris said when Alix finished telling her about it, "that the whole thing—everything but those cherubs—might really be authentic sixteenth-century work. Something valuable."

"Yes, I'll go along with that if we remember that 'might' is the operative word there. The fact that Geoff didn't see him paint it doesn't mean he *didn't* paint it, it just means that *maybe* he didn't . . . or maybe he did, and we have no way of knowing which it was, at least not at this point."

"At *this* point!" Chris repeated excitedly. "That reminds me: I need to make a quick call. If things work out, we just might find out which it was before this day is done." She'd hit the Connect button while she was talking and quickly began speaking to the person on the other end.

"Dr. Norgren's office, please . . . Oh, hi, yes, it's me. Are you going to be able to fit us in? Five o'clock? Yes, we can make that easily. Thank you. But listen, there's news. We just heard from Alix's father, who now remembers that all he personally saw Tiny painting was the cherubs, not the—"

That was the last Alix was able to hear. A kid on a toy motorcycle had chosen the sidewalk directly in front of their bench to demonstrate to a friend the excruciatingly realistic engine-revving racket his tiny machine could make, and Chris first turned away from them (and from Alix) to continue speaking, then had to get up and move a few yards farther onto the lawn.

It was five minutes before she rejoined Alix on the bench, by which time the kids had moved on to entertain other park-sitters trying to have a quiet afternoon. "What was that all about?" Alix asked. "Are we supposed to be somewhere at five? It's after four now, you know."

"Worry not, I've taken care of it. We'll get there in plenty of time."

"Get where? What's up?"

"Don't look so suspicious. Everything's good—better than good. The thing is, I took you at your word when you said you didn't mind my looking into this thing a little on my own, so I got hold of Christopher Norgren, who's now the senior curator of paintings at the Legion of Honor here—"

". . . and used to be at the Seattle Art Museum."

"Right, the same. He's really an old pal of mine. He and his wife used to be regulars at Sangiovese, so I got to know them pretty well." This was a reference to the upscale, art-themed wine bar that Chris owned in Seattle's hip Belltown district. By now it had become a weekly destination for Geoff too, who held court there for an hour or two every Thursday, never failing to draw an attentive, admiring audience of artists and would-be artists to Sangiovese's Fireside Niche.

"So anyway," Chris went on, "I told him we were in Frisco and if he had the time we'd really appreciate it if he'd have a look at the mirror himself and pass along any insights. So naturally, he promised he'd try to fit us in. I was supposed to check with him this afternoon and I just did. Five o'clock. He's got a meeting till then, and he has to be at some kind of dinner thing at six, so he's really shoe-horning us in."

"That's great, Chris, I remember what a nice guy he is. But what's he supposed to work from? This crumpled copy of the magazine? He couldn't—"

"Hey, come on, give me more credit than that. While you were snuffling up coffee at Sea-Tac, I was busily trying to locate the photographer who took that picture, in which endeavor I was unsuccessful. But employing the perseverance for which I am so well-known, I *was* able to contact his studio and to convince his assistant to email an ultra-high-resolution image of the mirror—not the whole magazine cover, just Tiny's mirror—to the Legion. Which she did, but the esteemed Dr. Norgren has not yet had a chance to get to it himself, so we're all going to look at it together."

"Good going, Chris, that's wonderful." Alix jumped up from the bench. "But let's get going. We need to find a taxi."

"I told you, that's already taken care of too. Uber Black to the rescue." She pointed at the ebony town car pulling to a curbside stop, not thirty feet away, at the nearby corner of Columbus and Union.

"Chris, you're amazing."

Chris mouth-shrugged and waggled her fingers. *Nothing to it.*

"Good afternoon, ladies," said the smiling driver through his open side window. "My name is Harold. The Legion of Honor, is it?"

"If you please, Harold," Chris said. "And then I'd appreciate it if you'd wait for us in the lot. We shouldn't be more than an hour."

"My pleasure," Harold said, starting up.

"Chris, can I ask you a question?" Alix said as they settled in. "Well, two questions?"

"Ask away."

"Well, I could see that that giant bag of yours has about a zillion pockets, most of them with zippers. Why do you just dump everything in the middle instead of using them? Just curious, that's all."

Chris considered. "You know, that is a very good question," she said nodding. "Hm. Now, what's number two?"

Alix laughed. "I was thinking about that ringtone: 'Starting Over.' It really couldn't be more perfect for my father. I missed the point before."

"Thank you, I thought so."

"And what's my ringtone?"

"Actually, I haven't settled on the one I want for you so I'm using a temporary one, just for the time being."

"Which is?"

"Wait a minute, I'll play it for you." The phone was still in her hand from the earlier calls, so no complicated excavation efforts were required. She hit a couple of buttons and the speaker emitted four notes of a slow, stately melody.

Alix, who knew opera, recognized it after the first two notes and laughed with pleasure. "I'd say that ought to do until when—or if—something better comes along."

It was the "Treulich Geführt" chorus from Wagner's *Lohengrin*.

Or in common parlance: "Here Comes the Bride."

CHAPTER 18

Alix had been to the museum's curatorial offices in the past, before Norgren had arrived there from Seattle, so she knew where to find them.

"Good God, what's down there, the crypt?" Chris exclaimed, looking dubiously at the dimly lit staircase before them. It was tucked into an inconspicuous concrete-block nook near the gift shop, and led uninvitingly down to an even dimmer basement landing. "The dungeons? Is that where they keep the heretics chained to the walls?"

Alix laughed. "It's where they keep the curators, but it's not as bad as it looks. Or at any rate they don't keep them chained to their desks."

But before they could start down, they were hailed by a pint-sized, middle-aged woman pushing a cart loaded with a thermal jug and coffee fixings, a carafe of what looked appealingly like white wine, a glass bowl of mixed nuts, and several mugs and stemless wine glasses. "Ms. LeMay? Ms. London?"

"That's us," Alix said.

"Dr. Norgren is waiting for you in the boardroom. He thought it would be better. It's back down at the other end of the hall. Come along, I'll show you. I'm on the way there myself."

"Mm," said Chris, "those goodies—are they for us?"

"Unless Dr. Norgren intends them all for himself, I suspect so, yes."

The Legion's boardroom turned out to be small but handsomely furnished, with just enough space for a gleaming, oval, eight-person conference table and big, comfortable-looking executive chairs. Behind the table, Christopher Norgren, fit-looking at fifty or so, with only a few silvery strands glinting through his slightly thinning blond hair, stood up. His trim mustache, which had turned completely white, still looked good on him. "Chris, Alix, it's great to see you both." Considering that he was going to be staying beyond the normal working day to help them out, his smile seemed relaxed and genuine. "It's been too long."

"Thanks very much, Mrs. Lesnevich," he said, taking the tray and setting it down. "This was over and above the call of duty."

"You bet it is, and don't think I'm going to let you forget it."

As she left he came around the table to greet the newcomers, hugging Chris, who responded with vigor, but correctly reading Alix's less demonstrative nature from her posture and settling for a friendly handshake. And very friendly it was. She owed him a lot. It was Christopher Norgren who had really launched her career as an art consultant by recommending her to Chris two years earlier, when Alix, living in the off-putting shadow of her father's notoriety, was having a hard time finding clients.

Afterward, she had stopped by his office in the Seattle Art Museum to thank him, and they'd wound up going out for gyros at a nearby Greek hole-in-the-wall restaurant. They'd talked for nearly an hour and she'd liked him right away. He'd struck her as perhaps the least self-important art museum curator she'd ever met; this in a profession in which an unassailable sense of self-worth sometimes seemed like a prerequisite. It would have been nice to get to know him better, but within a month he'd left for his current position here at the Legion, so this was the first time she'd seen him since.

He waved at the tray. "Coffee? White wine?"

"Wine would be lovely," Chris said.

"For me too," Alix said. "Only half a glass, though. And some coffee would be nice too."

"It's a Riesling," he said, pouring the wine, including a little for himself.

"We appreciate your going to so much trouble," Alix said.

"Not at all, it's a special occasion." He waved them into a couple of the big chocolate-brown leather chairs and handed them their drinks. "Unfortunately, I don't have that much time. Well, we'd better get down to it." He sat down across from them with a laptop on the table in front of him and got his fingers going on the keyboard.

As the usual succession of Microsoft's desktop followed by a zillion dialogue menus flashed across a screen set in the wall at the head of the table, Chris took her first sip of the wine. "Hey!" she exclaimed. "This is *good*!"

He raised his head to look sardonically at her. "And what did you expect? This is a classy joint we got here, lady."

"No, I mean *really* good. It's Alsatian, that's obvious . . ." She took another delicate sip and closed her eyes. "Clos Sainte Hune, am I right?"

"Yes," Norgren said. "That's astonishing, Chris."

"Astonishing," Alix agreed.

Chris grinned at them. "It's a knack. 'Connoisseur's taste buds,' we call it."

By now Norgren had found the image he was looking for and it popped up on the screen: Tiny's mirror, much enlarged but as clear as could be.

"Oh!" said Alix.

"Ah," said Norgren.

"What?" said Chris.

But Alix and Norgren were looking at each other. "So it *is* old," Norgren said.

Alix nodded. "Yes, centuries old."

"So Tiny *didn't* paint those cherubs?" Chris asked confusedly. "But didn't Geoff say—"

"No, the cherubs are new, all right," Alix explained, "but they were painted on top of an existing painting, a really old one."

"Which you two are so sure of, because . . . ?"

"The *craquelure*," said Norgren.

"*Craquelure*," agreed Alix, "right." Wonderingly, she shook her head. "How strange. I've had it all these years and looked at it a million times. But I never really *looked* at it before. It took this blowup to make me see it."

"Um, *craquelure*," Chris echoed. "Sorry, what is that again? Is that all those little cracks?"

Norgren seemed surprised that Chris, as a collector, wouldn't be more familiar with the term, but Alix understood. At Chris's request, her art education at Alix's hands was proceeding backward in time. They were still deep in the Post-Impressionist period at the tail end of the nineteenth century, and not enough time had passed since then for there to be much in the way of serious *craquelure* to consider.

"Yes, the cracks," Alix said. "The paint—or sometimes it can be the varnish—dries and shrinks over time, but the canvas or panel it's on can't shrink along with it, or at least not as much. Well, the paint can only shrink so much until eventually it gets to the point where the stress is too much for it, and—"

"It cracks," Chris said. "'Crackles,' I should say."

"Not only does it crackle," said Norgren, "but it does it in predictable patterns. Paint on canvas crackles differently from paint on wood, for example, and the way it crackles on an oak panel is usually different—subtle but discernible, if you know what you're looking for—from craquelure on poplar. And this pattern sure looks to me to be typical of poplar, which would indeed be most likely to have been the wood used by the northern Italian Mannerists. It's not that complicated. The stability and relative permanence of the wood's medullary rays in the context of atmospheric—"

Chris politely held up her hand. "That's okay, I'll take your word for it."

Norgren laughed. "A wise decision."

"And those cherubs haven't started crackling yet," Chris said, "so therefore, they're *not* old, but the background is." She nodded to herself and thoughtfully plucked a couple of cashews from the bowl. "Yeah, I get it."

"Right," Norgren said, peering a little more intensely at the image and blinking, "and I can see—I think can see—some irregularities in their surfaces that indicates that the craquelure underneath is starting to come through."

"Yes, they're there, all right," Alix said numbly. She was still dealing with the fact that she—the Art Whisperer, no less—had lived with a piece of art for two decades without being aware of its most obvious physical features. Not until someone else pointed them out to her—from a *photograph*. Well, if nothing else, it had taught her a lesson. Never again would there be any incredulous and condescending rolling of her eyes (mental, though it had been) at the amazing obliviousness occasionally displayed by her dimmer clients. She was one of them now.

All of them sipped a little, ate a little, looked at the image, and pondered.

"Italian Mannerist, of course," Norgren said.

"Absolutely," said Alix, thinking back to her talk with Geoff about Italian Mannerist clouds and French Rococo cherubs. Studying the image now, she added: "Probably Roman school, or maybe Venetian, but Roman would be my guess. Dr. Norgren?"

"Yes, Roman. Apparently a fragment cut from a larger panel."

"Oh, yes, obviously."

"Alix, I can't help wondering—" He hesitated. "You must have looked at the back of it time and again. Did that not tell you anything that raised questions in your mind? Guild brands? Sale markings? The condition of the wood?"

"No, I've never seen the back. It's covered with felt, and there was no reason—so I thought—to take it off."

"What about the edges of the panel? Could you tell if they were relatively recently cut, or—" When she began to shake her head he stopped and sighed. "No edges. It was already framed when he gave it to you."

"I'm afraid so. Hey, now, what do we have here?" she said softly, standing and walking around Chris's chair to get closer to the screen. "Dr. Norgren, are you able to enlarge the bottom any more without blurring it? Just the area below the mirror?"

"I don't know. Let's give it a try." He went to his keyboard again and a rectangle appeared enclosing the desired area, a cherub-free section of gray-blue sky and dull, purplish clouds. A little more keyboard prestidigitation and the segment enlarged in quick stages. On the actual mirror, the final area that was included would have been about eight inches wide by three inches tall. On the screen it was four times that and only marginally less crisp.

Alix studied it. "What do you know," she murmured inscrutably. "How about that?"

"Alix—" began Norgren.

Chris smiled at him and shook her head. "You just have to wait her out. She'll get around to telling us. Eventually. Maybe."

"Take a close look," Alix said. "What do you see?"

"Nothing," said Chris. "You're standing in front of the screen."

Alix moved to one side. Norgren, carrying his coffee, got up and walked nearer, but it obviously didn't help. He shook his head. "What are we supposed to be looking for?"

"Look at the clouds," Alix said. "Look at the one down near the left edge, the one that has kind of a brownish-greenish-orangey cast. It's quite faded and the craquelure makes it especially hard to pick out, but if you sort of narrow your eyes to—"

"Why, it's not a cloud!" Norgren exclaimed. "It's another cherub, isn't it? Most of his body. He's got his little arms raised—"

"Will someone please clue me in?" Chris said. "I don't see any little cherubs, I don't see any little arms, I just see weird clouds."

Alix placed a fingertip on the screen. "Here, look. This is the left eye, see? And the right eye here."

Chris was shaking her head. "No, I don't see."

Alix moved her finger. "This feathery orange blob here, that's his hair, now do you see? Painted pretty sketchily, but it's there. And his arm—"

"Oh, there it is, I see it, yes!" Chris said. "Wow, it doesn't exactly jump out at you, does it?"

"And those two darker little peaks on either side of his head? Those would be the tops of his wings," Alix said.

Chris got up to join them nearer the screen. "But it's completely different from the other ones."

"That's right," Alix said, "and that's what makes it important. For the Mannerists, the cherubs—*putti* is probably a better term—they weren't meant to jump out at you. They weren't solid, living bodies, but something between clouds and fleshly beings."

"A lot of historians think they weren't meant to be consciously seen," Norgren put in.

"Well, they sure succeeded with this one," Chris observed.

"What's more," Alix said, "it's not at all the kind of cherub that Tiny painted, the kind that didn't show up for another couple of centuries—the cute, rosy Cupids with the rosebud lips, those fat, naughty little messengers of love with their little bows and arrows."

Chris nodded. "You're right about that. No one would call this one rosy."

"Or naughty," Norgren said. "Nothing mischievous about this little guy. Look at his eyes."

Chris was puzzled. "Okay. So he's looking up at something that we can't see, something above him and off to the side. So?"

Alix explained: "Those raised eyes, that's a classic sixteenth-century expression of adoration, Chris, or ecstasy—*religious* ecstasy. From Donatello in the 1400s right through the Renaissance, and the

Mannerists, and the Baroque, right up until the Rococo itself, cherubs were strictly religious figures, the *cherubim* of the Bible—the third order of angels, I believe."

"Second order, if I'm not mistaken," Norgren gently corrected.

Alix went back to her chair with a hangdog smile. "Rats, that's what I get for showing off. I should have quit while I was ahead. All right, I admit it, Mannerism and the Baroque are not my fortes."

"If they're not," said Norgren, "I would love to hear you talk about your fortes sometime." Eyeing the image, he crossed his arms, then raised one hand to tap his lip with the side of a finger. "And so we have to ask: Even if we were to assume that Tiny somehow *did* paint the background—that he came up with some terrific new way of success-fully faking those cracks—then you still have to wonder: Why would he have put in that particular cherub, which doesn't go with any of the others?"

"And the answer," Alix said, "has to be that he didn't. Didn't put in that one cherub, any more than he painted the clouds and the sky. They were all already there, and apparently even he didn't spot that old, faded one."

Chris returned to her chair too. "'Nough said. I'm convinced."

Norgren was slowly shaking his head. "You *are* something, Alix. I could have stared at that 'cloud' for two solid hours and never realized what it really was."

Alix laughed. "Don't feel bad. I've been looking at it for twenty years and didn't spot it until today."

When she saw him steal a furtive glance at his watch, she jumped to her feet. "Thank you so much for everything. We've taken a lot of your time, and I know you've got someplace else you have to be."

"Yes, a dinner session with our advisory board's subcommittee on acquisition spending limits." He winced as he said it. "Chris, I wish you'd called me last week. I'd have saved tonight to take the two of you to dinner. I'd sure rather be doing that instead."

Chris too had arisen. "I'm really sorry about that too. Dinner would have been on us, though. Look, any time either of us can help you out in any way . . ."

"Thank you. I appreciate that. I really do need to get going now. Come on, I'll walk you out and over to the parking lot."

"Let me ask you one more question," Alix said to Norgren as they went down the now-deserted corridor, heels echoing off the floor. "You've agreed that it's sixteenth-century Italian, early Mannerist, and Roman school. I don't suppose you'd care to try to pin it down any more than that? Any particular artist, for instance?"

"Sheesh," Chris said. "You don't want much, do you? All he had to work from was one photograph on a *magazine cover,* which he got to see for all of twenty minutes. Give the guy a break."

"But it was a really good photograph to work from," Norgren said, "and, actually, it did give me some ideas, but . . . well, it'd be awfully presumptuous of me to come up with the name of the artist. I mean, really, I'd be on pretty thin ice, wouldn't I, to—"

Alix grinned. "But you're going to take a crack at it anyway, am I right?"

"Since you insist," he said, smiling back. "Just don't take it as gospel." He stopped with his hand on the door's panic bar. "If I had to guess, I'd say it's by a follower of Daniele da Volterra's, very likely one of his students."

It took a second for Alix to place the name and then she laughed. "*Il Braghettone?*"

"The same."

"*Il Braghettone,*" Chris repeated, frowning.

"It was da Volterra's nickname," Alix explained. "'The Breeches Maker.' He got it because he's the poor guy the pope stuck with the job of painting over the genitals in Michelangelo's *Last Judgment* with fig leaves and loincloths and such."

"Oh, he must have loved that," Chris said as they stepped through to the outside and began walking across the big Neo-Renaissance courtyard.

"He hated it," said Norgren. "He was a huge admirer of Michelangelo's and thought the ceiling was just fine the way it was, but the pope was the pope."

"And what about Michelangelo? I bet he wasn't too crazy about it either."

"He was dead at the time," Alix pointed out.

"Good thing for him," Chris said.

Once outside they walked past the larger-than-life bronze cast of Rodin's *Thinker* that was the centerpiece of—in fact the only statue in—the grand courtyard. It was the first time Alix had seen it without a crowd of visitors around it, mostly snapping pictures of their friends and relatives taking *Thinker*-like poses at the base of its plinth. Norgren sneaked another look at his watch. "Well, my car's over there in the staff parking lot. I'd better—"

"Let us walk over with you," Alix said. "I'd really like to talk just a little more. I'll make it fast, I promise."

"Sure," Norgren said, but picking up the pace so that Chris had to lengthen her stride to keep up with him and Alix was practically sprinting. "What do you want to talk about?"

"You said 'follower' of da Volterra," Alix puffed. "You don't think it could have been da Volterra himself?"

"*Could* have been? Sure, the work is competent enough, but it's like coming across something that has a Rembrandtesque quality to it. Any curator worth his salt is going to hope it turns out to be by the master himself, but you don't jump to the conclusion that it is. There was only one Rembrandt, but he had dozens of students whom he taught to paint the way he painted, and thousands of imitators who were pretty good too. So, absent other evidence, the simple odds tell you it was most likely one of them. Da Volterra had some pretty decent students and apprentices too—Michele Alberti, Giulio Mazzoni, Jacopo Rocchetti . . ."

"Yes, that's all true," Alix said, even though, of the three, Mazzoni's name was the only one that rang a bell, not that she could remember why it should; probably, he'd assisted da Volterra with the Sistine Chapel work. "But da Volterra, as good as he was, was no Rembrandt. I doubt if he had dozens of students."

"Oh, I wouldn't say—"

"Well, he certainly didn't have thousands of imitators."

"That's true enough," Norgren said agreeably. "Well, here's my trusty little Acura." He was anxious to be on his way, with the ignition key already in his hand, but he paused at the door. "You know, there's one thing we didn't get to talk about. Assuming we're right about the panel being the real thing, then—"

"I know," Chris said. "Then where did Tiny get it?"

And after a moment of silence, Alix softly asked: "And *how*?"

Nobody had any answers.

CHAPTER 19

The drive from the Legion of Honor to their downtown hotel through San Francisco's evening rush hour was one frustrating stop-and-start after another, and for the first quarter-hour of it they had their heads down, prowling separately through cyberspace, Chris on her iPhone and Alix on her iPad Mini.

Chris came up first, with a pensive look. "You know, there's something funny about all this."

Alix glanced at her. "Gee, ya think?"

"No, seriously." Chris dropped the phone into her bag. "Now, for the last fifteen minutes I've been bouncing around the auction databases seeing what I can find on da Volterra and his students—Art Nexus, Hislop's, FindArt, and so on. There hasn't been a lot of action on da Volterra himself, but what *has* been sold averages in the low five figures; anywhere from two or three thousand to twenty or so. The biggest sale was a *St. John the Evangelist* that went for a hundred thousand at Semenzato's in Venice in 2001, but that's, like, five times more than anything else, before or since. And as for those followers of his—Mazzoni, Alberti, and so on—there's *nothing*. For at least a hundred years, not a one has sold at any known auction. But if one were to come up for sale, it'd have to go for a lot less than one by da Volterra himself, wouldn't you say?"

"Yes, you're right, and I see what you're getting at, Chris. It does seem like there's been an awful lot of fuss over it, even if it is authentic."

"Chump change," Chris agreed. "That's all it would go for. Low five figures at most, probably even less. So . . . what's going on?"

Alix shook her head and spread her hands. "Don't ask me."

Chris grumbled something and looked out her window. "Where the heck are we, anyway?"

Alix looked out her own window. "Golden Gate Park," she said. "There's the de Young Museum. Slow going."

The driver heard them. "Yeah, I guess I should have taken Geary, after all. Sorry about that. Fulton's usually better. Should be there in fifteen minutes or so, though."

"No problem," Chris told him and got her iPhone out again. By the time they were dropped off at the curb in front of the Inn's modest canopy, she had lined up a superfast United flight at ten-thirty the next morning that would have them in Monterey before noon. They agreed to meet in the hotel lobby at seven-thirty to take care of checking out. Then they would leave their luggage with the concierge and walk to one of the nearby restaurants for a hearty breakfast—eggs, meat, *protein*— and thus, for what was likely to be another busy day, be better prepared than their oat fudge bars had left them that morning.

First though, there was this evening's dinner to be decided on. "I don't know how I can be hungry again after that colossal sandwich at lunch," Alix said, stretching upon getting out of the limo. "I thought I'd never want to eat again, but I sure do. And I know you're ready to eat."

"Now how would you know that?" Chris wanted to know.

"Because: when are you not ready to eat?"

Chris lifted an eyebrow as if she were trying to decide whether or not this required objection on her part, but after a beat or two the eyebrow came down and she responded with a judicious and tolerant nod. "That's a point."

"You know this area better than I do," Alix said. "Any recommendations for where to go?"

"Well, what do you feel like, French? Chinese? Steaks? Sea—"

"How about plain old American comfort food? It's been a long day."

Chris's face lit up. "I was hoping you might say that. Hamburger, fries, chocolate shake, something along those lines?"

"*Exactly* along those lines."

"Wonderful. Believe it or not, there's a place right around the corner, at Sutter and Powell. Lori's Diner. Straight out of the 1950s. Great burgers."

• • •

Lori's Diner was as advertised, with leather-topped chrome stools at the counter and red vinyl booths along the wall. A motorcycle was mounted atop the cold drink refrigerator and a jazzy, two-tone Edsel convertible stood near the back looking all ready to load up the kids up for the Saturday night sock hop at the high school gym. A black-and-white-tile floor and Elvis belting out "Blue Suede Shoes" on the jukebox made the picture complete.

And naturally the waitresses, one of whom came to their booth with menus and glasses of water, wore black rayon waitresses' uniforms with little white aprons.

"Evening, folks," she said, handing them their menus. "Today's dinner specials—"

"Oh, we don't need menus," Chris told her. "We know what we want. Alix?"

"I'd like a hamburger and fries, please," Alix said, "and a chocolate shake."

"What kind of hamburger?"

"What kind? Oh, maybe I'd better look at the menu after all."

"Not necessary," Chris said, gathering both menus up and handing them back to the waitress. "We'll both have the Big Bopper with fries, and a chocolate shake for me too."

"Big Bopper?" Alix asked warily.

"Trust me," Chris said.

"I guess I'll have to."

"Trust me, you're gonna love it," said the waitress, heading off.

Alix still looked as if she had something to say about Big Boppers, but Chris had something else on her mind. "Alix, I have a question about the mirror. At one point there at the Legion, the two of you referred to the mirror—I mean the panel it was on—as a fragment."

"Right."

"Well, I didn't want to ask about it then—I was pestering you with more than enough questions—but did you mean that literally? It's a *piece* of a larger panel?"

"Right."

"So there's . . . or there *was* . . . a panel somewhere that must be missing a piece?"

"Probably more than one piece. If it followed the usual pattern, probably all the corners were cut off. And as for the center . . ." She shook her head. "Well, that might be gone altogether. Destroyed, I mean."

Chris had begun to lift her glass to her mouth, but it went back to the table before she got it there. "Now you're really losing me. *Cut* off? We're not talking about some kind of accident? Somebody cut it into pieces on *purpose?*"

"Yes. I'm sorry, Chris, I thought you understood."

"I do not understand. Kindly elucidate."

"Well, it's been an unfortunate practice for a lot of years, sad to say—centuries. Thieves steal paintings from an old palace, or church, or museum, but if the paintings are even moderately well-known, trying to sell one of them to anybody is next to impossible because—"

"Because if the potential buyer was familiar with it, he might know it was stolen?"

"Right. Imagine trying to sell the *Mona Lisa* if you were an art thief. Is there anybody in the Western World who wouldn't recognize it and know it should be in the Louvre? You would certainly recognize it, wouldn't you?"

"What kind of a question is that? Of course I'd recognize it."

"How?"

"How?"

"How would you recognize it? From the smile? The face . . . ?"

"Well, yes, sure, and the hair, the head in general, and the clothing, and the pose, with one wrist over the other . . . at least I think it is . . . and a whole lot of things that, taken together—"

"What's in the background?"

"Background?"

"Yes, background. What's behind her?" Alix smiled and waited. Three seconds passed . . . four . . . five . . . "Excuse me, I didn't quite get that?"

"Uh . . . draperies?" Chris offered weakly. Alix merely continued to smile. "Roman columns?" Chris tried. On the jukebox now, the plangent voice of Johnny Cash was sinking deeper and ever deeper into his Ring of Fire. "Okay, not draperies, not columns," Chris said. "I give up, what?"

"A pretty blue lake with a winding path leading to it," Alix said. "Trees, hills, a patch of pale blue sky . . ."

"You're kidding me, a lake? A path? I thought . . . I don't know what I thought." She whipped out her smartphone and pulled up an image of the painting. "Whoa, will you look at that! All the times I've seen it, even in the Louvre itself, and I never knew there was a lake, or any of it."

Their shakes had come, each served in a ribbed soda-fountain glass and topped with a thick blob of whipped cream and a maraschino cherry. Beside the glasses were second helpings in the frost-coated metal beakers they'd been mixed in. So for a couple of minutes conversation was replaced by discreet slurping and murmurs of gratification.

"And so," Alix went on when it came time to top her drink off from the beaker, "if you were a thief and you'd somehow managed to steal the *Mona Lisa*, what would you do with it? Nobody would buy it from you. Even the crookedest fence in the world wouldn't touch it, because, what would *he* do with it? And with every police agency in the universe hunting for it, simply having it in your possession would be a tremendous risk."

Chris was engaged in using a long-handled spoon to shovel up the slippery gobbet of semi-solid ice cream at the bottom of her glass, but she nodded to show she was following along.

"So if he wanted to get any profit out of it at all," Alix continued, "what he'd do would be to cut out that part of the painting—it'd be the upper left quarter—frame it, and see if he could sell it as an authentic, sixteenth-century, miniature landscape. Which, of course, it is. It wouldn't bring him in even a thousandth of the worth of the full painting, but the full painting couldn't be sold, and at least this way there'd be something in it for him. Of course, to be on the safe side, he'd then have to destroy the rest of the painting as quickly and thoroughly as he could."

"And you think that's what happened with this painting, this panel."

"Possible. More than possible."

"Hm." Chris shook her head. "No, I don't buy it. Why go to all the trouble and the risk of stealing a famous, well-guarded painting like the *Mona Lisa* in the first place if that's all you're going to get out of it?"

"Well, the *Mona Lisa* was just an example. Nobody in his right mind would steal it—although somebody once did steal it, but that was back in 1911 and he *wasn't* in his right mind. But the thing is, if Chris Norgren is right and Tiny's mirror is part of a panel by a follower of da Volterra, it's sort of famous, but not *that* famous, and probably wasn't that well-guarded either. And since I'm still guessing, I'd bet that it had more chunks that could be sold separately than the *Mona Lisa* does, because the *Mona Lisa* is a portrait. Other than that upper left corner, I can't really think of anything but Mona's image itself that could pass for a complete, saleable painting on its own."

"Except that it would be unsaleable," Chris said.

The Big Boppers now arrived, and they turned out to be fat hamburgers with the usual trimmings—tomato slice, onion ring, lettuce, and relish—but with the addition of two thick bacon slices crossed on top and the whole thing drenched with melting cheddar cheese. The rest of the plate was hidden by a steaming heap of aromatic French fries.

"Whew," Alix said, having lifted the top half of her hamburger bun to have a look at the inside.

Chris grinned at her and shrugged. "I just thought that maybe we were a little weak on our saturated fat minimum daily requirement. Don't worry, you can handle it."

CHAPTER 20

In the end, Chris could but Alix couldn't. Even after leaving almost half of the Big Bopper and a dozen French fries on her plate, she was uncomfortably stuffed as they left the diner.

"Okay, final question," Chris said. "Can you handle one more?"

"Please. Maybe it'll get my mind off my stomach."

"Why are the two of you so sure that it's only a fragment of a bigger panel and was never an independent smaller painting in itself? You talked about a miniature landscape before, so why not a miniature skyscape? It's kind of attractive, in a somber sort of way."

"Yes, it is, but there's no focus to it, Chris, no design, no organization. There's no center, just a bunch of floating clouds and one off-center half-cherub that's—"

"But how do you *know* there's no center? If there is one, it'd be behind the mirror, wouldn't it? So we can't see it; the Virgin Mary or some saint, or something?"

"Well, yes, that's the sort of thing that would very likely be the focus of this kind of painting, but we don't have to be able to see what's in back of the mirror to know that the focus isn't there."

"Maybe *you* know, Alix, but I sure don't."

"All right, remember that faded cherub down near the left-hand bottom corner, the one that Tiny *didn't* paint, the one that was part of the original?"

"Sure, the one with his eyeballs turned up. In adoration, as you pointed out."

"Right—up and to the *left*, as *you* pointed out."

"Okay, so?"

"Well . . ."

She had to stop while the Powell and Mason cable car came racketing down Powell Street a few yards from them, clanking and clanging away like a fire engine in a circus clown act, and just as packed.

"So," she went on once it had passed, "what's he looking at?"

"Who knows? We can't see it. It's off beyond the edge . . . oh, I see what you're saying. The only way that makes sense is if that's where the focus of the painting is—the saint, whatever. Meaning that what we've got is only a piece of the original whole, probably something down near the lower left corner . . . no, the lower right corner, since the little guy is looking up and to his left." She scowled. "Do I have that right?"

"It's the way I see it."

As they came up to the Inn's entrance Chris glanced at her watch. "Early yet. What would you think about a nightcap? They don't have a bar here, but there's the St. Francis right across the street and they have a great one."

"Yes, it is a nice one, but I'll pass. I'm too stuffed."

"Coffee, then?" They were in the lobby now and Chris was pointing to a couple of urns in a corner seating area.

"Yes, that might hit the spot."

Just as she said this her telephone rang. Alix checked. "It's Jamie. I should take this."

"Definitely," Chris said. "It's midnight in DC. I just hope nothing's wrong." She gestured at a couple of armchairs. "You grab a seat and take the call. I'll round us up the coffees."

"Okay—but don't look so worried. Jamie's a night owl. Midnight's early for her. Probably nothing at all." She sank into a soft leather chair and hit the Talk button.

◆　◆　◆

"Alix, Jamie here. I've done some checking on Tiny for you, and well . . ."

"Uh-oh, there's a problem, isn't there? I can hear it in your voice."

"A teeny-weeny tiny one, yes. It seems—"

"—there's a warrant out for his arrest. I knew it. Oh, boy—"

"No, nothing as serious as that. It's just that it turns out the man doesn't seem to exist."

Alix breathed a sigh of relief. "Well, I can't say I'm surprised. Tiny does do his best to stay below the radar."

"No, I don't mean we couldn't find him. I mean the man . . . does . . . not . . . exist."

Alix had reached for one of the coffees that Chris had brought and was moving it toward her mouth, but that stopped her. She put the cup down on a glass-topped side table. "I'm afraid you'll have to explain that a little more."

"Alix, it turns out that in all of these United States, only one person named Beniamino Guglielmi Abbatista was born between 1950 and 1970. He came into this world on April 30, 1958, and resided with his parents in an apartment at 1134 Jerome Avenue in the Bronx, on the ground floor of which was Caruso's Barbershop."

"Yes, that all sounds right. What's the problem?"

"The problem is that the little guy died of bronchopulmonary dysplasia on December 4, 1958, at the age of eight months, and was buried in St. Raymond's Cemetery, where, presumably, he still resides."

"*What!*" Alix very nearly knocked the cup over.

Chris stared at her, concerned. "Alix . . . ?"

"Tiny doesn't exist!" Alix whispered.

Chris blinked. "Oh, is that all," she said. "You had me worried for a minute."

"You understand what this means, don't you?" Jamie said.

"Not really, no. If he's not Tiny, then who is he?"

"Oh, I'd say he's still Tiny, he's just not Tiny *Abbatista*. But exactly who he is . . . sorry, that I don't know."

"But how could he—"

"It's not that hard to pull off, Alix, and back then it was even easier."

It was particularly easy when you had access to the parish records of a sizable Catholic church, she explained. And St. Raymond's was one of the biggest and oldest in New York. All you had to do to find yourself a new identity was to go through their records until you located somebody who'd been born about the same time you had, and would thus have been about the same age you were—but who'd conveniently died as an infant, thereby handily eliminating any alternative paper trail that might trip you up, such as Social Security number, work history, etc. The backup information that you needed to go along with your new ID was right there in the records for you too: address, parents' and siblings' names, and more. As for a fake Social Security card and things like a birth certificate, they could be easily made to order, then as now.

"And you think that's what he did?" Alix asked. "But wait, he's been in prison—more than once. Wouldn't this have come out the very first time they arrested him? Don't they check things like that?"

"My dear, naive child, I hate to shake your confidence in our criminal justice system, but no, it probably wouldn't have come out. Why would the police have checked local birth records?" She snorted. "And even if they had, good luck with digging out the info. Remember, it's only the last few decades that those records have been computerized and put into a central data bank. As far as the police would have been concerned, he had a legitimate name and he had a Social Security card; that would have been enough. I'm sure he had an official-looking birth certificate too—maybe even the real one. Now, if he'd been accused of a really significant federal crime, it might have been different, they might have done some—"

"But the whole plan—thinking it up, searching through the records, finding someone to fake the Social Security card and everything, and then seeing it all through—it sounds a little . . . well, complicated for the Tiny I know."

"He wouldn't have needed to do all that himself, Alix. All he had to do was find somebody to take care of the whole thing for him. They're out there: contractors, you might say, who lay it all out, sub-contract the various elements to specialists, and pull the whole thing together. For a fee, of course. Not generally a lavish one, I should add, since the clients they deal with don't tend to be from among the one-percenters. Mostly, they're illegal immigrants these days, but there are plenty of other people—crooks, deadbeat dads, fugitives—who are in the market for new identities too."

"Wow," Alix said softly. "This is really . . . unexpected. Is there anything else you can tell me?"

"I wish I could, but the truth is, I'm stymied. I've got a few irons in the fire, a few people here at the Bureau to talk to, but at the moment, about all I can say is that whoever he is, he isn't Benny Abbatista. Who he really is . . . sorry, not a clue. Yet. I should be talking to Ted again pretty soon. Maybe he'll have some ideas. That's okay with you, isn't it? We're not talking about anything official."

"Sure, I wish you would. And listen, you can mention this to him too: Whoever Tiny turns out to be, I've got a really good lead on where he is, and that's Monterey, so my friend Chris and I are flying there tomorrow morning. We'll have a lot of places to check, so it might take awhile, but if he's there, we . . . will . . . find him."

"And do what, when you do?" Jamie asked with a rare note of concern, or perhaps even disapproval in her voice.

"Nothing dangerous, I promise, not that Tiny would ever hurt me. If the guy is in trouble, and he obviously is, we want to do what we can to help him out. Please don't worry about us, and don't let Ted worry either."

"It's not Tiny that worries me," Jamie said, "it's whoever the guys are that he's running from."

"Why would we be in any danger from them?" Alix asked. "Why would they want to hurt us?"

"I don't know."

"How would they even know where we are, or who we are, or that we're even looking for him?"

"I don't know."

But even as Jamie said this, Alix realized she was forgetting the man she'd spotted in Washington Square only a few hours ago. They *were* being followed, and it was surely in hopes of being led to Tiny; what else could it be? *Were* they in any danger? The stab of concern that accompanied this thought lasted only a moment. If the Sudoku-playing young man with the smudged glasses and the brown baseball cap was all they had to worry about, then there wasn't anything to worry about. Chris, who'd intimidated him simply by standing over him, could handle him with one hand tied behind her back; maybe both.

"On my honor," Alix said, "I will stay miles from any possible trouble. Also, I want you to know that I really appreciate what you've done. Thank you."

"Okay, kiddo, I'll take your word for it," Jamie said with a sigh. "As if I had any choice. Look, take care, and I'll call you if I come up with anything else."

◆   ◆   ◆

Naturally, Chris was avid to hear everything, and Alix took a few minutes to fill her in while they sipped their coffee and Chris nibbled at some of the shortbread biscuits that had been set out between the urns.

"That," Chris said, "is absolutely fascinating. It makes Tiny even more interesting than he was before. An international man of mystery."

"Mm. It's amazing, really, when you think . . . ." She let the rest of her sentence die away. "Oh, my God," she murmured.

Chris, with a cookie halfway to her mouth, stopped and goggled at her. "Now what?"

"Chris, I've been so stupid . . ."

"How? About what?"

"I should have known, I should have realized . . ."

Chris let out something between a sigh and a growl. "I wonder if you have any idea how much time I sit around wondering what you're talking about before you decide to let me in on it."

"Since I was a little girl," Alix said, continuing to talk to herself more than to Chris, "I've heard him talk about being born in the Bronx over a barbershop, so why would I not believe he was born in the Bronx over a barbershop?"

"I don't know. Why would you not? And what difference does it make if he wasn't; if he was born over a barbershop in Springfield, Illinois, or over a butcher shop in Lexington, Kentucky, or, or . . ."

Alix finally focused on Chris. "Because, although his English is fine now, twenty-five years ago, when I was five or six years old, he spoke it—and wrote it—as if he had just gotten off the boat the day before: 'Good-a morning to you, Ahlix. Today we gonna havva some-a nice-a-day, yes?'"

"Okay, but didn't you once tell me his family didn't speak it at home? Wouldn't that explain it?"

"So he said, yes. But as a boy, wouldn't he have spent most of his waking hours outside the apartment—at school, or running around with his friends? Why wouldn't he have picked up the language from them? Immigrant kids do it all the time. Nobody has to teach them."

"Yes, I know that, but—"

"And he was always singing Italian songs and using Italian words because he couldn't find the right ones in English. Chris, I think maybe he *had* just gotten off the boat. I think maybe he *was* born in Italy. Never mind 'think.' I'm sure of it. All the pieces fit."

Chris thought it over and slowly nodded. "You're right. Wow." The cookie finally reached its objective, and she chewed for a few seconds before saying, but with obvious reluctance: "But you know, I can't help wondering why your father never told you about this. He's his oldest friend—they go back practically to the time Mr. X became Mr. Abbatista. He *has* to know."

"Well, yes, all right, he might," Alix said uncomfortably, "but obviously Tiny didn't want it known and Geoff was honoring his wishes." She frowned. "What, you don't buy it?"

"No. Maybe there was no reason to tell you before, but—no offense, Alix, really, but shouldn't he have told you yesterday when you told him you were going to be looking for Tiny? It seems kind of pertinent, wouldn't you say?"

"Yes, but . . . oh, gosh, he *tried* to tell me. We were on Occidental Mall. He came right out and said, 'You know, Alix, there are some interesting things you don't know about Tiny's past.'"

"And?"

"And I said, like the supercilious brat I am, that I didn't need to know about his past, thank you very much."

"You shut him up."

"That I did. One more thing I need to apologize to him about. We do a lot of apologizing to each other, we Londons."

"Oh, I wouldn't worry about it. You know Geoff doesn't hold a grudge. Water under the bridge."

"The London bridge," Alix said with a smile. "More water under it than any other bridge in the known world."

"In any case," Chris said, laughing, "now that we've come up with this, what now?"

"Now I get ahold of Jamie again," Alix said firmly, her excitement building. "Now we might start getting somewhere."

CHAPTER 21

With Jamie, it was full steam ahead; no convincing necessary. "That makes a lot of sense," she said, cutting Alix off before she'd finished. "Okay, first thing in the morning I'll put in a call to my buddy in Homeland Security and see what he can tell us. He owes me one."

"Homeland Security? What does Homeland Security have to do with it?"

"Homeland Security includes Customs and Immigration now. I'm hoping Jock can get into their records from the eighties, the late eighties, and come up with a list of anyone who arrived during that time who might fit Tiny's description: male, Italian, about thirty, art background, with a history of trouble with the *carabinieri* or the Mafia, or who had 'questionable' associates. That kind of thing."

"Also he's huge. Bet he weighed a good two-fifty, two-sixty, even then. Don't forget that."

"Right. I've got a good feeling about this, Alix. I think we've actually got a chance of finding out who he really is."

"And if we do, Jamie, remember, you promised—well, sort of promised—that we'd keep it to ourselves. For our eyes only, right? It makes me nervous to have Homeland Security involved. I don't want to get the guy deported."

"Don't be nervous. Now get off the damn line. Even I have to get some sleep. Talk to you when I have something to tell you."

◆ ◆ ◆

"That's all very interesting," Chris said when Alix had filled her in. "But I don't exactly see how finding out his real name, which it looks like he hasn't used for most of his life, would help us find him."

"Good question. I don't really know either, but it can't hurt." Suddenly worn out, Alix covered her mouth with the back of her hand to stifle a yawn. "I don't know about you, but I'm heading up. I'm bushed."

Chris shook her head as if she couldn't believe it. "Alix, it's a quarter after nine. My ninety-one-year-old grandmother used to stay up later than that. You are absolutely the earliest-to-bed person I know."

"Yes, and I'm also the earliest-to-rise person you know. I bet I get half a day's work done before you even manage to crawl to the kitchen for your first cup of coffee."

"I wouldn't be surprised. Ah me, I am so glad my workaholic days are a thing of the past. Well, goodnight."

"Good night," Alix said, but she continued to sit there, her eyes unfocused.

Chris peered at her with that curious, head-tilted look of hers. "Alix, are you okay? Is there something wrong?"

"What? Yes, sure, I'm okay. Well, I'm concerned about Tiny, of course—"

"Right, and so am I, but there's something more than that that's eating at you. You were distracted all through dinner, and even now—"

"I was? I thought I was pretty sharp."

"I suppose, but I know you better than you do. Oh, hell, I don't mean to pry, but you're starting to worry me, so if there's anything you want to—"

"No, honestly," Alix said, "there's nothing. Well, nothing other than that I can't make those Golden Oldies we were listening to at Lori's stop running through my head. 'These boots are made for walkin','" she sang through clenched teeth, "'and that's just what they'll do . . .'"

Chris laughed and gave up. "Yeah, sure, that could be it. All right, kiddo. I'll shut up about it. You go ahead and head up. I think I'll grab another cuppa down here and do a little web-surfing. See you in the morning."

"Good. Seven-thirty sharp, right? You won't be late? I know it's early, but we won't have all that much time before the flight."

"But of course," Chris said, as if surprised by the admonition. "You know me."

Alix, at the elevator, stifled the flip response this so patently called for. "Thanks for everything, Chris," she said warmly. "You were great today."

Chris shrugged this off as she pulled down the lever on the coffee urn. "'Night, Alix."

"'Night, Chris."

But as the elevator doors closed, Alix could still hear Chris's voice: "'These boots are made for walkin' . . .'" she was singing. "Dammit, now you've done it to me!"

◆　◆　◆

There had been no chance to unpack, so Alix opened her suitcase, shook out the creases in the clothes she'd wear the next day—she was feeling too lazy to iron them; maybe in the morning—and hung them up in hopes that gravity would do the job for her, then attended to her end-of-day toilette and got ready for sleep.

She was in a strange mood as she tossed the surfeit of pillows and bolsters onto an easy chair—and then onto a second, when the first one overflowed. Between Geoff and Chris—and probably Ted now—it seemed she no longer had any private thoughts. They were all too sharp for her. Chris had seen right through the show of good spirits and lively conversation she'd put on (or thought she'd put on) during dinner. She did indeed have something on her mind, and it had nothing to do with who Tiny Abbatista was or wasn't. It was that last question she'd raised at the Legion of Honor:

How had Tiny come by that damn panel? (Funny—yesterday it was a treasured possession. Today it was a "damn panel.")

She hadn't brought it up again at dinner because she was in a peculiar and uncharacteristic mood. She didn't want to have a logical discussion about it, or to be talked into or out of anything, or to be agreed with or contradicted; she just wanted to keep her stew of feelings to herself. And at the moment, the ingredients that had risen to the top and were bubbling away weren't worry, or puzzlement, or anxiety; they were an unhappy mix of anger, resentment, and, above all, a sense of having been deceived.

For how *could* Tiny have gotten hold of it? She had come up with three possible scenarios and she didn't like any of them. The most likely one was the one she wanted least to think about: that he had stolen the panel from some church and cut that piece out of it himself; that her beloved Uncle Beni, with his deep and oh-so-sincere (and oh-so-often-expressed) appreciation for the Old Masters, had callously destroyed an irreplaceable work of art by a gifted sixteenth-century painter. It was more than deception, it was betrayal, and it was almost too much for her to deal with.

Of course, it was also possible that not Tiny but someone else, some gang, probably, had committed the original theft and that, one way or another, Tiny had gotten the panel from them. As far as Alix was concerned, that didn't make a lot of difference. She could forgive a past that involved art theft (why not? She'd already talked herself into forgiving forgery, or as near as made no difference), but the willful destruction of art? No. Never. In her world it was the unforgiveable sin.

The only other alternative she could think of was that the panel had been stolen and cut up by others and the segment that Tiny had used for the mirror had been a throwaway, a piece of unsaleable scrap from the cutting-up process he had found somewhere. That was the possibility she liked best, but it was the one that was hardest to take seriously, an unlikely and too-convenient rationalization for a set of distasteful facts.

One thing was for sure, she thought with a certain amount of sullen satisfaction: if it turned out that he'd really cut up that damn panel (there it was again; that "damn panel"), then he'd do better to worry more about *her* finding him than about whoever else was chasing him, because if she got to him first she'd wring his neck for him herself.

Well, metaphorically.

CHAPTER 22

In the morning, their plans for a steak-and-eggs power breakfast were set aside and they went instead to a creperie, very popular, very *sans pretensions*, that Alix knew and favored, just a block down Post Street at the corner of Taylor. As always there was a line waiting to order at the counter, but things moved quickly and by eight they had gotten their meals and, thanks to a dash and a last-second twist worthy of an NFL running back by Chris, they had snared a table in the very act of being vacated. They were about halfway through their orange juice and crepes (cheddar, mushroom, and crab for Alix; apple, cinnamon, brown sugar, and whipped cream for Chris) when Alix's phone rang. She grabbed a quick slug of the coffee and hit the Talk button.

"Hello?"

"News!" crowed Jamie Wozniak. "He's from Italy, all right, and his name is Santo Mamazza, born in August 1959 in a tiny village named Pieve de Teco in the middle of nowhere."

"That's incredible, Jamie. How did you come up with it so fast?" *Santo Mamazza,* she was thinking, trying it out in her mind, and the imaginary words forming in her throat didn't feel right. No, she decided on the spot, however this turned out he would continue to be Beniamino, her *Tio* Beni. He didn't even *look* like a Santo.

"Oh, it's all in who you know," Jamie said airily, "and lucky for you, I know everybody.

"Okay, here are the facts. Your friend Tiny, or rather Santo Mamazza, flew from the Genoa airport to JFK on November 30, 1987, supposedly to visit his family in New York, all perfectly legal, except that he never returned. Mr. Mamazza was described as twenty-nine years old, brown-haired, brown-eyed, weight 265 pounds, height six feet, four inches (converted from kilograms and centimeters), occupation 'plasterer.' Exactly four days later, 'Beniamino Abbatista,' physical description virtually identical, made his first recorded appearance (since his burial in 1958) when he filed for a New York State driver's license. After that, we don't hear anything from him until—"

"Jamie, I'm sorry, I have to go."

"What—"

"Thanks so much. I'll call you back."

She'd jumped from her chair so quickly she had to grab it to keep from knocking it over. "Chris," she said urgently, "we still have an hour before the car picks us up. Can we go back to the hotel now? I think I'm on to something."

"I can see that," Chris said as she stood up. "Your face is flushed, you look like you just found, I don't know, Aladdin's lamp."

"I *have*, in a way." The laughter that suddenly bubbled from her was choked off by her excitement. "Hurry."

"Well, tell me, already," Chris said as they got out onto Post Street. For once, it was Chris who had to hurry to match Alix's stride. "What are we doing? Why are we going back? What did Jamie find?"

"Well, mainly, we now know Tiny's real name—Santo Mamazza."

"I'll be darned. That'll take some getting used to. But I'm still a little lost. Why is that so exciting?"

"That's not what's so exciting. What's exciting is—well, I'm not a hundred percent positive yet. Look, do you have a copy of that high-resolution photo of the mirror? Can you email it to me?"

"You already have it. I had it copied to you when it was sent to Chris Norgren."

"Great. All right, give me twenty minutes and then meet me down in—no, better yet, I'll just come over to your room. Chris, I'm telling you, if I'm right about this . . . Wait'll you see!"

Chris shook her head. "Whatever did I do for excitement before I met you?"

· ◆ ·

"Do you always tidy up your own bed in the morning, or is this because you knew you'd be having company?" Alix asked.

"The latter. Strictly for show. I hope you appreciate it."

Chris's room was a near mirror-image of Alix's, simple but elegant, with a gas-log fireplace, and new-looking, unfussy furniture done in complementary red and beige fabrics. They sat down at the coffee table, Chris in a corner of the beige sofa, Alix in the red armchair next to it.

"Now, then," Alix said, producing a few sheets of paper she'd brought in with her. "I had these photos printed up for us at the desk."

"This is gonna be good," Chris said. "I can feel the vibes."

Alix put one of the sheets on the table. "You recognize this, of course."

"Well, sure. That's the bottom part of your mirror, the part below the glass. It's the same enlargement Chris Norgren put up on the screen. What'd you do, blow it up from the magazine cover?"

"Yes, from the hi-res photo you sent." She laid a second sheet beside the first. "And what about this one?"

Chris picked them both up, looked from one to the other, and scowled. "Alix, you have to admit I've been very patient. But if it's all the same to you, do you suppose you could dispense with the trick questions and just get to the damn point?"

"This *is* the point. It's the same photograph, wouldn't you say? Well, except it's in black and white. Right?"

Chris sighed. "Right."

Alix shook her head. "Wrong. It's an enlargement I made from . . . *this* photograph."

The third and last sheet was laid on the table. It was a religious painting, in the center of which a saintly, hooded female figure was standing among clouds and surrounded by what appeared to be other saints, male and bearded, all of them backlit by an explosion of rays from the sun. Other than this center, the rest of the picture was sparingly painted, consisting of dreary clouds and a few wispy, wraithlike, vaguely creepy Mannerist cherubs.

"Which I got from the Art Loss Register," Alix continued.

"So it's a stolen painting?" Chris asked. "Or missing, at any rate." The Art Loss Register was the world's main repository for documentation and photographs of stolen and missing art.

"Stolen, in this case. Chris, did you ever hear of the Palazzo Giallo theft?"

"No, I don't think so. Uh-uh, no."

"Happened in Genoa, in the 1980s. It was pretty famous at the time—"

"Oh, wait, is that the Cellini one? The, what was it, the famous pendant he made for King What's-his-name of France?"

"Right, for Francis I; the Odysseus pendant."

"And, if I remember, it's never been seen or heard of again, correct?"

"Correct. Which is strange to begin with, because in Italy, the ransom demand usually comes about five minutes after the stuff has been taken, but not this time. Anyway, the loot also included a few less well-known items, three sixteenth-century paintings—one of which is this one, the *Assumption of the Virgin* by Giulio Mazzoni."

"Mazzoni. Didn't Norgren tell us he was one of the artists who might have painted the panel your mirror was on?"

"He did, and he was right. Observe." With a mechanical pencil she drew a rectangle around the lower right quarter of the image, the full painting. "This little part here, as you see, is—"

"—the same as the enlarged area we were looking at at the Legion this afternoon—from *your* mirror."

"From my mirror. And that little orange-haired cherub looking up and to the left? You can barely see him, and only you know what you're looking for, but at least now we can see what he was looking at: that glowing Madonna in the center."

"Yes." She took the pencil from Alix and put a small oval in the center of Alix's rectangle. "And here's where Tiny put your mirror . . . covering nothing very important."

"That's right. This whole segment has nothing important on it, which is why I think it was a piece of scrap left over from cutting out the saleable parts."

"Do you . . . do you think the whole painting was cut up and sold in pieces?"

"It's a reasonable guess. Unfortunately."

"And probably everything else too," Chris put forward solemnly. "And the pendant—that was probably melted down. And that's why nothing was ever heard of again."

Alix shuddered. "Let's not go there right now."

Chris dropped the pencil on the table and stared disbelievingly at the photo of the entire painting. "Alix, this is really incredible. Your mirror's panel was cut from *this* painting. All these years, you've had a part of the Palazzo Giallo theft right up on your wall in plain sight. It's a wonder nobody ever stole it before."

"Well, remember, this particular piece isn't all that valuable. It's the Cellini pendant everybody's interested in. Besides, nobody who might have known what that panel was ever had any idea I had it until—"

"Until they saw it on the cover of an international art magazine," Chris acknowledged, "thanks to yours truly."

"Not your fault, Chris. Besides, it's been . . . interesting."

"Interesting," Chris echoed with a one-note laugh. "Let's just hope it doesn't get any more interesting. But Alix, I don't get it. Yesterday, when we were talking to Norgren—hell, half an hour ago, when you were talking to me—you didn't know what was going on. Now, suddenly, you know exactly what painting it came from, and where and when it was stolen? What . . . how . . . ?"

"It was Chris Norgren that got the wheels turning, I think. As you said, he mentioned Mazzoni as one of the candidates who might have painted the panel and I knew even then there was something familiar about the name, but I couldn't think what. And then this morning, Jamie told me about how Santo Mamazza disappeared from Genoa on November 30, 1987, and Beniamino Abbatista made his first American appearance on December 4. Well, the Palazzo Giallo theft was November 28, 1987, not even a week earlier—I did have to look that part up—and so it all came together."

"*What* came together?"

"Mazzoni, Genoa, the theft, the dates—Tiny running to America just two days after the theft. It was pretty hard to miss, actually."

"Yeah, for you, maybe. Good job, pal. Hey, we've got to get ready to go."

Alix checked her watch. "Car won't be here for almost thirty minutes. Gives me time to call Jamie and pass this on to her. I'll meet you in the lobby after."

Alix suspected that it was no more lost on Chris than it was on her that there was now a new issue that neither of them had chosen to touch.

It was virtually certain now that Tiny had something to do with the Palazzo Giallo theft. What was it?

◆ ◆ ◆

Alix called Jamie and was told that Ted had concluded his assignment and she could call him on his regular cell phone if she liked, which thrilled her. But her room, with its unmade bed and pulled-out drawers and stuffed wastebasket, struck her as too disheveled for a conversation with her new husband, so she went downstairs and across Powell Street, to Union Square, which was fairly quiet at this time of the morning, especially because the day was misty, and San Franciscans, unlike Seattleites, stayed inside when it got wet. She sat on the broad rim of one of the concrete planters that held a cluster of the square's famed palm trees and made the call.

"Ted? It's Alix. Jamie said—"

"—it was okay to call me now, and it is. She told *me* you and Chris were—"

"—on our way to Monterey, yes. We have a flight—"

"—at 10:30 this morning. As for me, I'm still in Geneva, but—"

"The assignment's over! I know! When can we—"

A burst of laughter from Ted cut her short. "Hey, isn't it supposed to take more than a week before married couples start finishing each other's—"

"—sentences for them?" Alix said, laughing along with him. "Just think, in a year or two we won't have to talk at all. We'll know what each other is thinking before anything gets said."

An open-sided red and tan "San Francisco Highlights" sightseeing bus, tricked out to resemble a trolley car despite its rubber-tired wheels, rolled by, filled with glum, wary-looking Asian girls in school uniforms, while an accompanying guide up front gestured at nearby buildings and rattled enthusiastically on. The passengers looked so low, and hearing Ted's voice had made her so joyful herself, that she gave them a wave and a smile. A few of the girls waved gingerly back with giggles and shy smiles of their own, but most continued to stare morosely ahead.

"Perish the idea," Ted said warmly.

"I'll second that. Listen, sweetheart, I don't have much time and I have some new developments to tell you about." She launched excitedly into them, and managed to cover more or less everything in five minutes, hardly pausing to breathe: Tiny's real identity, the identification of her mirror's panel as being a piece of the Mazzoni, and the inclusion of the thirty-year-old Palazzo Giallo theft in the mix.

"Good God," said Ted. "That's incredible. How did you come up with all that?"

"Well, Jamie helped a lot."

"I'm sure she did, but I'm impressed all the same. Very." He paused, probably giving her a chance to bask in the praise, which she did. "Alix, did I ever mention Gino Moscoli to you?"

"Yes, your friend in Genoa, the art squad captain."

"That's right, the man I asked to interview Alessandro Ferrante after your place was broken into, and a really nice guy. Believe it or not, Gino headed up the team investigating the Palazzo Giallo theft, and it's stuck in his craw all these years."

"That was almost thirty years ago. He must have been awfully young."

"He was. But now he's old, and he's never given up on it. I think it's practically an obsession with him and probably the only reason he won't retire—he's got some health problems now. Oh, and something else? He's convinced—been convinced for years—that your Ferrante's the man who carried out the robbery, and he did it on commission for the Mafia, although Moscoli's never been able to prove it. They've been playing cat and mouse for decades. They're almost friends by now, at least as Gino tells it."

"Ferrante stole those things all those years ago," Alix said, mostly to herself, "and now he's interested in the mirror. Which just happens to go missing."

"Yes, raises a lot of questions, doesn't it? But"—he paused again, but this time it was a pause of hesitation, not an intermission—"what you've learned brings up some questions about Tiny too. I know he's a sensitive subject to you, but I have to ask."

Even though Alix had known this was coming, she felt a wall of defensiveness form around her. Hackle-raising time. "Ask, then," she said curtly.

She heard him take a breath. He wasn't enjoying this either. "Alix, nobody knows the guy better than you do. The obvious question is, how did he come by that piece of the panel? We now know, thanks to you and Jamie, that he arrived in the States—from Genoa—just a few days after the theft, which does suggest . . . Well, do you have any indication at all, anything he might ever have said, that suggests he might have been involved in the robbery?"

"No."

"Ah."

"Ted, I'm not saying he *wasn't*. Maybe he was, I don't know. I didn't know him then. But I do know that if he did, he's a very different kind of man now. And anyway, who knows what the circumstances were?"

"True, but his circumstances hardly—"

"What I *am* saying is that it's *not* possible that he cut that chunk, or any other chunk, out of that painting or any other painting. One of the things that you don't understand about the man is how much he loves art—reveres it—especially from the time of the Old Masters."

"Well, for a man who loves art so much—"

Again, she talked right over him. "The idea that he would *ever* have cut up a precious sixteenth-century painting to sell the pieces separately is . . . is . . . as likely as me cutting one up. Or you, for that matter. You can just absolutely, unconditionally forget that as a possibility, damn it!"

She hadn't intended to sound off like that, and at first she was taken aback by her own heat, her bellicosity, but she quickly grasped that it wasn't Ted she was bawling out but herself. Those doubts about Tiny with which she'd tormented herself the previous night, they had been—what, some kind of stupid intellectual exercise to prove to herself that she was capable of not letting her feelings, her deep affection for the man, get in the way of looking hard-eyed at the facts and what they implied?

But now, in the misty, jeweled San Francisco morning, things were clearer than they'd been last night. All right, he had been in Genoa at the time of the theft and had left—and never gone back—very shortly after. Maybe he *had* had something to do with the robbery, that she could envision. But beyond that, she had nothing else to go on but her feelings, her intuitions, grounded as they were in the two decades she'd known him. And those feelings told her exactly what she'd told Ted: Tiny would never—*never*—mutilate a work of art, let alone one that had existed for four centuries.

Her little tirade had apparently startled Ted into a momentary silence. For a couple of seconds there was nothing from his end. Then, in a tentative, extremely un-Tedlike tone, he offered: "Umm . . . I think maybe I hit a nerve there?"

It made her burst out laughing, and the apology that followed was effusive, heartfelt, and thoroughly muddled. "Ted, I'm so sorry! I was so . . . I mean, that was totally uncalled-for . . . honestly, I can feel myself blushing with shame. You know, Tiny means so much to me . . . I guess I just got carried away."

"Oh, maybe a little," he agreed, and she could hear the smile in his voice.

"I love you, Ted."

"I love you too, babe."

Alix laughed happily. "I think this is what Chris calls smooshie-mooshie talk."

"And she's right. Let's have no more of it. Back to business, if you please. Uh-oh. Wait. Stop. Halt." She could tell that he'd gotten up and was moving about. "I just heard that there's a limo from the Spanish embassy waiting for me downstairs." From the rustling sounds she could picture him shrugging into one of his sport coats. He bought them off the rack at Brooks Brothers, but they fitted him as if they'd been hand-cut for him by a bespoke Savile Row tailor. *Forty-four long,* she heard herself saying under her breath, relishing the idea that his jacket size was something she should be aware of.

"The paintings we captured were from a museum in Barcelona," he went on, "and there's a celebration or presentation or something I'm supposed to be at in twenty-five minutes and I need to get going. You can call me later if you want. Otherwise, I'll call you soon. Oh, one more thing: This secret marriage business is getting kind of awkward. It's almost like being undercover; I have to lie to people. We need to do something about it, and soon."

"Such as tell Geoff, you mean. Yes, I know. And I will. Just give me a few more days to figure out how I want to do it."

"Okay. 'Bye for now. I lo—"

"Yes, I know. I love you too."

They were both laughing as they hung up.

•   •   •

She was still glowing a few minutes later as she sat in the lobby with Chris, awaiting their ride to the airport, but Chris wanted to talk about the Palazzo Giallo and all that had come from it.

"How much crazier can it get? Ferrante, the guy who called you a couple of weeks ago about the mirror—that is, about what we now know to be a piece of a sixteenth-century painting by Somebody Mazzoni—this is the very guy who stole it in Genoa thirty years ago? And probably had the piece re-stolen a few days ago from your condo?"

"That's right."

"But look, if he's got all the rest of the loot—I mean, the *Cellini,* for Christ's sake?—why would he even give a damn about this Mazzoni thing?"

"Chris, I do not have a clue."

"Oh, that's helpful. What?" she asked, seeing the pensive look on her friend's face.

"It just occurred to me." She turned to face Chris more squarely. "It wasn't the panel Ferrante was so interested in at all—it was Tiny! Of course! It should have been obvious from his questions. Why did it take so long to dawn on me?"

Chris blinked. "Tiny? Why?"

"Well, maybe because he doesn't know where the loot is himself, and he figures Tiny has to know where the Mazzoni—the rest of the Mazzoni—is. And if Tiny knows that, hances are he knows where the rest of the loot is as well, and that's what he's really after. Especially the Cellini pendant, that's the big one. Does that make any sense?"

"But Ferrante's the one who stole it. How can he not know where it is? What, he just happened to misplace it somewhere?"

"I don't know. Though these people we're talking about are thieves, after all. Maybe someone stole it from *him*."

Chris nodded. "What you're saying makes sense, but there's something that doesn't fit. If it's the Cellini that he's really after, why did he steal Tiny's mirror? What good would that do him?"

"I'm beginning to think it might not have been him."

"Oh, come on, I don't mean Ferrante himself. I don't think he flew over from Italy to do it, but it must have been someone he hired."

"Not necessarily."

"Well, who else would it have been?"

"Look, the magazine cover is where he saw the panel, right? And knew right away what it was."

"Right."

"And so what makes us think nobody else recognized it as well? You told me *Art World Insider* has a circulation of something like six thousand, worldwide, and I know it goes to a lot of libraries too, so we're talking about a *lot* of people, and who's to say there aren't a few more with inside knowledge about the theft? Any of them could have wanted that mirror, for . . . well, I don't know, for whatever reason they might have had. Or let's just go back to one of the early theories: A break-in by some opportunist who saw the magazine cover and figured it had to be worth something."

"Ah," Chris said, waggling a finger, "but who besides Ferrante would have known you were going to be gone for a week?"

"Hm." Alix's index finger tapped gently against her lower lip. "I guess I did let that little cat out of the bag when he called, didn't I? Well . . ." She shrugged. "I really don't know. I guess neither of us has all the answers yet."

Chris laughed. "If that isn't the mother of all understatements, I don't know what is. But we're getting there, slowly but surely."

"Ms. LeMay," said a desk clerk who had come up to them, "your driver is here. If you're ready to go, I'll have your bags taken out."

"Thanks, Les. We'll be right out." She jumped up, extended a hand, and pulled Alix out of her chair too. "Okay, now let's go to Monterey, do some digging, get hold of Tiny and find out what's going on with him. That's the most important thing."

"So it is," Alix agreed. "What's going on with Tiny."

Damn it, what *was* going on with Tiny?

CHAPTER 23

When he wasn't on the job, *Capitano* Gino Moscoli lived the simple, not unpleasant existence of an aging, self-sufficient widower who asked little more from life than that tomorrow be no worse than today and that no unexpected visitors, or events, or catastrophes disturb the comfortable routines he had established for himself over the years. Among these pleasant routines was a relaxed dinner in the Trattoria da Giovanni, which was conveniently located on the street level of the nineteenth-century apartment building in which he lived. Despite its fusty, shabby interior, this largely blue-collar café was, in fact, a prime reason he had settled, after the death of his wife, on this building as his home. Living here, his dinner was but a flight of stairs away. Moreover, since the restaurant had been right there since 1888, he'd reasoned, it was highly likely to outlast him, so that he wouldn't be troubled, ten years from now, in his advanced old age, to have to find another, less convenient café.

On this particular morning, he was, as usual, among the day's first customers, waiting in the entryway when the establishment unlocked its door at 6:45 p.m. so that he could take his usual table for one in the niche next to the fireplace, close enough to feel the dry, sunlight-like warmth on his cheeks from the gas logs in the wintertime. This being September, the fireplace would be cold, but still, this was his seat, and this was where he sat.

"As always, *signor* Moscoli?" asked the waiter.

"As always, Ettore," said Moscoli. That was another thing about the Giovanni. Here, wearing presentable but comfortable old clothes, he was not *Capitano* Moscoli, whose very presence in the same room, even drinking a cup of coffee, made people nervous; he was plain *signor* Moscoli, just a civil, nicely spoken old gent—a retired dentist or accountant, maybe—who lived upstairs, who was there virtually every evening of the year, who ordered the same thing every day, who kept to himself and made no trouble; a valued customer to be treated with courtesy and consideration.

"*Minestrone, spaghetti alla carbonara, calamari alla griglia,*" recited Ettore. Soup of the day, pasta of the day, main course of the day. Moscoli even had a standard, discounted price for this: €14, which he paid weekly.

"That sounds very nice," said Moscoli, as always.

He never ordered dessert, but every second day he would order a thin, black Toscano cigar, which the counterman would cut in two and then put the unused half aside for Moscoli's use the following morning, the way an attentive steward might hold a half-bottle of fine Barolo for the next day's dinner. It was a service no other customer received or would think of asking for. After finishing his meal he would light up his half-cigar, and sit back to half an hour of reading either newspapers from the rack, or magazines that he brought with him.

Finally, at his signal, there would be a cup of hot chocolate to finish—an idiosyncrasy of which Ettore patently disapproved (hot chocolate was not something which an Italian gentleman would be expected to order, and especially not after dinner) but which, out of deference, was uncomplainingly provided.

When the cigar was down to its last inch on this evening, his telephone rang. His face darkened. Telephone calls at eight o'clock at night were unlikely to be anything good.

"Gino, it's Ted. Hope I'm not bothering you at dinner."

"Not at all, Teo," he said truthfully. "What can I do for you? Have you finished your case?"

"Yes, that's done, and I have some good news for you—I hope you're sitting down—on the loot from the Palazzo Giallo."

"You've recovered it?" Moscoli's stomach clenched. He didn't know whether the prospect delighted him (found—at long last!) or dismayed him (yes, found—but by somebody else!).

"No, nothing quite as good as that—"

Moscoli's stomach relaxed.

"—but we have found a piece of it, a piece of the Mazzoni. Well, we haven't exactly found it, in fact we've lost it, but we—"

"Teo, I'm in a restaurant. It's a little noisy. Let me go upstairs to my apartment. Can you hold or shall I call you back?"

"I can hold. Take your time."

Filled with anticipation now, even shaking a little with it, Moscoli made for the rear stairway to the upper floors.

Ettore goggled at him. "*Niente cioccolata calda, signore?*" He had every reason to be astonished. If this were really so, it would be the first time in living memory. Moscoli never heard him. He climbed the flight of stairs like an automaton, his mind far, far away, in time if not in place.

November 1987. The theft from the privately owned Palazzo Giallo, so called because of its mustard-colored facade, had been dubbed the art crime of the century, but that dubious title had lasted only three years, until 1990, when the Isabella Stewart Gardner Museum in Boston had been robbed of three Rembrandts, five Degas, a Vermeer, and a Manet. Even the priceless Cellini pendant—one of the artist's very few works in gold that hadn't been melted down over the intervening centuries—couldn't hold its own against that stellar bunch. Interestingly, neither "crime of the century" had ever been solved.

The palazzo's owner, a flagrantly corrupt politician but a careless one (the palazzo, along with his other assets, had soon afterward been seized by the government and turned into a State museum), had never even bothered to insure his art.

The theft had been meticulously executed by a lone, ski-masked "gentleman robber" who had solicitously placed the frightened elderly caretaker into a closet, reassured him that he would not be harmed, and then gone efficiently about his business. The gentleman robber— Alessandro Ferrante, Moscoli was sure—had run a flawless operation, leaving not a single physical clue. Moreover, none of the stolen art had ever been heard of again. There had been no threats to destroy it, no ransom demands, no taunting letters to the police, no anything. The current prevailing theory was that it had gone straight to a Swiss bank, where it had been used by Ferrante's Mafia friends ever since, as collateral for one nefarious enterprise after another. Either that, or—as happened all too often—the tremendous publicity and attention from law enforcement had made the pendant unsaleable, even on the black market, and the Mafia had destroyed it or had it melted down for the gold rather than risk being caught with it.

Over the years, as new cases piled up, the Palazzo Giallo theft had necessarily dropped below the *carabinieri's* radar, but Moscoli himself had never been able to let it go, had pursued every so-called lead no matter how tenuous, all of them eventually proving fruitless. Moscoli's theory of what had happened to the loot differed from the conventional ones. He had come to believe that it had never left Genoa at all, but was still hidden away somewhere in the city for reasons he couldn't fathom. It was a theory that he kept to himself because he had little to support it other than the fact that, in all these years, there had not been a word, not even any minimally credible gossip, about shadowy international buyers, or of its passing through other hands in other places. Beyond that, he had nothing to go on besides gut instinct. Old cop that he was, though, he knew that gut instincts, while not to be considered as anything approaching evidence, were not to be dismissed either.

"Teo, are you still there? Teo? Teo!" He was on the telephone in his apartment with no memory of climbing the stairs or opening the door.

"Relax, Gino, I'm still here. Okay, I have a lot to tell you."

But he was only a few minutes into it when a palpably agitated Moscoli cut in. "This 'Tiny' person, this so-called Abbatista—he left Genoa on November 30, but under a different name, an Italian name?"

"Yes, I told you. Two days after the Giallo robbery, which makes us think—"

"His Italian name—you have it?" Even over the telephone, Ted could tell that he was holding his breath.

"Sure. Umm . . ." Ted had made a note of it but he didn't have his notebook with him. "Santo Something . . . Manini . . . no, Mammano? I'm sorry Gino, I have it at the hotel. I'll—"

"*Mamazza*!" shouted—shrieked—Moscoli. "It's Mamazza, Santo Mamazza!"

Ted heard a slap; Moscoli had whacked something in his exhilaration. "That's right, but how did—"

"Listen to me, hear me out." Moscoli lowered his voice now, down to a rapid, urgent whisper. "After the theft, among the few people who might conceivably have had some access to or knowledge of it at the time, there was one, and one only, who dropped completely out of sight."

"And that was Santo Mamazza?"

"Yes! He was a young apprentice frescoist at the church next door. Simply vanished, gone for good by the very next day. He was not a suspect because he had no criminal record. He was only newly down from the mountain villages, and he had no known connection to the criminal world. We assumed the whole affair had frightened him back to the mountains. Later, we did make some attempts to find him to see if he could provide any useful information, but we had no luck. So after a while we—well, we more or less forgot about him. But now everything has been turned on its head. Teo, if there is anybody in this world who can tell us where that loot is, or what has happened to it, it's this man Abbatista . . . Mamazza."

"You're probably right, Gino. And at our end, I think Alix and her friend are getting close to finding him, and when they do, I promise, you'll be the first to know. They've tracked him to Monterey—Monterey, California, not Monterrey, Mexico. They're on the way down there now."

"What do you think of their chances?"

Ted hesitated, but only for a moment. "I think they're good, Gino. Alix knows him about as well as anybody does, and these are a couple of very intelligent, very resourceful young women. Yes, if he's there, I think they'll turn him up."

Now it was Moscoli who held back. "Ah, Teo, I hope this is not an indelicate question—you appear to be on familiar terms with *signorina* London—but, well, considering her close association, her intimate association, with both her famous father *and* with Abbatista, and taking into account that the panel had been in her possession for so many years, isn't it possible that she herself might have played some . . . some unsavory role, or should I say some questionable role in the—"

"What, when she was two years old? Because that's about how old she would have been in 1987."

"No, no, of course not, but the art is still out there somewhere, and now there is this mysterious 'theft' from her flat, and I can't help speculating that she might—"

"Well, don't," Ted snapped. "Alix is so straight-arrow we did our best to get her to work full-time at the Bureau. She turned us down, but we still use her on a consulting basis. She's been about as vetted as anybody could be. We trust her implicitly, and for damn good reason, so don't even *think*—"

He stopped, brought to a halt by a stab of remorse. It was the first time he'd ever spoken like that to his respected and much senior colleague, and now, ashamed and embarrassed, he emitted a sheepish little laugh. "Gino, forgive me, I had no right to talk to you like that. You had every reason in the world to—"

Moscoli was equally taken aback. "I didn't . . . I meant no offense. It's only that I know next to nothing about the lady. I had no idea that she was in such good standing with the FBI."

"And with me. Personally," Ted said, then sighed. "She's not a *signorina*, Gino, she's a *signora*. She's my wife. Maybe I should have mentioned that before."

Moscoli laughed. "Maybe you should have."

"Yeah, I know, but, well, you see, we just got married a week ago and Alix wants us to keep it to ourselves until she figures out how to put it gently to her father that her new husband's one of the cops that got him convicted, and I guess trying to keep it a secret has given me kind of a short fuse, so that when you, when you—"

"Say no more, my friend. I understand." And then, with great formality: "*Congratulazioni. Tanti auguri per una vita felice insieme!*"

"Thank you, Gino."

"And that is the last I will ever say on the subject, until, and if, permission is granted. All right now, I hope you will tell the two excellent ladies that I wish them well. And at my end, I believe it is time for me to have another little session with Alessandro Ferrante in the morning, but this time it will be in *my* office. I will telephone you afterward. Goodbye, goodnight, *buona notte*, thank you!"

Ted couldn't help smiling. He had never heard the old cop more animated. Not that Ted wasn't excited himself; if all this led to the recovery of the Palazzo Giallo loot, it would be the art retrieval of the year, of the decade. But his excitement was mixed with unease. It was now obvious that Benny Abbatista had been involved in the famous theft, and unless some Italian statute of limitations applied, this then was probably going to end with his going to prison. On Abbatista's account he had no concerns, but how would Alix take it? Ted had already had a part in the conviction and jailing of her father. Now was he going to do the same thing to Tiny, her beloved *Zio* Beni? Oh, boy, he thought, good thing her mother was dead.

Otherwise, he'd probably find some reason to lock her up too.

CHAPTER 24

Unlike Moscoli, Alessandro Ferrante took most of his meals with others, in trendy dining spots, but when he was alone he too had his favorite restaurant, the stately, darkly glowing old Caffè Vanni, which was not only virtually tourist-free but also served, in his opinion, the city's finest *stuzzichini*, Italy's far more elegant version of *tapas*. Here, in this oasis of order and urbanity, he was at his most tranquil and assured.

But not today. "The *stuzzichini*, they are not to your satisfaction today, *signor* Ferrante?"

Ferrante, lost in thought, in worry, in self-recrimination, jumped. "What?"

"I'm so sorry, I didn't mean to startle you, *signore*."

"No, that's all right, Eduardo. No, they're excellent, as always, but I find myself not very hungry this afternoon. You can take them away."

"Another glass of Prosecco?"

"What?" Ferrante looked at his glass, surprised to see that it was empty. He could remember taking only that first small sip. "That would be nice, Eduardo," he said.

"Right away, *signore*."

Ferrante returned to his anxieties, with which he was well supplied. It had occurred to him belatedly—only this morning—that since Fausto Martucci now knew the name of the detective agency Ferrante was using, he, or Don Rizzolo himself, was perfectly able to communicate directly with di Stefano Investigations any time they chose. Which meant that he was now superfluous, an annoying, untrusted, unliked middleman whose services were no longer required. Add to that the fact that he had so flagrantly let the don down (again), and the implications were all too clear.

Since talking to Fausto the previous day he'd been vacillating over what to do, but sitting here in the quiet café, he had finally come to his decision. He would have to run. He had lived in Genoa all his life, and he was an old man now, nearing seventy. To think of living elsewhere sat like an icicle in his heart, but as things now stood, Genoa was no longer safe for him.

Now, with a second Prosecco in front of him, its bubbles slowly disappearing as it sat untouched, he formulated his plans. He had two hundred thousand euros in a bank in the Channel Islands, another hundred thousand in negotiable securities in the stock market, twenty thousand American dollars in a local safe deposit box, and he could probably convert another ninety thousand euros to cash within the next few hours. Trying to sell the gallery business couldn't be done without Rizzolo's learning of it, so he would just walk away from it. With what he owed on it, there would be as much gain as loss. All together, the money wouldn't be enough for him to live in the manner he was used to for very long, but it was more than enough for him to make a simple life for himself elsewhere, someplace far away from Genoa. An out-of-the-way mountain village up in South Tyrol, perhaps, that was more Swiss than Italian, where as many people spoke German as Italian and the Mafia showed up only in the movies and jokes. Maybe he'd go to live in Switzerland itself, if they would let him do it.

But no matter how he tried to talk himself into it, the idea of spending the rest of his life in a foreign country made him ill. He was Italian through and through, more than he'd ever realized before. As for living a "simple life," well, he really didn't know how to do that and had no desire to learn. And so he would stretch his luck a little to give things one last chance to satisfactorily resolve themselves here in Genoa. If they did, if "Tiny" were actually found and detained, they would never kill him. They'd be congratulating him instead. And he'd be enjoying the rewards that came with being in the good graces of the don.

He'd heard this morning from di Stefano Investigations that the women had flown to Monterey, which surely meant they believed they would find "Tiny" there. London was a capable, intelligent woman, and he would simply hope—and pray—that she led di Stefano to him before the day was over. It was early Thursday morning there now. He would give her until the very end of the day, midnight, Monterey time, to succeed. That would be 9:00 a.m. Friday in Genoa, more than twelve hours from now. If he hadn't gotten good news from di Stefano by then, he would be on a plane as soon as possible after 9:00 a.m. Between then and now, he would arrange his financial affairs as well as he could and book his flight to Basel, a city he knew well.

Twelve hours. That was still enough time for things to work themselves out. And in the meantime, he felt himself relatively safe. The Mafia did not generally come calling in the night, but to make himself still more secure, he would return neither to his gallery nor to his condominium. The night would be spent in an airport hotel.

He was feeling better than when he'd sat down, and could even sense a stirring of optimism. If things actually worked out . . . "Eduardo," he called. "I believe I'll have a plate of *stuzzichini*, after all."

"And a little more Prosecco to go with it?"

"Yes . . . no, let's have champagne instead. Do you have *Veuve Clicquot*?"

◆　◆　◆

Chris, displaying her impressive research skills during the drive to San Francisco International and the short flight to Monterey, determined that there were forty-two seafood restaurants in Monterey—not quite Waldo's "million," but formidable enough. None was owned by a Costantino or Valentino, or any variant thereof. One of them, however, the Starfish Grill, in the heart of downtown, just off Cannery Row, listed a day shift supervisor named Tino Calomino, and it was there that they began. They took a hired car directly there from the airport and had the driver then drop their bags off at the Monterey Plaza Hotel, where they were staying.

The high hopes with which they entered the Starfish were soon dashed. Tino Calomino was there, all right, serving from behind the counter, and Alix, having had a little coaching from Chris, made a more artful inquiry than she had at Zappa's. But Tino, who turned out to be Panamanian, not Italian (making it a little unlikely that he was Tiny's cousin), just shook his head. He knew nothing about Tiny or anyone who might conceivably be Tiny.

"Well, that certainly went well," Chris said brightly as they left.

"That's only one," Alix said. "Forty-one to go. We'll find him." She wished she felt as optimistic as she was trying to sound.

Around the corner from the Starfish, on the Row, they found a bench and Chris produced two identical, annotated maps she'd printed up from the Internet. From them, it was clear that a majority of the city's seafood restaurants were gathered right there, in the touristy part of the city, many of them within a few doors of each other. They decided it would be simpler, and probably faster, to walk from one to the next rather than jump in and out of a hired car that would then have to go searching for a place to park. They would begin north of downtown, at the far end of the Row, and work back toward the hotel, which would cover fifteen restaurants, including the Starfish. At the Plaza they could have a restorative bite and a cup of coffee at number sixteen, Schooners, the hotel restaurant. Afterward, assuming they had yet to turn up Tiny, a ten-minute walk would take them to Fisherman's Wharf, along which another eleven were clustered, giving them altogether twenty-seven of the forty-two. The fifteen that were left were scattered around the city; they could cover those the next day if they had to, either singly or as a team. And if that didn't do it . . . well, they'd deal with that contingency when and if it came.

◆ ◆ ◆

A pleasant chat with two good-looking women put most men in a cheerful frame of mind and Tino Calomino was like most men. He was whistling softly to himself as he clipped yet another fish-and-chips order to the ticket wheel for Gussie to fry up in the kitchen. When he turned to the front again and glanced through the plate glass windows, his attention was immediately caught by two men who were crossing the street toward the Starfish. They were an eye-catching pair, one of them small-headed and darty—ratlike—the other a real gorilla, with a mean, stupid face, a neck that was thicker than his head, and biceps that would burst the sleeves of his bomber jacket if he ever decided to flex them. Because the small one was wearing jet-black sunglasses, Tino thought that he was seeing a blind man being assisted by a friend or whatever he was, but after watching them walk a few steps, with the little guy always a foot or two in the lead, his impression changed: more like watching a trained bear being led by his keeper.

Tino was hoping they'd veer off before reaching the Starfish. Two months ago the restaurant had been robbed and he had had his nose broken and his cheek split open by the butt of a gun. His nerves were still on edge, and the gorilla had him spooked. *Prison*, was his immediate thought. *Where else does a guy who looks like that get so bulked up?*

At the door they stopped to talk, and after a few seconds the big one clumped away down the street, looking angry, and it was only the little guy who came in, heading for a stool at the end of the counter. Tino exhaled his relief.

"Hi, buddy, what can I do you for?"

"Just a cup of coffee, please, no cream, no sugar." An odd voice, almost a soprano. Like Mickey Mouse's, but with a European accent: French, maybe, or Italian. Not German, definitely not Spanish. He had on a tie and a beige linen suit that was wrinkled but struck Tino as being the kind of suit you'd see on a movie star or sports celebrity. *Yeah, Italian,* he thought now. He was older than he'd seemed from a distance, perhaps in his late fifties, with short, thinning hair and a lined, crepey face.

"No problem." Tino wiped his hands on his apron, went to the carafe, poured a mugful, and with a smile, set it on the counter in front of the newcomer.

"Thank you." Returning Tino's smile, he drew the mug toward himself. There was something unsettling about the smile—it was too tight, as if his thin lips would split if he tried to stretch them any more. *I wish you'd take those damn glasses off,* Tino thought. *They make me nervous. Who wears sunglasses inside a restaurant anyway? And you ain't no movie star, not unless you're that guy from those Nightmare on Elm Street movies.* He was starting to think he wasn't any crazier about this guy than the gorilla he'd left outside.

"No charge for refills, just ask," he said, and started to move away toward another customer who'd just sat down.

The man stopped him by laying a hundred-dollar bill next to the mug. Tino stared. "Whoo, for a cup of coffee? Is that the smallest you got?"

"I am afraid so."

"Ah, don't worry about it. I could probably change it, but it'd wipe out my cash drawer, so what the hell, just go ahead and enjoy your coffee. It's on the house."

"Thank you, but you see, I don't want any change. What I would like is the answer to a question."

"Question?" Tino repeated nervously. "Look, mister, I don't know what you want, but I don't think I can—"

"Oh, I think you can. It's a simple question." He took off his dark glasses slowly, one earpiece at a time, and Tino flinched. The guy had one hell of a stare, dead-eyed and intense at the same time. A Clint Eastwood stare, as if he was trying to come to a decision: *Let's see, should I just kill you now, or would it be easier to do it later?* The gash of a smile was still on his face, unchanged, but it didn't look like a smile anymore.

The sheer psychic force of it backed Tino up. This was one scary character. "Hey, mister, I'm just trying—"

The man slid the bill across the counter toward him but kept his hand on it. "The two ladies who left a minute ago, they were asking about somebody, yes?"

"Well . . . yes, but I didn't know the guy they were looking for."

"That's all right, I was hoping you could give me his name." He slipped his glasses on again, which improved things a little.

"All you want is his name?" Tino echoed stupidly. He was still nervous, but at the same time he was having a hard time keeping his eyes off the money. "Umm . . . it was Italian, lemme see . . . Oh, jeez . . . oh, Benjaminio, something like that, and the last name . . . oh, Christ . . . Abbatosta, Tostaleone, something like that. No, it was . . . wait a minute—she wrote it down!"

He reached into the plastic garbage can at his feet, fumbled among the food scraps and used paper napkins, and came up with Alix's soiled business card. "Here. I tossed it, see, because like I told you, I didn't know the guy."

The man turned the card over to the back. "'Beniamino Abbatista,'" he read off in that weird Mickey Mouse voice. "Very good. And this number we have here? Is that a telephone number?"

"Yeah, I was supposed to call her there if I thought of anything. It's the hotel she's staying at."

"And which one is that?"

"Monterey Plaza," Tino said, feeling guilty about it, but she hadn't said it was any kind of a secret, and anyway, all the guy had to do was call the number himself to find out, so what was the point of keeping it from him? Besides, Tino didn't have that hundred bucks yet.

The man studied the card a little longer and put it into an inside jacket pocket. He stood up without ever having touched his coffee.

"So is that all you want to know?" Tino asked. "Did I—did I do okay?"

The man put his sunglasses back on, picked up the bill, placed it in Tino's palm, and closed his fingers around it. "You did fine, my friend." He smiled again and Tino shivered.

CHAPTER 25

The ratlike one with the bone-freezing stare was Fausto Martucci, Don Rizzolo's top lieutenant. The gorilla was a fearsome enforcer by the name of Giuseppe "Beppe" Balboni. They were both in Monterey at the wish of Don Rizzolo. Beppe's job was to handle this "Tiny," to get the information they needed out of him, to chastise him adequately and appropriately for all the trouble he'd caused them, and then to dispose of the body. At all of these tasks he had in the past proven proficient.

Martucci's job was to handle Beppe. That, and to deal with the Americans when necessary (Martucci's English was good, but Beppe was barely literate in Italian), and to do whatever thinking was required.

Martucci, while not a lawyer (Rizzolo had more than enough of those), served as his *consigliere*, the man whose counsel he sought more often than anyone else's, and the "arranger" with whom he trusted his most sensitive and important business matters. Unusually for a *consigliere*, he had come up through the ranks, proving himself first as a *picciotto*, a "little man," a low-lever enforcer, and then a crew chief, a *caporegime*, where his administrative abilities first caught Rizzolo's attention. He was very literally a "little man," small and slight. Not much to look at, but there was something about him—something in his manner or his strange, squeak of a voice, or the simple intensity of his personality—that could put the fear of God into people who needed it put into them.

Beppe, by contrast, was a mountain of muscle, an effective, fiercely loyal enforcer whose medium was action, not words. He was something of a loose cannon, thin-skinned, dangerous, and unpredictable—more so when he'd been at the *vino*, which was all too often. But there wasn't much his *caporegime* could do with him, given Beppe's special relationship with the don. Beppe had permanently won Rizzolo's respect and gratitude when he'd been tried for murder two decades ago, had been convicted, and had then served fourteen years in prison, contemptuously ignoring the authorities' threats and enticements through it all, refusing to implicate Rizzolo, on whose orders the victim had, of course, been killed. Beppe—who seemed content, even happy to remain a simple *soldato* after all these years—was as strong, and volatile, and dangerous as a chained elephant. His nickname was *l'Animale*, although the only two people known to have said it to his face now bore somewhat rearranged faces of their own.

The two men had arrived at Monterey Regional Airport at 10:00 a.m., two hours before the women's expected arrival. Their trip had taken twenty hours, including a change of planes in San Francisco, and they were travel-weary in the extreme. With two hours to wait for the women, Beppe had suggested a couple of morning glasses of Chianti. Instead, Martucci ordered them hefty, American bacon-and-egg breakfasts. Beppe accepted this (it had been made clear to him by Rizzolo that Martucci was to be obeyed, no arguing), but he did it with ill grace, openly, pointedly sulking.

After twenty straight hours of keeping Beppe out of trouble in crowded airplanes and crowded airports, Martucci had needed a few glasses of wine more than Beppe did, but settled instead for some predictably lousy American coffee. In the few hours since then, things had not gotten easier. For the first time he was feeling some sympathy for Beppe's unfortunate *caporegime*. Being the Animal's keeper was no picnic.

Nonetheless, progress was being made. They'd learned "Tiny's" name, they were on the women's trail, and even if they should lose them they knew where they were staying. All in the space of fifteen minutes. *E fin qui ci siamo.*

So far, so good.

• • •

For Alix and Chris, things went faster and easier than they'd anticipated, the only problem being that they didn't have any success. Still, by 3:00 p.m. they'd covered all twenty-seven of the walkable seafood places, and they decided to tackle the remaining fifteen in what was left of the afternoon rather than waiting till tomorrow. But since they were scattered about the city, it was going to take longer to get to them all, so they divided the list and split up, using taxis. If either one of them came up with a lead to Tiny, she would call the other and they would proceed from there. If not, they would meet at seven on the patio of Schooners, the Monterey Plaza's restaurant, to regroup.

Alas, no telephone calls were required, and at ten minutes past seven Alix sat waiting at an umbrella-shaded table on the outdoor terrace of Schooners Coastal Kitchen and Bar, which was perched on concrete pillars twenty feet above the hypnotic slap of the surf below. The evening sun was golden and glorious, the huge expanse of the bay a wonderful, luminous butterfly blue. Below, and not a hundred feet away, seals lay on the rocks on their backs, their flippers raised, giving themselves up to the sinking sun. Alix gazed out at it all, but it was purely out of a sense of duty. How could you sit in so much beauty without being grateful for the privilege?

And so she did gaze, but gratefully, no. She was at her lowest point since finding that old photo of Tiny on her closet shelf. With Chris this afternoon, they'd joked about a plan B, but neither of them had suggested what it might be. The trail they were on had now petered out and died, and there wasn't any other trail they knew of, so where was there to go from here?

Given the rotten mood she was in, the appetizer and wine she'd ordered both tasted rotten, the Chardonnay watery and insipid and the barbecued chicken wings too garlicky. She took an occasional glum sip of the first and pretty much just pushed the second around her plate with a cocktail fork. She was restless and cranky. Where the hell was Chris? You'd think if she was going to be late, she'd at least have telephoned.

But as she stewed over these grumpy thoughts she spotted Chris striding forcefully along the hotel's main terrace on the level above, and she immediately cheered up. It was hard not to smile at the sight of this tall, striking woman dressed as gaudily as good taste—reasonably good taste—and expensive clothes allowed. Apparently, she had stopped in her room to change from the sedate, skirted business suit she'd worn for the day's interviews to more typical, marginally outrageous Christine-garb. This evening it was a particularly fantastic combination: an elbow-length black tunic patterned with brightly colored, embroidered tulips and worn over a red turtleneck, along with black suede hip-huggers, and high-heeled black velvet ankle boots. A long, gold-link hip belt dangled its loose end down the outside of one thigh. With those heels she stood an Amazonian six-five, and Alix watched heads, male and female, swivel as she passed. Somehow, she got away with these outfits of hers, bizarre as they might be. The fact was, she looked smashing in them.

Alix, still wearing what she'd had on for the afternoon—a favorite outfit: pale-blue summer sweater, big and loose, with push-up sleeves, faux-designer white jeans, and sandals with one-inch heels—suddenly felt a little dowdy, but she was used to that when she was with Chris by now and it didn't bother her. Chris was Chris, Alix was Alix, and she was happy with both facts.

"Chris, hi!" she called, and Chris waved back from the top of the concrete stairway that led down to Schooners. As she started down, her phone rang. It took her all the way to the bottom to find it in that cavernous shoulder bag of hers, and she stood to one side at the foot of the steps to answer it, just a few feet from Alix's table.

"Yes, hello, Viv . . . Oh, great, glad to hear it. Really? That's wonderful, give him my love and tell him I'll be there next week." She hung up. "That was my aunt Viv," she told Alix as she dropped the phone back into the bag. "My uncle just had a hip replacement. Operated on this morning, home this afternoon, starting therapy on a portable set of stairs tonight, can you believe—*Whup!*"

Two men had come barreling down the stairs behind her, shoving and pushing like a couple of rowdy kids, except that these weren't kids and one of them was huge, and they had obviously been into whatever they were drinking for some time. They were paying little attention to where they were going, and they didn't see Chris right in front of them, still fooling with her purse. The big one lurched sidewise into her and sent her sprawling to her hands and knees onto the tiled deck. The purse went flying, spewing its varied contents.

"*Scusi, scusi,*" mumbled the big guy, reaching clumsily down to grab her arm, but only making it harder for her to right herself.

"It's okay, I'm all right," she said, getting to her feet with a small assist from Alix, who had jumped up to help.

"Chris, are you really all right?"

"Yes, really, I'm fine. Where's my—oh, there," she said, spotting her purse a couple of yards off. The big one's playmate, an older man and much smaller, had stooped beside it, and Alix's first thought was that he was making off with it, that this whole thing was a staged robbery.

"Hey . . ." she began, but then she saw that what he was doing was gathering up the stuff that had popped out of the bag and dropping it back in. She watched with extra care to see that the wallet went in with the rest of the things, which it did, and after which he brought the bag to Chris, holding it out to her in both hands.

"I'm so very sorry, *signora,*" he said earnestly. "You're not hurt?" The accent was northern Italian, Alix thought.

"No, I'm perfectly fine, please don't worry about it. It was an accident."

"My friend and I, we've been celebrating, you see. His wife, she is back in Italy, she has had a little baby girl, and . . . well, I suppose he may have had a drink or two too many—or three," he added with a quick, little rictus of what seemed to be a smile.

Or four, Alix thought, or five. And *you* might have seen where you were going if you weren't wearing those sunglasses.

"Beppe," he said sternly, *"chiedi scusa alla signora." Apologize to the lady.*

Beppe glared at him, waiting a pointed two or three seconds before he complied. *"Mi scusi, signora, mi dispiace molto."* The words were right, but he delivered them with something between a leer and a smirk. Alix, her attitude darkening, wondered if he hadn't managed to get in a grope and this was his way of letting Chris know that it was no accident, and that he'd enjoyed it very much, and how about doing it again sometime?

"That's all right," Chris said, but her voice had hardened; she didn't know Italian, but she knew offensiveness when she heard it. She turned to the other one. "Thank you," she said, "I appreciate—"

Meanwhile, the glowering Beppe was off to the side, grousing as if to the air. "Why don't you watch where you're walking?" he muttered in Italian. "Stupid—"

Alix's temper, held in check till now, flared. "She *wasn't* walking," she said angrily in Italian. "She was standing perfectly still. *You* were the one who walked into her—make that *staggered* into her. If you weren't so, so smashed—"

She realized that Chris had put a hand on her forearm and she glanced up to see one of those cautionary, furrowed-brow looks of hers that was every bit as clear as words: *Alix, do we really want to get into a fight with these characters?*

No, we do not, Alix thought after a millisecond's consideration. She closed her mouth and left unspoken whatever else she was going to say.

Before Beppe could respond to Alix his companion moved to stand in front of him, as if to block him, although how he could have done it was a mystery. The top of his head barely came up to Beppe's chin, and his chest looked about as thick as Beppe's neck. "*Andiamo,*" he said—*Let's go.* It was an order, not a suggestion, and when Beppe didn't move the older man actually jabbed him with a forefinger—hard—in the chest. "*Andiamo!*" he commanded again, but this time it was more like a threat, or at least a warning.

Beppe, surly to the end, took his time responding, but eventually turned, and up the steps he started.

The other man turned back to them, spread his hands and shrugged, as if to say, "Well, what can you do? When he's sober he's really quite a nice fellow." Then he followed Beppe, helping him along with a shove in the small of the back. Beppe turned his head and complained but all that got him was another forceful shove with the flat of the hand. Alix and Chris watched them until they were gone.

"Well, that was exciting," Chris said. "He's got a lot of nerve, that little guy, I'll say that for him. I kept thinking old Beppe was going to lose it and just break him over his knee."

Alix nodded. "It was like watching a lion tamer in a cage with a lion who wasn't in the mood. Any minute you expected him to get his head chomped off. You're really all right, aren't you?" she asked as they took chairs at Alix's table.

"Sure," she said, but quickly followed it with "Oh, no! Damn!" She was looking down at the back of her hand, held at table height, a few inches from the table's rim.

"Oh, Chris," Alix said, "your knuckles—they're really scraped."

"What? Oh, who cares, that's nothing, but look at this." She raised one knee into Alix's view. The black suede had been deeply scuffed, revealing the pale, smooth leather beneath. "Damn!" she said again, but with more vigor. "I could kill that guy."

"You're lucky he didn't kill you. I don't know if I've ever seen anyone else who made Tiny look like a midget."

"Yeah, I know, the man's a monster. But let us speak of serious things . . . What do you think of the outfit?" She held out her arms and turned side to side in her chair so Alix could admire the piratical cut, the embroidery.

"Well, it's quite . . . striking . . . and very colorful . . . and, um . . ."

Chris laughed. "It's Ukrainian style. According to *Vogue*, and I quote, it's the latest in 'au courant street-style bait.'"

"Is that good?" Alix asked.

Chris shook her head. "You are truly hopeless. So what's with the chicken wings? Something wrong with them?"

"No, they just didn't appeal to me. Help yourself."

Chris did, quickly disposing of two, and signaling to the approaching waitress that she wanted a glass of whatever Alix was drinking.

"I gather that you didn't have any luck either," Alix said, hoping that perhaps Chris had a surprise in store for her.

She didn't. "Nope," she said glumly, "and we've hit every single seafood place in the city. So what's plan B again?"

Alix tried another sip of her wine. Still too bland, she thought. "I don't know, Chris. I can't stand the idea of giving up, but what options do we have?"

"Well, let's give it one more day."

"To do what?"

"Never fear, we'll think of something tomorrow. It's been another long, busy day today and we're tired now. Oh, besides, I do have a surprise waiting for you tomorrow."

Alix brightened. Hope flickered again. "About Tiny?"

"Afraid not, but I think you'll like it. Too late to give it to you now. I want you to see it in daylight. What do you say we get up early tomorrow and take a couple of hours off for recreation in the fresh air. Might clear our heads and help us come up with something."

The waitress was back with Chris's wine, and to take their orders. They decided to make a dinner from the bar menu's "small bites" appetizer list: pork belly sliders, chorizo skewers, cheddar quesadillas, and half-a-dozen oysters on the half-shell. "Oh, and what the hell," Chris added, giving her menu to the waitress, "may as well throw in one of those little pizzas. Or do you think that would be too much?"

"Not for me, honey, and I'm guessing not for you either. And what about you, ma'am, would you like another Chardonnay?"

"I think I'll have a lemonade instead, please," Alix said, handing over her half-full wineglass.

By the time they'd finished dining (Chris having had three of the four pizza slices), they were both in a fairly optimistic mood and looking forward to the next day, although they had yet to come up with a workable plan.

Later, as Chris was getting off the elevator at the second floor (Alix's room was on the third), Alix propped the door open with one hand. "I can't believe it," she said. "You never said another word. You're really not going to tell me what this surprise thing is, are you?"

Chris responded with a complacent, close-mouthed grin. "Nup."

"Not even a hint?"

"Not even a glimmer, not even an intimation, not even an allusion, not even—"

Alix sighed. "Sleep well, see you in the morning," she said, letting the door slide closed.

CHAPTER 26

A ll in all, the mafiosi had had a better day. After their success at the Starfish, they'd continued to tail the two women, splitting up when the women did, with Martucci staying with Alix London and Beppe trailing the other one, the big one. Martucci had ruled out any further follow-up interviews with restaurant staff, partly because he was concerned about being spotted, but mostly because it was no longer necessary; safer to just stay with the women and let them do the work and lead them to *signor* Beniamino Abbatista.

At a little before 5:00 p.m., Martucci had received a telephone call that made things even easier. The caller was a courier who had driven down from Milpitas in the Silicon Valley with a little device that had to be ordered before leaving Genoa because, while it was supposedly legal in Europe, it had proven unavailable. In America, on the other hand, it was illegal but available—if you knew the right people, who knew other right people, who knew other right people. Which, it should go without saying, Martucci did.

This device, known to the trade as a micro audio recorder-transmitter, was manufactured in a residential garage in Milpitas by two graduate students in computer systems engineering at nearby Northern Pacific University, who used their circuitry skills and intuition (and their access to NPU's testing laboratories) to assemble components from Japan, China, Israel, and Germany into a remarkable eavesdropping tool with the same weight, size, and look of a credit card (with front and back customizable).

Slipped into a wallet or a purse, or just about anything, it could pick up whispers up to six feet away, which could be listened to, either live or recorded, anywhere in the world by simply calling the thing's SIM card and putting in the approved code. It was voice-activated, and had an astounding battery life of thirty hours at full-time usage. The narrow six-foot range could be a drawback, but then how far from their wallet or purse did people get when they were talking to someone else?

Now, with one of these recorders safely in the big one's purse (despite the drunken, belligerent Beppe's nearly making a mess of it), they wouldn't have to follow the women around the next day to learn what was going on. They could just listen in, relax at the hotel and get over their jet lag, maybe unwind for a while in the rooftop Jacuzzi. The problem would be keeping Beppe away from the bar.

And then there was the gun; that was worrisome too. *Nessuna pistola*, Martucci had firmly told him at the start. *No guns.* Beppe had responded with an offhanded shrug and an unpleasant laugh. *"Mi bastano le mani,"* he'd said. *All I need are my hands.* That was back in Genoa, but today Martucci had discovered that Beppe had a gun, after all, a pocket-sized 9 mm Beretta Nano that he'd somehow gotten through security, or more likely had picked up here one way or another, despite Martucci's effort to keep him in sight at all times.

Martucci had confiscated it the minute he'd seen it, though not for long. Fausto Martucci was known for his ability to intimidate just about anyone, but a flushed, enraged, wild Beppe with a few glasses of wine in him was another thing altogether, notwithstanding Rizzolo's instructions to obey Martucci. Martucci took the prudent course and backed off. Perhaps he could return to the subject in the morning and make Beppe see the light, make him see that having a firearm brought far more in the way of dangers than advantages.

But he doubted it. Who, other than Rizzolo, had ever made the Animal see the light about anything?

• • •

"There are two gentlemen here to see you, *signor* Ferrante."

"Ah." Ferrante was on one knee going through the bottom shelf of the two-level wall safe in his office, and he did not look up. Except for a barely perceptible stiffening, he knelt as still and solemn as a sculpture of a man at prayer.

So it had come to this, after all.

"No appointment?" he mumbled, his head still bowed. Less a question than an expression of resignation. It was 7:00 a.m. Friday. He had waited too long.

"No, *signore.*"

He nodded. "All right, ask them to wait a few moments and then bring them in."

"I'm not sure I can do that. I . . ." Filomena hesitated. "I think they may be Don Rizzolo's men."

Yes, Filomena, I think so too. "Do your best, Filomena. Just for a minute or two. Joke with them, perhaps, or flirt if you have to."

Filomena's mouth turned down. Joking and flirting were among neither her job responsibilities nor her gifts. "I'll try, *signore.* Shall I make coffee?"

"I don't think so, no."

When she left he closed the safe, stood up, and slipped on the subtly pinstriped charcoal suit coat that was draped over the back of his chair, buttoning the middle one of its three buttons so that it would drape smoothly. He went to the corner grouping of armchairs, where there was a mirror. In front of it he tinkered with the faultless knot of his silk tie, brushed invisible specks from the shoulders of his jacket, and smoothed back the already impeccably groomed, silver wings of hair at his temples.

Staring into the mirror, he shook his head at himself. "How could you *let* it come to this?" he asked softly. The aristocratic, strangely calm countenance looked soberly back at him, but offered no answer. "Well, never mind," Ferrante said with the slightest of smiles, only a little forced. "The question is moot."

Indeed, he knew perfectly well that his arrival at this lamentable point was his own doing. Like some groveling schoolboy eager to ingratiate himself with the master, he'd run to Rizzolo to boast about how quickly he'd recognized the mirror on the magazine cover for what it was, and about his oh-so-brilliant plans for tracking this "Tiny" down.

How much wiser he would have been, Ferrante thought now that it didn't matter anymore, to have simply kept his mouth closed, to have gone about the task without telling Rizzolo. If in the end he'd succeeded, he would have been back in the game, a major player again. If he'd failed, he would have been out a few thousand euros, that was all. The don would never be aware that he'd even tried. But he hadn't kept his mouth closed, and now here he was.

Even so, he wouldn't have been here but for a small memory lapse. It might have been all that Prosecco and champagne at Vanni the night before, but whatever the reason, it wasn't until thirty minutes ago that it occurred to him with a start that his passport was still in his office safe, which was why he was there now, half an hour before his self-imposed deadline and two hours before his flight to Basel.

Finding Filomena in the gallery had been a shock. He'd thought she always came in at eight, an hour before he generally did. She was equally surprised to see him there so early, but he'd come up with some story or other and hurried up to his office. In ten minutes at most, he would be gone again.

But, as he now knew, it had been a terrible mistake, his final one. What he should have done . . . well, never mind what he should have done. It didn't matter anymore. You waited too long, he told himself again.

When he heard the door to his office open, he turned from the mirror with a sigh.

"Don Rizzolo would like to speak with you, *signor* Ferrante."

Until this moment he'd been oddly serene, philosophical, even. It was as if he were at a play, a Greek tragedy, watching the ineluctable circle of Fate come closed. It had been *interesting*. But now, seeing these two big, blocklike men right here in front of him, filling the vestibule of his office, it took only a few seconds for sweat to pop out on his forehead and his upper lip. His heart wrenched painfully in his chest. His head was suddenly crowded with a thousand foolish, jumbled thoughts of escape. "Yes, of course," he said. "Just give me five minutes to finish up here, and I'll drive directly over."

Their hard-eyed smiles were as good as words. *You should know by now, signor Ferrante. When Don Rizzolo says he wishes to speak with you, he doesn't mean at your convenience, he means now, always.*

Ferrante somehow summoned up a smile of his own. "Perhaps it might be better if I came at once?"

"Perhaps it would," said one of the hoods archly, as if he were making a joke, which in a way he was.

"Of course. I'll go immediately. My car is right out in back—"

"No, that's not necessary, *signore*. We will be driving you there."

Ferrante had the feeling that he was physically shrinking, that he was shriveling up into a little ball. His body was near to collapsing and yet his mind had to make its little jest: *Yes, but will you be driving me back?*

·   ·   ·

They drove to Porto Antico, the busy, tourist-oriented strip along the Genoa waterfront where the enormous *Princess* and *Celebrity* cruise ships berthed to let loose their hordes of day-trippers. Ferrante sat in back with one of the men, the other sat directly in front of him in the front passenger seat, while a third man, who hadn't come up to the office, drove. In front of the giant aquarium they pulled to a curbside stop in a no-parking zone. The windows were then rolled down.

"Why are we stopping here?" Ferrante wanted to know, although, having already asked several questions that brought only silence, he didn't really expect an answer, and he proved right. Still, he tried again. "What happens now?"

This time he got a response from the one beside him. "You get out."

Ferrante's breathing stopped. "You want me to get out?"

The driver turned, a man with a face as scarred and leathery as an old suitcase. "Open the door," he said, as slowly and distinctly as if he were speaking to someone having a hard time understanding the language, "and get out. Find a taxi, go to the airport, and don't ever show up in Genoa again—*ever*."

Indeed, Ferrante was having a hard time comprehending, but it wasn't that he didn't understand, it was that he couldn't believe what he was hearing. They were letting him *out*? *Here*? It made no sense. Surely they wouldn't kill him here, right in front of the aquarium. Even at this time of the morning there were people all over the place. But surely they wouldn't simply let him leave either. Well, would they? If so, then what was the point of the whole thing? And why let him off in the center of town, why not drive him to the airport themselves? He was too confused, too upset, and too desperate to think it through, but the farther he got from them the happier he would be. If they wanted him to go, he would go.

He opened his door and stepped out, his neck and shoulders hunched and rigid, as if that might stop a bullet. His heart was pounding so hard each beat shuddered his frame.

"I can just leave?" he mumbled over his shoulder. If the muzzle of a gun was six inches from the back of his head, he didn't want to see it.

"*Cazzo*, will you go already?" The voice was fed up and bored. "We're doing you a favor, don't blow it."

Was it really possible, then? Ferrante's legs were trembling with the effort it took to keep from breaking into a run, but Alessandro Ferrante, even *in extremis*, was not about to scuttle away from a bunch of gangsters like some terrified beetle afraid of being stepped on. "Thank you, gentlemen," he said politely, and reached up to straighten his tie—

The sensory pathways of the human nervous system seem to transmit pain instantaneously; touch a hot griddle and you know it in a hurry. But they do so far from instantaneously. A little over three hundred feet per second is about as fast as they can go. A .38 Special caliber bullet, on the other hand, leaves the muzzle of its barrel at over eight hundred feet per second. Fired into a human skull from three feet away, it will destroy the brain faster than the brain is able to tell itself about it.

Thus, for Ferrante, there was no shock, no pain, no sense of blackness descending. There was only that hand at his tie and then nothing. No hand, no tie, no Ferrante. No more world.

CHAPTER 27

Having had a reasonably good bacon-and-eggs breakfast from the buffet breakfast at the Holiday Inn Express Geneva Airport (one of the few decent Geneva hotels that served an American breakfast *and* came in under GSA per diem limits), Ted was at the elevator, waiting to go to his room on the seventh floor, where he planned to finish packing for his flight to Ronald Reagan International Airport. He was about to press the Call button when his waist tickled; the telephone on his belt was vibrating.

"Ted, it's Gino Moscoli. I'm glad I caught you before you left."

"Just barely. How did it go with Ferrante?"

"It didn't go at all. Ferrante's dead."

"You're kidding me!"

"Why would I—"

"No, I know you're not kidding me. It's just an expr— I just . . . What happened, exactly? Do you know?" He stepped farther along the corridor to get himself out of range of fellow guests at the bank of elevators.

Ted was surprised to hear what was surely a grim chuckle from Moscoli. "I'll say we do. We know exactly when it happened, where it happened, and how it happened. We have depositions from a dozen people who witnessed it, snapshots from two, and a video from one."

It had been less than two hours ago. The witnesses were mostly tourists strolling along the Genoa waterfront, and what they saw was a black Maserati sedan with four men in it come to a stop outside the aquarium. A well-dressed man stepped out of a rear door, stood for a moment, and then crumpled. Some people saw a black-sleeved arm extend from the front passenger window and shoot him in the head, some did not; but everyone heard the shot. Some also heard a second shot, some didn't. All of them were shocked at how casually it was done. The whole thing had taken only five or six seconds. Done in front of all those people, it was, in effect, a public assassination.

"Mafia," Ted said. "I know you have an active cell there."

"Oh, definitely. Neither Ferrante's money nor his identification was taken. Even his passport was on his person."

"To make sure there'd be no doubt about who he was."

"Yes."

"Something to do with the Palazzo Giallo, do you think?"

"Yes, I do think that. I'll tell you the truth," Moscoli said with a sigh. "I'm sorry to see him come to an end like that."

On the surface, it seemed an odd reaction from a tenacious cop. He was totally convinced the murdered man had masterminded the theft and had been unsuccessfully pressing him for almost three decades to find out what had happened to the vanished hoard. But Ted understood that over the years they had developed a not-so-grudging respect for one another, and perhaps even a mutual affection.

"In any case," Moscoli continued, "the investigation of the murder falls to the *carabinieri* general command; my focus continues to be the art."

"I appreciate you calling to let me know about this, Gino."

"Ah, but that's not at all why I've called," Moscoli said, brightening. "I've called to tell you that I shall be flying to Monterey on the chance that your 'very intelligent, very resourceful' young women really will locate Mr. Abbatista, because I would like very much to be there when they do. And I wondered if you might be able to cancel your flight to Washington and join me instead. We'll cover your passage."

"Do you mean today?"

"Time waits for no man."

"Sure, I'm game if it'll be of any help, you know that. So I assume you are now counting on Tiny as the best lead we have to the loot."

"The *only* lead." Pause. "The only living lead."

"Yes, but shouldn't we be talking—"

"No time for talk now. I've already talked too long. You should get going."

"All right," said Ted. "I'll cancel my flight to DC right now. But how do I arrange to connect with you?"

"Happily," Moscoli said with a touch of smugness, "the *Comando Carabinieri per la Tutela del Patrimonio Culturale* has already made provisions. I am at this moment sitting in solitary splendor in the luxurious cabin of our newest Gulfstream intercontinental jet, which is now beginning to roll down the runway and which will then proceed northwest toward Geneva at nine hundred kilometers an hour, and which will arrive at Geneva Airport to pick you up at ten o'clock. If you go to the Alitalia check-in desk in Terminal One, someone will be waiting to escort you through Security and take you to the plane. The direct flight to Monterey is expected to take nine hours, so with the nine-hour time difference, we'll arrive there at 10:00 a.m. *their* time."

"Wait, wait, wait. I'm supposed to be there by ten? That's not even an hour from now."

"Then you'd better get moving, hadn't you?" Moscoli said tranquilly.

CHAPTER 28

In the morning, Chris told Alix that getting to the surprise she had waiting for her required a walk of a mile because it couldn't be moved, so what about stopping first for a couple of breakfast burritos at Papa Chevo's Taco Shop just down the block from the Monterey Plaza?

Alix was all for it. After the previous night's tapas-style dinner, she was hungry for something more solid and burritos sounded good.

"So what are you frowning about?" Chris asked as they stood at the counter to order.

"I'm trying to figure out what you just said. It can't be moved?"

"That's right. Well, not by me, anyway."

Alix was itching with curiosity—Chris's "surprises" could be pretty extravagant—but because they'd soon be seeing this one, she let it go. Instead, their breakfast conversation again went back to Tiny and how to find him, and again the results were dispiriting. It had occurred to Alix that when Tiny told Waldo that he would be working in Monterey, he might have been referring to the Monterey Peninsula as a whole— not only the city of Monterey itself, but Carmel, Seaside, Pacific Grove, Pebble Beach, and whatever else there was. Chris immediately whipped out her phone, and, using the fingers of just one hand (the other continuing to operate her fork) she came up with a new seafood-restaurant total before either of them was halfway through her chorizo-and-egg burrito: sixty-two restaurants in all.

"Of which we've already been to forty-two."

"Right," said Chris, "leaving just twenty more. Piece of cake."

"Except these are scattered all over a pretty big area. I can't say I'm looking forward to getting to them all, but . . . Chris, frankly, I'm starting to lose heart. What makes us think they're even telling us the truth? Maybe we already hit the right one but didn't get told."

Chris popped the last of her refried beans into her mouth. "You know what I think?"

"No, what do you think?"

"I think we should go see my surprise."

◆　◆　◆

Monterey has two large public wharves. Old Fisherman's Wharf, the smaller of them, is crammed with restaurants and tourist attractions, is in every tourist guide (and on the cover of most of them), and is the closest thing to a mandatory destination for every visitor who sets foot in the city. Half a mile to the east lies the less romantically named Municipal Wharf Number 2, which is also known as the Commercial Wharf. Understandably, it appears in no tourist guide and is thus visited by few tourists. Alix herself, who had been to Monterey once before, hadn't even known it existed, so she was puzzled when Chris led her onto it.

"What—" she began, but stopped when her phone made its unobtrusive, almost embarrassed signal. "Just let me see if I need to take this," she said. "Oh, it's Ted—"

"Then you need to take it," Chris said. "And you need to give him his own ringtone so you know when it's him, is what you need."

"You're absolutely right. You need to show me how."

Chris stepped a few yards away to give her some privacy, leaned on a railing, and looked out at a small marina that was nestled at the foot of the wharf and filled with boats. Alix hit the Talk button.

"Ted, darling!" Alix said. "Where are you calling from? Are you still in Switzerland?"

"No, as a matter of fact," he said, with a happy laugh that thrilled her, "I'm practically in Monterey. We're forty minutes out and I can see the Peninsula from here. Hey, is that you, in the red pullover?"

"No, green. Ted, this is wonderful! Are you coming to see me?"

"Well, between us, that was a considerable inducement, but no, the official reason is that we—Gino and I—would really like to talk to Tiny about the Giallo thing, and we figure you two are our best bet for getting hold of him." He paused. "Ah, I sense a chill in the air."

"I didn't think it would carry forty miles, but obviously it did. Ted, you know I respect what you're doing, but you can't expect me to just lead you to him. I owe him a lot. I'd certainly try to convince him to talk to you, but I'm not going to help you get your hands on him if he doesn't want it to happen. I'm sorry, I just can't."

"Alix, we don't want to 'get our hands on him' at all. Tiny is the only link we have now to the theft. We need his help, and right now you and Chris are our best bet to reach him."

"The FBI is after Benny Abbatista because they need his *help*? Well, that's a switch."

"Look, Tiny doesn't have anything to fear from the US government, and Gino told me the Italian statutes of limitation ran out a long time ago and they have no interest in charging him with anything at all."

"Oh, I'm glad to hear that, but what do you mean he's your only link? What about Ferrante? What did he have to say to Gino?"

"Nothing. Ferrante's dead."

". . . He's *dead*?"

"Yes, killed, murdered."

"Oh, my," she said, abruptly sobered. "This is getting kind of serious, isn't it?"

"You bet it is. Some interesting developments have come to light in the last few hours, baby, but look, I'll fill you in when we get there. Hey, Gino's making all these extravagant Italian gestures at me. I think they mean he needs to talk to me. I'll call you when we've landed. Bye, honey."

"What's up?" Chris asked when Alix came up to her. "You look . . . I don't know what you look. Funny."

Alix quickly summarized what Ted had told her.

She'd been looking interestedly out over the marina as she spoke. "Chris, I thought this was a commercial wharf. Those aren't fishing boats."

"No they're not. The Monterey Yacht Club keeps its boats here. It's not technically part of the wharf."

"Oh. Ohmigosh, will you look at that!"

"At what?"

"Right down there on the left. See the big one with the red, white, and blue sails? Look at the boat alongside it."

"The white one, the catamaran?"

"No, the other side, the sleek black and gray one. With the blue and red stripe up the middle?"

"Oh, yes. Ooh, very nice."

"I'll say it is! That's a Lancia Powerboat!"

"Mm. Hey, isn't that the kind you got to drive while you were on that cruise in the Med? You liked it, as I recall."

"I *loved* it. It was the most thrilling ride I ever had." Alix smiled. "Well, maybe not quite as thrilling as that time in the Lamborghini, but—"

"I should hope not," Chris said. "I wound up in the hospital in Española, New Mexico, if you remember. And that gorgeous car practically got totaled."

"Yes, but that wasn't my fault and you know it. You don't have a lot of options when you're on a narrow road with a cliff wall on one side and a giant truck is doing its best to scrunch you into it from the other side. There's not much you can do about it when things like that happen, and they do happen."

"To you they maybe happen. To normal people, no. Except when you're with them."

"Oh, come on, be fair. You were the one who rented that car, you were the one who asked me to drive, and *you* were most definitely the one who wanted to see how fast it could go."

Chris glanced at Alix from under lowered eyebrows. "Oh, right," she said archly, "and you didn't?"

As a matter of fact, Alix did. She had been even more eager than Chris to see what that magnificent (before she wrecked it) automobile could do on a wide-open desert road. She was, to put it bluntly, a speed freak. As personalities went, Alix's was among the more consistent and integrated. As anyone who knew her could tell you, she was conservative in her dress and manner and not given to exhibitionistic displays or flashy behavior. But nobody's personality is a hundred percent consistent, and in Alix's case, the outlier, the chunk that didn't fit, was a passion for speed. She loved fast cars, fast boats, fast anything.

And she had a previously unsuspected knack for handling them.

She discovered this—to her surprise—in her early twenties, when she met the son of the elderly master restorer with whom she was studying in Florence. The middle-aged Gian-Carlo Santullo had been an amateur racecar driver in his youth and still maintained a garage full of the cars he'd raced. To be polite, he had taken his father's star student out for a hair-raising ride in his Alfa Romeo Spider one Sunday morning and Alix had come away from it flushed with excitement. Gian-Carlo had been equally pleased with her response and had offered to teach her sports-car etiquette, skills, and rules of the road.

A year later, she had progressed to the point at which she was given free access to most of his cars on those weekends, and there were many of them, that she was his father's guest at their home in Ravello. From then on, the highlight of her week became the heavenly Saturday morning hours she spent cruising down the Amalfi coast in Gian-Carlo's wondrous Ferrari, or Lancia, or Lamborghini. Even now, when she thought of it . . .

"Hello-o? Anybody home?" Chris was jiggling a key ring three inches from Alix's nose. "Do you want to drive that thing or don't you?"

"What?" It took a moment for Alix to grasp what was going on. "You don't mean—"

"I do mean. This thing here will turn on the ignition to that thing there—"

"The Lancia? Are you serious?"

"—which has been rented from its owner for the next two days and is yours to play in as much as you like."

"But Chris—renting a Lancia! It must have cost—"

"It did, but let's have none of that. We have an arrangement, do we not? Just say thank you."

Alix smiled. "Thank you."

Their arrangement had become necessary because Alix refused to charge Chris for her consulting services, but also insisted on picking up her own tab on the many things they did together, which left Chris feeling that she wasn't contributing her fair share. So instead, Chris was "allowed" to come up with an occasional gift, as long as it wasn't *too* extravagant. This one, Alix thought, was probably pushing the envelope, but she certainly wasn't going to argue.

"Thank you, Chris," she said again. "This is fantastic."

"You're welcome. It's all gassed up and ready to go." She handed the keys to Alix. "What do you say we take it for a spin before we get back to work?"

Alix hesitated. "We'll give it two hours, all right? Then I think we'd better get back to Tiny."

"Agreed. Come on, I'm anxious to get going. It's been too long since the last time I risked my life."

•   •   •

Other than the double-levered throttle in place of the gear shift lever, the controls on the Lancia were much the same as those on the same brand's automobile, so handling them had come readily to Alix's mind when she'd driven a Lancia Powerboat the first time, even if some of the smaller, more esoteric dials were still a mystery to her. To build up her confidence—particularly with that double throttle—she thought it best to refamiliarize herself with it by trying it out in the quiet inner bay for a while before taking it out and letting it do its thing. They were cruising slowly alongside the wharf, with Chris marveling at the boat's furnishings: "These seats are fabulous. Smell the leather! Wow, look at that paneling—how do you even polish mahogany to a shine like that? Wow, did you see . . ."—when Alix slowed and then reversed a few yards.

"Chris, did you see that?" She was practically shouting.

"See what? What's wrong?"

"Look!" She pointed at a sign above a rolled-up pull-down door, behind which was a dingy concrete-block interior with floor-to-ceiling freezers along the back wall, a large wire rack with a few cartons scattered on its shelves, and a stairway leading up. The stairway had what looked like gallon bottles of bleach lined up at the edge of each step. A full-sized, red, green, and white Italian flag was tacked to a cabinet on another wall.

Puzzled, Chris shook her head. "What am I supposed to be looking at?"

"The sign, dummy! Read the sign!"

Chris read it, half aloud.

COASTAL SEAFOODS

CRAB, SHRIMP, SQUID

WHOLESALE ONLY

EST. 2001

PROP: CELESTINO PALUZZI

"Celestino!" she exclaimed. "Tino!"

"Right!"

"But this isn't a restaurant, Alix, it's a wholesaler."

"True, but Waldo didn't say 'restaurant,' he said 'seafood place.'"

"Are you sure?" Chris looked doubtful.

"Yes. 'Seafood place.' Which this certainly is."

"Yeah, but he meant *restaurant*." She frowned. "Or at least I thought he did."

"So did I, and maybe he did," Alix said, "because he *thought* that's what Tiny meant."

"But we don't know what Tiny actually meant, or even what he actually said, and Waldo probably doesn't remember either. Maybe . . . what?"

"Why are we arguing about it? Let's just go in and ask. It'd take less time." Alix was already maneuvering the boat into an empty berth along the wharf.

No one was in the warehouse, which smelled about the way you'd expect a wholesale seafood distributor to smell, so they climbed the splintery wooden steps to an upstairs office, which was nothing fancy, but nicer than they'd anticipated: a neat row of filing cabinets, a stack of cardboard file cartons in the corner, a nautical map of the central California coastline, and a gigantic old maple desk with two up-to-date computer monitors. In front of the desk was a low table with a chess set on it, at which a man sat, deeply absorbed in playing a game against an iPad.

"Hello?" Alix said from the doorway. "Excuse us, we—"

The man, a grizzled old-timer who had a three-day growth of stubble and was wearing a frayed denim shirt and dungarees, and could have served as a model for a picture of the Ancient Mariner, held up his hand. "Give me a minute," he said, tapping with one finger on his only remaining rook. A moment later, he gave it up, sitting back with folded arms and scowling at the tablet. "They did it to me again," he said with a shake of his head. "I can't believe it. Hoist by me own petard. Again."

Chris offered a friendly smile. "Whatever a petard is."

"It's a bomb devised by the French in the sixteen hundreds, mostly to breach walls," he said absently, and then finally looked up at them. "If it goes off prematurely, the soldier placing it gets blown up in the air—'hoist,' which was the past participle of *'hoise,'* which is an archaic form of the current verb 'to hoist.' The actual phrase, which is of course from *Hamlet*, is 'hoist with his own petard.'" He stood up, smiling.

"Wow," Chris said, "did I just get blown away."

Alix simply stared mutely at him. *Will you ever learn not to judge people by their appearances?* she was asking herself. Grizzled he was, she saw now, but hardly ancient, probably in his early sixties, and with a clear, lively intelligence in his eyes.

Their reactions made him laugh. "I used to teach seventeenth-century lit at UC Santa Cruz," he explained. "Until I found my true passion."

"Which is?" Alix said, because it seemed to be expected.

"Squid, naturally. How can you ask? Now, how can I help you ladies?"

"Are we speaking to Mr. Paluzzi?" she asked.

"Tino, yes."

"My name is Alix London, Mr. Paluzzi—"

"Tino."

"—Tino, and I really need to get in touch with my uncle, Beniamino Abbatista."

Tino turned serious, chewing at the inside of his cheek and shaking his head. "Sorry . . ."

But Alix, with plenty of practice the day before, kept going. "Sir, I know he doesn't want to be found because he thinks he's in trouble, but he's *not*, and that's part of what I want to tell him—if I can only find him."

"I hope you do find him, Ms. London—Alix—but I don't see what I can do to help you."

Chris chimed in. "Tino, let's be honest here. We *know* Tiny's working at a low-profile job in Monterey, in the seafood industry, and a friend or a relative named Tino helped him get the job. So—"

Tino, obviously a man who laughed easily, did so again. "So here you are, in Monterey, at a seafood wholesaler's, talking to the owner, who happens to be a fellow named Tino. And you suspect there could be a connection, do you?"

"It does seem possible," Alix said.

"Mm." Tino shrugged, tipping his head first one way, then the other. "I suppose I could ask around for you, see if anybody knows him. I don't see how that would hurt."

A shiver ran up Alix's spine. It was the first real flash of hope she'd had since they'd started looking. *He knows!* she thought. "Tino, how about this? If you do find someone who knows him, then perhaps he could pass along to Tiny that I'm trying to find him, and leave it to Tiny to follow up if he wants to. If he doesn't, then that's that . . . but he will! Could you do that?"

"I could do that."

"That's wonderful! Thank you so much. Here's my card with my phone number, and we're staying at the Monterey Plaza if he wants to get hold of us there."

Tino took the card and examined it. "Sure."

"We won't bother you any more now—you've been more than kind—but if you could let us know one way or the other, we'd really—"

"I have some free time right now, ladies, and I am not about to subject myself to the humiliation of another checkmate by an idiot machine that's only capable of binary calculations. So why don't you two take a little walk on the wharf, perhaps stop in for a cup of coffee at the Sand Dab, and come back in half an hour or so? I'll see what I can do."

CHAPTER 29

The life of *Doryteuthis opalescens*, the common California market squid, is no bed of roses. They are as close as makes no difference to the bottom of the marine food chain, barely above plankton and krill. Just about everything they run into would like (and will probably try) to eat them. Against this multitude of predators, they have but one defense, the release of clouds of bluish-black ink in hopes of concealing themselves.

It is not the world's most effective defense mechanism to begin with, and is of no use whatsoever against an enemy for which evolution has not prepared them: the voracious purse seines—vast, ringed nets—used by most of the world's squid boats. If their brains were just a little bigger, they might get at least a little solace out of realizing how unpleasant they make life for the seamen tasked with manhandling these great, slimy, squirmy, dripping, heavy nets—a ton would be a relatively meager haul—from the winches that lift them out of the sea and onto the decks of their boats. From the decks the squid are pumped down into the refrigerated holds, there to begin their transition to calamari.

The work is not merely arduous but odious as well, not least because of the mucus-laden gouts of ink that the squid spurt in every direction in their desperate, hopeless effort to defend themselves.

It was after one such exhausting battle aboard the *23 Squiddoo*, fifteen miles northwest of Monterey and five miles out to sea, that Tiny Abbatista, aka Santo Mamazza, stood on the deck with his four crewmates as they sluiced themselves down and took off the blue foul-weather gear they had put on over their sweats for protection, and plucked off the fiery, agonizing strands of jellyfish that always managed to get through. Tiny stood a little apart from his joshing and cursing crewmates. He'd only come aboard a few days ago, under somewhat odd circumstances (Why was it so sudden? Why hadn't they gone through the usual hiring channels?) and he seemed inclined to keep to himself, a favor they willingly granted.

Frankie, the sixteen-year-old son of the boat's captain and owner, who had begun to go out with them occasionally (but had yet to offer to take part in the work), came aft, treading gingerly on the slimy deck. "Call for you, dude," he said, holding out a cell phone to Tiny.

Tiny stared at it as if it might attack him. "For me? Are you sure? Who is it?"

"Paluzzi."

"Tino Paluzzi? Are you sure?"

Frankie snorted with impatience. "Dude, what is your problem? You don't want to take it, don't take it."

"No, I'll take it," Tiny said, putting out his hand. He held the phone a cautious six inches from his ear. "Hello?" he said warily. "Tino?"

◆ ◆ ◆

"You're all set. He wants to talk to you," said the beaming literature professor *cum* squid wholesaler Celestino Paluzzi. "He's out near the top of the bay, working on a netter, the 23 *Squiddoo*, but he's on a break, and he says this would be a good time to call him."

"Thank you so much, Tino," Alix said. "I can't tell you how grateful we are."

"And I'm equally grateful to you, Alix. He hasn't confided in me as to what the problem is, and I haven't pressed him—you know how he can be, I'm sure—but I can tell you this: when I said your name, I heard the first smile in his voice since he arrived. Here, I wrote the number on your card. Oh, but be sure and ask for Paolo; he's going by Paolo Zamboni while he's down here."

Chris was shaking her head and laughing as they walked back out onto the wharf. "*Zamboni?* I swear, Alix, this guy has more names than a character in *War and Peace.*"

• • •

"Ah, can this really be *il mio tesorino*?" Tiny said huskily when he was handed the phone, and whatever doubtful feelings Alix was having about him dissolved on the spot. *My little treasure.* She felt suddenly as if she were four years old again, and Tiny's big palm was ever so affectionately patting her head, and from his immense height, he was smiling and murmuring, "*Il mio tesorino,*" and she knew that with him there, there was nothing in the world that could harm her. Emotion so flooded her throat that she had trouble speaking.

"It's me, all right, Tiny," she whispered. "*Zio* Beni."

"Are you all right? How did you find me?"

"Yes, I'm all right, and I'll tell you how we found you when we see you. We *will* get to see you, won't we?"

"Who's 'we'?"

"Chris. My friend. You know Chris."

"Does Geoff know I'm here?"

"Nobody else knows, Tiny, just us. Now: Are *you* all right?"

"Oh, yeah, sure, everything's fine."

"Is that right? Everything's fine? And that's why you disappeared without a word and I had to ask for Paolo Zamboni to talk to you?"

Low in his throat, he chuckled. "Well, hey, that's kind of a long story. I didn't have much choice. I know I probably worried everybody—"

"Oh, a little, maybe."

"—and you're probably wondering what the hell's going on, but I think it's better, you know, for the time being—"

"To tell you the truth, Tiny, we already know an awful lot about what's going on."

"You do, huh? Don't worry," he said off to one side, "I'll be there in a minute. I still got ten minutes coming." And then back to Alix: "Okay, what do you think is going on?"

"It's a long story. How about waiting until we get together? Only when will that be? We've got our own boat here, a pretty snazzy one; we're sitting in it right now. How about if we just come out and get you?"

"You mean right now, this minute? Well, I don't know . . . No. No way, no. We still gotta process the catch down in the hold. It's kind of lousy work, and I don't like to leave the other guys to do it. Give me, say, three hours, okay?"

No, it wasn't okay, Alix thought, but she also thought it was unwise to push Tiny, who still sounded a little skittish. She didn't want to lose him again. "Yes, all right," she said. "Where are you? Can you give me the map coordinates?"

"Yeah, give me a minute."

"He's game," Alix said to Chris with her hand over the phone. "I think it's all going to work out."

"Never doubted it."

"Alix?" Tiny was back. "Okay, you got a pen and paper?"

Alix made scribbling motions to Chris, who went rummaging in her purse and came up surprisingly quickly with a miniature notebook that had a toothpick-sized pen attached with a little chain.

"Yes, let's hear them."

"Okay, if you're still near Paluzzi's place, then we're about fifteen miles north of you, way out in the bay. What?" he said to someone on the *Squiddoo*, and then to Alix, "Okay, north-northwest, I guess. Here's the GPS coordinates." He read them off with painstakingly slow clarity, while Alix repeated them for Chris, who punched the location into the digital chart plotter built into the Lancia's console: 36° 51' 43.1964" north, 121° 56' 43.7856" west.

"All right, Tiny," Alix said, her optimism beginning to sprout again. "Look for us in three hours. And don't worry, we've got good news for you. You'll stay right there, right?"

He laughed. "Where am I gonna go? I'm lucky if I can dog paddle twenty feet."

"That's great," Chris said when the call ended. "We should go in and thank Paluzzi, and then maybe get that cup of coffee we were talking about. And then maybe you ought to call Ted instead of waiting for his call. I think he'll want to know we actually found Tiny for him." She smiled. "We did, didn't we? Congratulations, partner."

"We sure did. I wonder how happy Tiny is going to be with that, though. He's not exactly going to be wild about the idea of meeting up with the FBI."

"Well, he's going to have to get used to it sometime, isn't he, given his favorite little girl's somewhat, shall we say, intimate relationship with a certain member of that organization."

"Oh, boy," murmured Alix. Worries about Tiny had washed that particular difficulty, which applied to Geoff as much as to Tiny himself, out of her mind, but now it came roaring back. "Honestly, I just don't know how I'm ever going to deal with it."

"Coffee," said Chris. "I am in dire need. There's that place where Tino said we could get some."

A few minutes later they were coming out of the Sand Dab with their lidded take-out cups, and Chris was ramming her wallet back into that jammed bag of hers, which was slung over a shoulder, when she suddenly stopped with a scowl on her face. "Now what the heck is this?" she said, pulling out a slim, green and white card, the size of a credit card.

"It's not a credit card?"

"Not for anything I have credit for."

"A gift card of some kind?"

"Well, yes, but I'm pretty sure this is one of the few I don't have. Besides, it feels . . ." She handed it to Alix.

"'Starbucks, $50,'" Alix read. "'When you need a lift.'" She hefted it in one hand. "It's awfully heavy, isn't it?" She rapped one edge of it on the wharf's railing. The result was the unmistakable clink of metal on metal. "What in the world—"

Chris grabbed it from her. The reverse side looked normal enough too, with the SKU bars and the space for a signature, but she used a fingernail to scrape at one of its corners. In a few seconds the corner came loose and she was able to pull off the entire rear of the card. Underneath was a metal surface covered with electronic circuitry.

"Damn it!" she cried, skimming the card out over the water as hard as she could. Like a flat pebble it skipped twice, flipped over, and sank some twenty yards offshore.

"What—" Alix began.

"It's a micro recorder!" Chris cried. "A bug! Absolute state of the art. How did it get into—" They looked at each other for a second, then nodded.

"The gorilla who slammed into you last night," Alix said, expressing both their thoughts. "The little guy put it in while he was supposedly being a gentleman and picking up all your stuff."

Chris nodded. "Of course. They were tracking us, hoping we'd lead them to Tiny, just like that dweeb in Frisco."

"These two aren't dweebs, though," Alix observed soberly.

"No, not by a long shot. Those are hard men, Alix. They were Italian, weren't they? Good God, I bet they were Mafia; they *looked* like Mafia." She jerked her head. "And we *did* lead them to him. They heard us talking to him. They know where the *Squiddoo* is just as well as we do, down to the last degree, minute, and second, which means they're probably on their way right now trying to beat us to him. We have to hustle if we want to get to him first. Let's go!"

"No, wait, there's no problem; we'll get there first. They'll have to find out where you get a boat first, and then go and get it, and sign for it and all, and whatever they get isn't going to be as fast as ours, which is sitting there waiting for us about twenty feet away. We can wait another minute. I should warn Tiny."

"Tiny, listen to me," she said when he came onto the telephone a moment later. "You're in trouble. I just found out. There are a couple of guys after you. These do not look like nice guys. Both from Italy. They know where you are and they're going to want to get at you to find out where the loot is. That Cellini pendant is worth millions now. I'm sure you know that."

"What loot? What Cellini pendant?"

"Oh, please, let's not . . . well, never mind. Look, Chris and I will be right out to get you; we've got a boat that can beat whatever they have. And, listen, Tiny, someone from the FBI art squad just showed up here in Monterey. I know him, um, really well, and he's a good guy. If it's all right with you, let me—"

"*WHAT?* The FBI?"

"Believe me, this is someone you want on your side. And he's got a *carabiniere* with him, another good guy, and I know they'll—"

"The *carabinieri*? Are you kidding me? You keep those guys away from me, Alix. I don't want them anywhere near me. I'm telling you—"

"Okay, okay, calm down, it was just an idea. Fifteen miles? Shouldn't be much more than twenty minutes. We'll be in a speedboat: black and gray with a blue and red stripe. Keep an eye out for us."

"Yeah, I will, I will. But no FBI, no *carabinieri*!"

"I hear you, Tiny. We're coming."

"Okay, I'll be ready. I just have to get my stuff together."

"Right, sit tight, we're on our way."

"No FBI!"

The moment she ended the call she called Ted, barely giving him time to say hello. "Ted, I think we may have a situation developing, and we can use your help."

"Situation—?"

"Just listen. We're going out to get Tiny. He's on a squid boat. Here are the GPS coordinates."

"Alix, what—"

"Write them down," she ordered and gave them to him. "We're heading out in a Lancia Powerboat and I'm pretty sure we can beat the Mafia there, but if you can make it out too—"

"Well, yeah, I think I can hitch a ride . . . hey, wait. Mafia, did you say? *Mafia*? Whoa, whoa, whoa, now you just hold on—"

"Just do it, please. 'Bye, Ted." With a flurry of protestations and questions jostling each other in her ear, she disconnected.

Chris was looking at her with a combination of perplexity and amusement. "'Just do it'?" she repeated. "Well, I can see who's wearing the pants in this family. That didn't take long."

"No, it's just that if we got into a real conversation he'd be doing his manly thing and telling us to stay the hell away and let him handle it, that it was dangerous, etc., etc., etc. And then we'd have a hassle and I'd end up either ignoring his . . . his directives, or else following them but resenting it. Seemed better this way. Let's go."

"You know," Chris said, "you just might be better at this marriage business than I was giving you credit for."

"Thank you." Alix dropped into the boat and started it idling. "Now how about untying us?"

Chris climbed out to unloop the rope from one of the few mooring cleats along the wharf. "Hey, I just thought of something," she said. "We've been assuming we'd get a head start on those creeps because we already have a boat and they'd have to go find one. But aren't we forgetting who these guys are? They're in a hurry to get him, they're not going to go find some rental agency and mess with signing papers, and IDs and all, they're just going to *take* the first boat they can steal. What if they did that the minute they heard those coordinates—just ran down to the nearest dock and mugged somebody and stole his boat? What then?" She climbed cautiously back into the bobbing Lancia.

"Then they have a twenty-minute head start on us, so we'd better get going." Alix shoved the throttle forward.

"Whup!" Chris was flung backward into her seat, the half-full coffee cup in her hand went flying over her shoulder, and the boat leaped forward.

CHAPTER 30

"T hat's it, all right!" Chris shouted to be heard over the engine noise. "I can read the lettering now: *23 Squiddoo!*"

She was peering through the binoculars she'd found on the Lancia at the clunky-looking aluminum boat, whose giant winch had finally come into sight a minute ago, and was now a little less than a mile off, according to the chart plotter on the console.

"Great." Alix, eager to get Tiny safely off the squid boat and onto theirs, itched to push the double throttle even farther forward, but their bow was already a good four feet in the air, the sea had gotten choppy, and she was afraid of capsizing.

"Can you see Tiny?" Alix herself could now see activity on the deck but couldn't make out whom she was looking at or what they were doing.

"No," Chris said. She was leaning forward, holding tightly to the top of the framework that surrounded the open-topped cockpit with glass. "No . . . *yes*! I see him! I see him, there he is! He's just . . . there's something going on . . . Now what? You're kidding me! I think . . . Alix, I think he just jumped overboard! He did, he jumped overboard!" She stared at Alix, who stared uncomprehendingly back.

"Overboard?"

Chris brought the binoculars back up to her eyes. "Yes, he's in the water, he's swimming toward . . . I don't know what he's . . . oh, I see, there's a buoy or something not far from the boat, out in front. Christ, Alix, I hope he can make it, he swims like a . . . Go, Tiny, go!"

Alix had quickly recovered her senses, and while Chris was talking she'd surveyed their surroundings. "It's that boat," she declared. "The white one out in front of us and off to the right, moving fast, heading straight for the *Squiddoo* . . . no, for Tiny, I think. Oh, my God, it must be—"

"It is!" Chris cried, having swung the binoculars around. "The two goons, the Mafia! They must have seen him jump too. What are they doing? Do they plan to run him down? Are they—"

Choppy sea or no choppy sea, Alix didn't see much choice. She jammed the throttle forward. The bow lifted up even higher and the Lancia bounded forward through the air, hitting the water so hard, stern down, that when it landed Alix had to struggle to regain control over the bouncing, careening craft. It took all of four, five seconds for her to get it plowing straight ahead toward Tiny and the *Squiddoo* again.

Eyes wide, Chris looked at Alix. "What are you going to do?"

"I don't know," Alix yelled back, leaning forward in an instinctive effort to get even more out of the Lancia.

"I mean, when we get there, what are you going to—"

"I *know* what you mean," Alix shouted back, teeth clenched and eyes slitted against the salt spray and the whipping of her hair against her face.

"Alix, they're practically on top of him now," Chris screamed. "My God, what are we going to do? We can't possibly get there in time to fish him out of the water!" She was frantic.

She was also right, Alix knew. The other boat, a yellow, fifteen-foot Wahoo, flimsy but fast, was already almost even with the *Squiddoo*, less than a hundred yards from the desperately flailing Tiny, and already slowing down. Chris and Alix were only fifty yards behind them, but with no possibility of reaching Tiny before the Wahoo did.

Their slowing down told Alix that they weren't trying to kill him. What they wanted was information from him; that was the point of this whole bizarre misadventure. But once they had the information—or if Tiny didn't have it to give—and he was no longer of use to them, then what?

No, she had to come up with something, do something to keep them from getting their hands on him. Once they had him, who knew what could happen?

Alix was as frantic and irresolute as Chris was, yet at the same time, in some small, quiet compartment of her mind, the situation and the possible alternatives were being calmly, logically analyzed, but at warp speed. It was a strange, split state of mind that she'd encountered only a few times before, always in crises (but nothing like this!), and she had learned that, with an effort, she could shut off the frenzied howling from the one part, and listen to the composed, unruffled advice from the other. And what it advised was to apply an elementary theory of boat propulsion, but one that had rarely—if ever—been employed to the degree that would be required here.

Alix waited another millisecond, hoping for something better, a plan B, but there wasn't one. It was plan A or nothing. She swung the Lancia around and aimed its bow straight at the Wahoo. "In for a penny . . ." she mouthed and shoved the twin throttles forward.

"Alix! You're not going to *ram* them? You'll kill—"

"Grab something and hold on tight," Alix commanded through clenched teeth.

"But . . . but . . ." Words failed Chris at that point, and she obeyed, dropping the binoculars and clutching the rim at the top of the console with both hands. Her face was white, drained of blood. Alix suspected her own didn't look any different.

The two men in the Wahoo now became aware of them, of these two crazy women bearing down on them. They had to realize there was no hope of getting entirely out of the way, but the little one, at the wheel, spun it away from them as hard as he could, trying to avoid a full broadside collision. Meanwhile big Beppe angrily jabbed his finger at them, then did it again.

No, not his finger. "Chris, he's shooting at us, get your head down!" Alix too hunched down and to one side, although there was something unreal about being shot at. Nothing seemed to hit the boat, and the roar of the engines blotted out the *pop* of the gun.

They were only thirty yards or so from the Wahoo now, and still moving at near top speed, and the little guy suddenly leaped from his seat, threw up his hands, and jumped over the side. But Beppe stood his ground and kept shooting, and now a round, ragged hole appeared almost magically in the windshield between the two of them. There was no sound, but the little glass chips were clearly visible as they flew into the cockpit. They both jerked away from them. Things suddenly seemed very, very real. Nevertheless, despite Alix's insistent, pushing panic, that logical little compartment of her mind was still in control (barely), and it was time to just hope for the best and put the plan into play . . . *now*!

With only a couple of boat-lengths between them before they collided, Alix snapped the wheel to zero and flew through a set of maneuvers—threw the left throttle lever to idle, then jerked it all the way back to reverse while jamming the right throttle lever forward as far as it would go—that shot the forward power of the starboard engine to its absolute maximum while the port engine roared back against it. Inches before ramming the Wahoo, the Lancia canted almost fully onto its port side (bringing a "Yikes!" from Chris) and wheeled in an astoundingly tight quarter-circle to port.

If they had been in a car, there would have been a terrific screeching of tires. Alix had automatically shut her eyes at the last second, anticipating a horrendous crash, but when she opened them a moment later it hadn't happened and they were skimming safely away with nothing but wonderful, blue, wide-open water in front of them. Now she looked behind her.

And she was greeted with a welcome sight. The huge wake—a curving, six-foot wave, really—that the Lancia had thrown off to its right when it turned had just plowed over the Wahoo, first jolting Beppe off his feet and then—wonder of wonders—tipping the Wahoo's bow way up and tilting the boat so much that it stood momentarily on its stern and then flipped completely over, dumping Beppe into the water to flounder alongside his thrashing partner. The plan couldn't have worked more perfectly. Alix had counted on the *mafiosi* helping out by trying to steer away from her, making the Wahoo even less stable. They had, and it was.

"Are we dead yet?" Chris said from her crouch.

Alix laughed. "Look."

Chris came up. "Oh, my," she said happily. "Did we do that?"

"We most certainly did," Alix said. "Now let's go get our man."

Tiny had somehow made it to the buoy he'd been headed for and he waved weakly at them, but the smile on his face couldn't have been broader.

Alix waved back and started putt-putting in his direction, hugely elated, but at the same time in a kind of adrenaline-based, blissful stupor, so that—

"THANK YOU, LADIES, WE'LL TAKE IT FROM HERE."

The booming, ear splitting order, seemingly from heaven itself, practically made *her* jump out of the boat. She spun around and was astonished to find herself looking up—far up—at the stainless white prow and diagonal red stripe of *87312*, the *Hawksbill*, Monterey's resident Coast Guard cutter, probably a hundred feet long. When in the world had that gotten there? How could she not have seen it before? But there it was, with a smiling young officer at the rail, apparently he who had issued the command.

"We'll get him out of the water," he said, and the loudspeaker thundered the words out at her. "We'll get them all. Promise not to miss any."

And now, among the other sailors at the railing, she spotted Ted. So this was the ride he had "hitched." He was shaking his head wonderingly, and laughing to himself, and murmuring something, and she thought she could she could read what it was on his lips:

"I swear, Alix . . ."

She chose to interpret it as a compliment.

CHAPTER 31

Alix and Chris stayed at the scene to watch the goings-on with the cutter. Ted, in the meantime, was able to lean down from the cutter's deck and tell her what would be happening afterward. The two goons would be handed over to Monterey PD—they had indeed "liberated" the Wahoo without permission, and then, of course, Beppe had been shooting at Alix and Chris, so problems lay ahead for the two of them.

"And Tiny?"

"No trouble as far as the law is concerned, but Gino has a lot of questions he needs to ask him. We'll get him dried off and cleaned up and then sit down with him and see what he has to say."

They both paused for a couple of minutes to watch the crew haul the *mafiosi* up out of the choppy, spuming water in wire rescue baskets. They both looked utterly dejected and miserable, a pair of half-drowned rats. It was a sight that cheered Alix's heart. As for Tiny, he was already safely aboard and swathed in blue Coast Guard blankets with a steaming mug in his hands.

"Ted," Alix called up, "I hope you're not going to take him to the police station. He's a stubborn guy, and that won't make him any more cooperative."

"No, no reason for that. He's not under arrest. It's all voluntary on his part. But we thought if we could get a conference room at the Monterey Plaza, that'd be perfect. Neutral, non-threatening . . ."

"Might work," Alix said, "and I think it might help if I were there. It'd make him feel more like he was among friends, don't you think?"

"No, ma'am, I do not think so; not by a long shot. Well, here we go," he called as the *Hawkbill*'s engines came alive. "I'll call you as soon as I can, babe. Thanks, you two, that was some show you guys put on."

But the cutter was already too far away for her to reply. The two women looked at each other, and Alix smiled. "That *was* a pretty good show, wasn't it?"

"Don't ask me, I had my eyes shut the whole time. But Tiny's safe, the bad guys are in tow, and"—she pinched her arms—"we still seem to be alive, so it must have been." She jerked her head. "I still can't believe you did that. You must have come within two inches of them before we swerved."

"Yes, I'm embarrassed about that. I was shooting for four inches. I must have miscalculated."

Chris laughed. "The amazing thing is, I believe you. Well, what now? Here we are, our job is done, our powerful engines are at the ready, and the open sea beckons."

"Tell you the truth, Chris, this whole episode really took it out of me. I feel like a damp dishrag. I think I'd just like to go back to the hotel and rest for a while. Everything seems to be well in hand."

Chris rolled her eyes heavenward. "*Thank* you for saying that. I was afraid you'd want to go scooting around some more and, let me tell you, I've had all the excitement I can take for one day. Maybe even for two days. And the sea's getting a little rough, isn't it? So turn this baby around and get us back."

◆ ◆ ◆

Two hours later, with Alix still fully dressed but soundly asleep atop the bedcovers, her room phone rang. With her eyes closed she groped for it with a groan and managed to pick it up.

"Hi, baby—"

Ted. Her eyes popped open and she swung her legs over the side to sit up.

"Listen," he said, "when you suggested sitting in with Tiny before, I may have been a little, well—"

"High-handed?" she suggested archly. "Overbearing? Pompous? Prematurely dismissive?"

"Yeah, I'll settle for that last one. The fact is, we can't get anything out of him. Where's the missing art? Shrug. The Palazzo Giallo robbery? He never heard of it. Is his real name Santo Mamazza? Shrug. What was his connection to Alessandro Ferrante? Never heard of him, and on and on. I'm not sure whether we've gotten through to him that the statutes of limitation on the theft have expired, so he can't get in any legal trouble over any of this. He doesn't seem to be listening real hard, though. And then just now, after not saying a word for ten minutes or so, he looked both of us straight in the eye and said flat out: 'I don't trust you, and I don't trust you.' So I was a little ticked off by then, and I said 'Well, who the hell *do* you trust?' And guess what he said."

"I'm on my way," Alix said, wriggling a foot into one of her shoes. "Where am I going?"

"We're right here in the hotel, conference floor, Big Sur Room 1. I think he'd be more comfortable if it was just you, not Chris."

"Probably so. See you shortly."

◆　◆　◆

The room, obviously used for breakout sessions during seminars and conferences, was small and relatively plain, but not intimidating. The three of them sat on folding chairs at a folding table, in the middle of which was a tray that held coffee makings for three, but only Tiny had one of the Styrofoam cups in front of him. He was wearing clothes that must have been picked up in the hotel gift shop. His red sweatshirt said "I ♥ Monterey." There was also a plate in front of him that now held only crumbs. Across from him sat Ted and *Capitano* Moscoli, who greeted Alix most civilly. Tiny didn't get up when she walked in but he smiled hugely, and the heave of his chest suggested a silent sigh of relief.

"Well, here I am," she said to all three of them. "How do you want to proceed?"

Moscoli answered. "I think it would be good if Mr. Abbatista"— Alix noted that he went along with Tiny's American name—"could hear from your mouth that we are not trying to put him in jail, and that he is in fact immune from prosecution in Italy. We are interested only in the missing art and we speak with him in the hope that he may have some information on it." He stopped and waited for Alix's response. Tiny watched her as well.

"As far as I know, that's all so, Tiny," she said, wishing she could have told him something a little less ambiguous.

It was good enough for Tiny, who relaxed still more. "That's a relief," he said.

"Well, damn, Tiny," Ted said, "we've been telling you that for the last hour. Why didn't you—"

"Because," Tiny said coldly, "like I told you before, I don't like you and I don't trust you. You neither," he added for Moscoli's benefit.

Ted released something between a sigh and a throaty growl, but Moscoli showed no reaction. "And now," he said, "I believe that Mr. Abbatista would be more comfortable if you would remain here with us at the table while we once again go over the questions that—"

"No, that's not what Mr. Abbatista would like," Tiny interrupted. "Mr. Abbatista would like you guys out of the room altogether, and Alix can ask the questions. I think she knows I'll be honest with her."

"I know you would, Tiny," Alix said, "but I don't really know what questions to ask. I'm not that familiar with the case."

"That's true, Tiny," Ted put in. "We need to be here. We'll keep our mouths shut while you're talking, I promise."

"Not good enough. You said I'm not under arrest, right? So I can leave anytime I want, right?" He pushed himself back from the table. "So . . ."

Alix had expected to find him demoralized and intimidated when she arrived, but he was obviously anything but. Really, she shouldn't have been surprised. When had she ever seen him intimidated (by anybody but Geoff)?

"Let's not rush into anything," Moscoli said, holding out his hand, and then to Ted: "I don't see why we can't accede to Mr. Abbatista's request"—he peered hard at Tiny—"as long as he understands that Ms. London will be free to pass on to us whatever information he provides."

"I got no problem with that."

"I have a better idea," Ted said. "I have a digital recorder in my case. Why don't I just put it down on the table and let it take everything down?"

"I got no problem with that either."

Alix was getting confused. "Then what do you need me for? What's the point of my being here at all?"

"The point is," Tiny said pedantically, as if it should have been obvious, "that I'm not going to sit here spilling my guts while these two characters sit there eyeballing me the whole time." He had the ability to shrug his shoulders the way a horse or a dog does, more a shiver of the skin than a shrug of the muscles beneath, and he did it now.

And so it was agreed. Ted and Moscoli got up and left, to return in half an hour, and Alix was left alone with Tiny, although before they left Ted called for fresh coffee to be brought in to them.

They sat there grinning at each other across the table until Alix got up and said, "Oh, what the heck, Tiny, give me a hug, will you?" He jumped up, came around the table, and enthusiastically obliged, lifting her half a foot off the floor, while she thought: Tiny, Geoff, Ted, and Chris . . . the only four people in the world from whom she was truly comfortable accepting an embrace. What did that say about her? Anything? Not something to worry about right now . . .

Ted had gotten the recorder going before he left, so Alix said: "What do you say we start at the beginning? Back in Italy, when you were still Santo Mamazza, when—"

"Oh, so you know about that," he said.

"Well, yeah! We've been looking for you a long time, and we've done a lot of research."

"What kind of long time? I took off from Seattle last week, not last year."

"Well, it sure seems like a year." She smiled. "But it was worth it: we found you."

He smiled too. "Yeah, you found me. I really appreciate that you came looking, Alix. You and your friend." He sat back, hands loosely folded on the table, waiting for her next question.

The coffee was delivered, along with a fresh plate of Danish pastries, and they both took a pastry. "So," Alix said, "let's hear."

"Okay," he finally said. "Nineteen-eighty-seven. I was just another big, dumb kid from this little village in the mountains—Pieve di Teco. Worked on and off with the road maintenance crews when I could to earn a little money for me and for my mother." He shook his head. "Seventy-eight years old and taking in other people's laundry. Ah, what the hell. Anyway, I had a few scrapes with the law, just minor stuff, but I was heading absolutely nowhere. But I guess I did show some artistic ability, and so . . ."

And so his Uncle Innocenzo, his mother's younger brother and the village butcher, had scraped together enough money to send his awkward, ungainly, unpromising nephew to the big city—all the way to Genoa, almost sixty miles—to learn a trade that might take advantage of his natural skills. He had apprenticed him to one Rafaello Della Rocca, a crabby, garrulous, old frescoist and restorer, a second-rate craftsman whose other students had all left him, but who was the only available *maestro* Innocenzo could afford. He was cranky and demanding, but Tiny, more out of a sense of obligation to *Tio* Innocenzo than anything else, had resolutely taken the abuse and stuck it out.

With Tiny's assistance, Della Rocca continued his long-running project of repairing the moldering murals in the decrepit, seventeenth-century church of San Carlo Borromeo. Unknown to Tiny at the time, the rear of this church abutted the rear of the Palazzo Giallo, while the fronts opened on different streets. Adjoining doorways in the backs of the two buildings had been constructed in the early nineteenth century to make passage to and from the church easier for the pious count who lived in the palazzo at the time.

There were two other important things that Tiny didn't know: First, that the passageway was a key element in the theft that was to come, and second, that his master, Della Rocca, had a sideline, at which he was known to art theft rings in Milan and Genoa as a man proficient at "altering" ill-gotten paintings in such a way as to maximize their potential profits while minimizing the risk that they could be traced to their source. In plainer language, he was skilled at cutting them up into frameable, saleable chunks, and doing it economically, that is, with minimal waste. It was through Ferrante's good offices, including a sizable donation (actually funded by the Mafia) to the Genoan diocese, that hired Della Rocca had been hired for the church work. It had been, as a matter of fact, the first step in Ferrante's elaborate, year-long preparations for the heist; both the old man and the proximity of the church were to figure importantly in its execution. And they did. Within minutes the loot had been hustled through the abutting doors and down into the church's dim, cobwebbed basement, all but abandoned except for stray cats and the occasional rodent that managed to elude them (never for very long). The atmosphere was thick with mold, musk, and the acrid smell of decades—maybe centuries—of ashy, dried-up feces. Here, in a dusty workroom behind a heavy, iron-studded oak door, Della Rocca had at once begun to plot the lines of his intended cuts, working through the night.

On the following morning, Tiny found himself troubled by the eighty-year-old Della Rocca's vagueness and shakiness, his more-than-usual crankiness, and his frequent absences from the moisture-damaged *Virgin and Child* they were close to completing. At one point, after Della Rocca had been gone from the scaffold for forty minutes, Tiny went in search of him. Earlier, he had seen the *maestro*, furtively come up the stone steps from the basement, and it was there that he went. The place alone was enough to give him the creeps, but they were greatly magnified when he heard Della Rocca's voice. Somewhere nearby, the old man was talking to himself, *crooning* to himself. He would ask a question—"Here, Rafaello?"—and answer it: "No, Rafaello, *here*, ha-ha, yes, precisely."

The hairs on the back of Tiny's neck stood up. "*Maestro?*" he called gently.

No answer, but the crooning stopped. Tiny, standing roughly in the middle of the basement, turned slowly around, and along the far wall he saw a sliver of light coming from under a closed wooden door. He went to it and knocked.

"*Maestro?*"

"Go away."

"*Maestro*, it's Santo. Are you all right?"

"Go away! Stupid boy, do your job. Do you need me with you every second?"

Half an hour later, Della Rocca, without a word about any of this, was back on the scaffold six feet off the floor, touching up the fresco. He was shakier than ever and at one point he gesticulated too vigorously while berating Tiny for insufficiently thinning a newly prepared pail of lime. After a wild few seconds of windmilling arms and teetering body, he was forced to surrender to gravity and tumbled from the scaffold. Tiny rushed to break his fall but couldn't reach him in time.

The old man lay on his back on the stone floor, dazed and mumbling. Tiny called 118 and in ten minutes an ambulance was there. At the hospital he was diagnosed with a hairline-fractured radius, shock, and concussion, for all of which he was treated. But they had missed a ruptured brain aneurysm, and at a little before one o'clock in the afternoon, without issuing another coherent sentence, he quietly expired.

In the meantime Tiny, not sure what else to do, had continued working on the *Virgin*, putting in some of his own touches and even daring to redo some of Della Rocca's work. By now, he had learned of the previous night's next-door theft and couldn't put aside the thought that Della Rocca's strange behavior was in some way connected to it. When word came of the *maestro*'s unexpected death, he put down his tools and returned to the basement. Two huge old locks now guarded the door to the room. He went back upstairs for the wrecking bar they used to break up old plaster walls, came back, and in another minute, was able to wrench the door open.

"*And?*" Alix urged, restraining herself from shouting it when Tiny stopped to thoughtfully swirl the few ounces of coffee that remained in his cup.

"And I guess that's when all the trouble started."

"Half hour's up," Ted said from the doorway, having entered with Moscoli. "Okay?"

"Sure, come on in, what the hell," said Tiny. Clearly, talking things out with Alix had improved his disposition. "But I'm not gonna go through it all again. You can listen on the tape recorder or whatever it is. I was just getting to the good part, the part everybody's so interested in, anyway."

"What happened to the loot," Moscoli said.

"Bingo. Have a seat."

"Wait a minute, Tiny," Ted said. "Before you get into that, answer one question for me, will you? When you jumped into the water . . . why'd you do that?"

"What do you mean, 'why'? I was trying to get away from those two goons, that's why. So I jumped out the opposite side of the boat."

"But what were you going to do? You can't outswim a speedboat."

"I know that, come on. I was heading for that buoy."

"Well, what for? What was your plan? Long-range, I mean. After you reached the buoy."

Tiny fidgeted and shuffled his feet. "Well, I'm not too great with long-range plans," he said, and Alix smiled, knowing how true that was. "It just seemed like a good idea at the time, okay?"

"A good idea at the time," Ted repeated, as though to himself.

"Can we get back to the loot now?" Moscoli suggested.

"Yeah," Tiny said, "but first I want to hear it from your mouth one more time. I can't be prosecuted for what happened, right? Nothing I say can, be, like, held against me."

"Absolutely," Moscoli said. "I can show you the statute. I'll put it in writing if you want."

"You bet I do."

Tiny and Moscoli locked eyes.

"And you need it right now, before we proceed?" Moscoli said.

Tiny regarded him narrowly for a long moment, then shrugged. "I'll trust you."

"Well, that's an improvement," Moscoli grumbled.

Tiny took a deep breath and went on. "Well, I walk into the room where Della Rocca was before and I turn on the lantern, and there they are, all three of the paintings, lined up on the floor along the wall."

"And the pendant?" Moscoli asked with evident anxiety. "The Cellini?"

"Yeah, the pendant too. That was just sitting there on a rickety old shelf. The pictures had these lines drawn on them; that's what Della Rocca was doing in there. Even back then, I knew what that meant, and, well, it shocked the hell out of me. I mean, Della Rocca was no prize, but chopping up four-hundred-year-old paintings? I couldn't believe it."

"Only the lines?" Moscoli asked quietly. "Then where did Alix's panel come from? Who cut up the Mazzoni?"

Tiny understood what he was really asking and took offense. "Well, not me!" he declared, and Alix silently cheered him on. *You tell him, Tiny!* "Della Rocca had already cut it away, just that one piece, the lower right corner, just waste. It was in the garbage can and I took it out and kept it. That's what I made the mirror from."

"Yes, but that was later, Tiny," Ted said reasonably. "You didn't know Alix then, so that couldn't have been the reason."

"No, I kept it because if I ever did tell the story—what I'm telling you now?—I wanted to have proof. Then later . . . well, I thought she'd like it."

"I loved it," Alix said. "Losing it was like losing . . . well, it really hurt." She smiled. "I was kind of hoping you'd make me another one sometime."

Tiny threw back his head and laughed. "I don't have to. I'll just give that one back to you."

"*You* have it?" Ted asked.

"I *took* it," Tiny said.

"*You* took it?" Alix said. "Why—?"

Tiny was still laughing. "Well, hell, after that magazine came out and these two guys started following me around I was afraid they'd come after you too, and I wanted to . . . well, you know, I wanted to . . ."

"Protect her," Ted supplied with a soft smile, and Alix could see his estimation of Tiny changing as he spoke. Her heart soared. Maybe these two were going to get along after all.

"Well . . . yeah," Tiny said, and now he was embarrassed. "So I figured if word got around that somebody stole it, well, then, she'd be safe. Sorry about the mess, Alix. I tried to make it look good, you know, but not do any real damage."

"Tiny," Alix said, "you did anything but damage."

"I understand all that, Tiny," Ted said, "but it only accounts for one piece of one painting. What did you do with the rest?"

"I hid it," Tiny said flatly, "and I'd be real surprised if it's not still there."

Moscoli, Ted, and Alix all waited for someone to ask the big question, and finally Moscoli did.

"Dove?" Where?

"About forty feet from where I found it. In the church, right next door to the palazzo."

"In the church? No, I don't believe it," Moscoli said. "We went over every millimeter."

"Inside the walls."

Moscoli energetically shook his head. "No. No. We examined the walls; of course we did. We applied X-ray, we used thermal imaging—"

"Not ten feet up, you didn't," Tiny said proudly.

"Ah . . . ten feet up?" Moscoli repeated dully.

"We were up on scaffolding, in the middle of working on that old fresco. Not far away there was a big, blank section of wall that was in bad shape, so Della Rocca had me plastering it over when I wasn't working with him, okay? Well. I moved the scaffold over there, got up on it, cut out a section of the wall and put the stuff inside, in a space between the beams. Then I put back the piece of the wall I cut out, spackled it in, and plastered over the whole damn wall so there wouldn't be any seams. Then I took apart the scaffolding and put it in the basement, and . . . well, that's it."

It was a long speech for Tiny and he broke off a restorative piece of his bear claw, downing it with a cheerful sip of cold coffee.

"Well, how about that?" Ted said slowly, with something like admiration. "What were you going to do with it? What were your long-range—" Alix smiled as Ted caught himself. "You hid them away because you were worried about getting into trouble?"

Tiny gave his great head a sharp shake. "Hell no. Because I didn't want that sonofa—sorry, Alix—that rotten, so-called politician who owned them to get them back, that's why. You know how he got rich enough to get that kind of art? He—ah, never mind, I guess I was just hoping things would change somehow, that . . . I don't know."

"But things *did* change, Tiny," said Moscoli. "We caught up with Gamberini a few years later. He's probably still in prison. The palazzo and everything in it were confiscated. It's a State museum now, and it's beautiful, and it's famous. And this art you hid? That would be part of it, but I wouldn't be surprised if it goes on show in Rome first, or maybe at the Pitti Palace." He paused to let Tiny take this in. "Tiny, how would you feel about coming back to Italy and showing us exactly where it is?"

Tiny was obviously taken with the idea but shocked as well. "But . . . you're sure I wouldn't get arrested right at the airport?"

Moscoli let out a great horse laugh. "Arrested? Tiny . . . Beniamino . . . Santo . . ."

Don't forget Paolo, Alix thought.

". . . you don't understand. If what you say is so, you'll be treated as a hero, not a criminal."

"A hero?"

"It would amaze me if you don't get a medal pinned on you down in Rome. You've safeguarded—and returned—a significant piece of the national patrimony."

"A medal," Tiny mused, a smile slowly forming on his face. Alix was surprised and pleased to see that this former embodiment of low-profile existence seemed to rather like the idea. "Would there be a ceremony? Could my uncle come?"

Moscoli stood up and held out his hand. "Mr. Abbatista," he said, "you can bring any damned person you want, and the State will cover the expense. This I guarantee."

Tiny was clearly overwhelmed. With the back of a finger he dabbed unobtrusively at his eye. Moscoli was grinning broadly. Even Ted looked pleased for him.

And for Alix, one wonderful thought reigned supreme: You didn't cut up the paintings. I knew you didn't. *I knew it!*

CHAPTER 32

In Italy over the next week-and-a-half, Tiny was not merely a hero but a celebrity. The opening of the cache was a national television event, and Tiny himself was the subject of a thirty-minute TV special on the entire affair: "The Man Who Outsmarted the Mafia and Saved a Cellini."

And a week after that, he was at the Quirinale in Rome to receive the Silver Medal for Distinguished Contribution to Culture and Art from the hands of the Minister of Culture himself.

Among the two dozen invited attendees were his aged Uncle Innocenzo, Gino Moscoli, and Geoff and Alix London. Tiny then went off to Pieve di Teco for his hero's welcome and a weeklong visit with relatives he hadn't seen since 1987, and the next morning Geoff and Alix boarded British Airways 571 for their flight to Seattle.

They arrived at 5:00 p.m. looking and feeling like anybody else who was stepping off a fifteen-hour flight. "Maybe we should skip the Sangiovese tonight," Alix suggested. "We've been up since 2:00 a.m. Seattle time, and you look tired. I know I am."

"Certainly not," Geoff said reproachfully. "It's Thursday. My public expects me."

"Well, we certainly wouldn't want to disappoint your public," Alix said jovially, but she was far from jovial.

There was a plan in the works that Chris had come up with the day before Alix had left for Rome. On their return, Alix would drive Geoff to Sangiovese just as she did most Thursday evenings, and Geoff would do his thing in the fireside niche. Then, when he was still glowing, they would sit down with him in a private corner, and Alix would tell him that she was a married woman and his new son-in-law was FBI special agent Ted Ellesworth, whom he had last seen testifying for the prosecution at his trial almost a decade earlier. With Geoff already in a good mood, and Chris as a moderating influence, things were bound to go reasonably smoothly, or as smoothly as could reasonably be expected. And most important, it would finally be, in Chris's words, a done deal: no more clandestine marriage folderol, no more secrets from Alix's father, no more constrictions on Ted.

Alix had readily agreed, but that was then and this was now, and it no longer seemed like such a hot idea. What was the hurry, after all?

Well, there *was* a hurry, though. As she'd said to Chris, Geoff was almost as "connected" as Chris was, with a grapevine that had few equals. And by now there were a lot of people who knew that she'd become Mrs. Ted Ellesworth: Chris, of course (who wouldn't tell); Moscoli, of course (who wouldn't tell); Jamie, of course (who wouldn't tell); Ted, of course (who wouldn't tell . . . except that he'd already told Moscoli); and then there was the county clerk in Maryland who'd issued their license; and the municipal court judge who'd done the marrying; and the jeweler who was working on her ring; and any people to whom they might have mentioned it.

And what about Tiny? He didn't know about the marriage, she was sure of that, but he'd seen how Ted and Alix had been when they were together, and although she doubted that he'd put two and two together, he must have passed on some of his impressions to Geoff, who'd spent time with him in Rome over the past day or two.

No, it couldn't be much longer before the information reached her father from others or he deduced it on his own, and she didn't want either of those things to happen. Telling him tonight at Sangiovese and getting it over with had everything to recommend it, and yet . . . she liked to think it was just the jet lag, but she wasn't ready to face it, not yet. Surely, it could wait another day. Better yet, two. Time to recover her strength and fortitude.

And so she'd suggested stopping off at Geoff's place so that he could shower and change after the long haul from Rome, and then at her condo so she could do the same, and he agreed, but with reluctance: "As long as we don't get there any later than eight at the *latest*." She was hoping, of course, that if she dragged things out long enough, he might tire and give up. Instead, he emerged from his speedy toilette, showered, shaven, smelling of Old Spice, and looking fresher than ever. So much for that.

Twenty minutes later, they were in Green Lake, and Alix was climbing the single flight of stairs to her condominium, lugging the larger of her two carry-ons. Geoff was still down at the car, having insisted on bringing up her smaller bag and laptop. The cold feet she'd been developing were now frozen solid, and as she turned her key in the lock she was thinking that, once behind the closed door of her bedroom, she could telephone Chris and call the thing off. It was cowardly and she knew it, but—

The key had been turned and her hand was on the door handle when the door was pulled open from the other side. Standing in front of her in a freshly pressed, light blue dress shirt with the sleeves casually but impeccably folded up on his tanned forearms, was a smiling, impossibly gorgeous man with a bottle of red wine and two wineglasses held easily in one hand.

Alix stood there, tongue-tied and stunned. "Uh . . ."

"Hi, sweetheart," Ted said. "Welcome home. Thought I'd surprise you." From behind him came the sweet, sad strains of a Chopin nocturne, and the air was filled with the peppery aroma of the Jamaican beef stew that was a specialty of his.

Laughing, he pulled the bag out of her numb fingers. "Looks like I succeeded, too." He stepped back out of the way. "Aren't you going to come—"

His attention was caught by the figure of a bearded, elderly man coming slowly up the steps with an overnight bag and a laptop sleeve. Ted froze.

Geoff continued up the stairs to the landing and handed the bag to him. "Young man, perhaps you'd take this?"

"Of course, sure." He looked helplessly at Alix. "I think we have some explaining to do."

"Geoff," Alix said awkwardly, "Dad . . . this is . . . well, the fact is . . ."

Geoff edged politely past them into the entryway, then turned to face them. "Alix, my dear," he said, his voice at its plummiest, "really, must we persist in this tedious charade? Don't you think it's time to properly introduce me to your husband?"

Alix goggled at him. "How did . . . how long have you . . ." but Ted just laughed and held out his hand. "It's a pleasure to meet you, Mr. London. Again."

Geoff shook his hand. "Yes, again," he said dryly, but with an amicable little smile of his own.

"And now that that's out of the way," Ted said, "the best stew you ever tasted is on the stove, there's more than enough for three, and I for one would really be happy if you would join us."

Geoff smiled at Ted, smiled at Alix, and said, "Young man, nothing would please me more."

Alix sighed. The world was right again.

Acknowledgments

Karen Stewart, Charlotte's sister, who alerted us to the idea that there had to be a story behind Tiny's mirror.

Randy Roberts of the Sequim Bay Yacht Club, who shared with us some of his boating knowledge. We apologize for a liberty or two we may have taken in the interest of smooth story-telling.

About the Authors

With their backgrounds in art scholarship, forensic anthropology, and psychology, Charlotte and Aaron Elkins were destined to be mystery writers. Between them, they've written thirty mysteries since 1982—garnering an Agatha Award for the best short story of the year, an Edgar Award for the year's best mystery, and a Nero Wolfe Award for Literary Excellence, among other honors. The authors revel in creating intensively researched works that are as accessible and absorbing as they are sophisticated and stylish. In addition to writing the first three Alix London mysteries—*A Dangerous Talent, A Cruise to Die For*, and *The Art Whisperer*—they are also the authors of the Lee Ofsted golf mysteries, including *A Wicked Slice, Rotten Lies, Nasty Breaks, Where Have All the Birdies Gone*, and *On the Fringe*. Charlotte was born in Houston, Aaron in New York City, and they now reside on Washington's Olympic Peninsula.